BREAKING
ALEXANDRIA
A NOVEL

D1522046

NEW YORK TIMES AND *USA TODAY* BESTSELLING AUTHOR
K.A. ROBINSON

Cover Designer: Romantic Book Affairs

Editor and Interior Designer: Jovana Shirley, Unforeseen Editing, www.unforeseenediting.com

Lyrics to "Mechanical Rationality" by Smile Empty Soul are used with permission from Smile Empty Soul.

Visit my website at: www.authorkarobinson.blogspot.com or www.facebook.com/karobinson13

ISBN-13: 978-1497305670

OTHER BOOKS BY

NEW YORK TIMES AND USA TODAY BESTSELLING AUTHOR

K.A. ROBINSON

THE TORN SERIES

TORN

TWISTED

TAINTED

THE TIES SERIES

SHATTERED TIES

TWISTED TIES

CONTENTS

CHAPTER 1

I groaned and rolled over to escape the sun shining through the window of Joel's bedroom. My body tensed as I realized for there to be sunlight, then it must be day. My eyes opened, and I grabbed my cell phone from the table beside the bed to check the time. *Shit.* It was almost three o'clock in the afternoon, and I had a ton of voice mails and missed calls. I couldn't believe that I'd slept this late. I was so fucked.

I sat up and pulled the blanket up to cover my naked body. I had snuck out of my parents' house last night after they grounded me for fighting in school again. I'd thought I could sneak back in this morning before they woke up, but that obviously wasn't going to happen now.

My eyes traveled to Joel as he snored lightly beside me. The sun was directly on his back, showing off the skull and crossbones tattoo that covered most of the area. His normally guarded expression was gone while he slept. Joel looked like the typical badass, but he was so much more. His body was covered in tattoos—and when I say covered, I mean, covered. There was barely an inch of him that didn't have ink with the exception of his face. His hair was a dark brown color, and he kept it just a bit shaggy. His eyes were a startling green color that made people stop and look twice. His cheekbones and overall face structure would make any male model jealous.

I smiled dreamily as I thought about our night together. At twenty-two, he was five years older than me, but our age gap never seemed to bother him. We'd been together for almost a year now, and I couldn't be happier. I'd met him at my cousin's graduation party two years ago, and I'd instantly developed a crush on him. He hadn't paid any attention to me, but when I'd started hanging out with some of his younger friends who were in high school with me, I'd finally gotten him to notice me.

I'd been drunk at a party one night and braver than usual. Girls much older than me had surrounded him, but I had shoved through them when I saw him and walked straight up to him. He'd raised an eyebrow when I stopped in front of him, but I'd simply hopped on his lap and kissed him until I couldn't breathe. After I had finished, I'd stood up and walked away.

We'd been together ever since that night.

My parents weren't happy that I was dating someone who was so much older and more experienced. The fact that he was covered in tattoos from head to toe hadn't helped my case any either, but I'd sworn to them over and over that Joel and I weren't having sex. Obviously, that was a lie, considering where I'd woken up just now, but they didn't need to know that.

Joel was trouble. I'd known that before I got with him, but I'd still taken a chance, and I was glad that I had. Everyone knew he was the son of the town drunk, and it showed. Joel had one hell of a mean streak. Even when he had been in high school, everyone had been terrified of him. He had been kicked out for fighting more times than I could count. On top of that, everyone knew he was the go-to guy if someone needed a fix. He'd later explained to me that he'd started selling drugs to help pay the bills that his dad never worried about. Joel was good at dealing though, and he'd stuck with it even when he could have left this town and started fresh.

He had already been living on his own by the time we met, and I was glad. I wasn't sure how I would have handled seeing the man who had abused Joel for years. I wanted to cause Joel's father as much pain as he had done to Joel. I knew it had been years since Joel had talked to his father, but it still bothered me.

"Joel, wake up. I need to leave," I said as I nudged his shoulder.

He groaned in his sleep and rolled over, but he refused to open his eyes. I sighed as I hit his shoulder harder. His eyes finally opened when I started smacking him on the stomach. He shielded his eyes as he rolled over to look at me.

"What?" he grumbled.

"I need to go home, like, right now. We slept in." I stood up and started looking for my clothes.

"You're already in trouble. Why hurry home to be yelled at?" he asked as he sat up.

He didn't bother to cover himself, and I couldn't bring myself to look away from his naked body. I loved the trail of dark hair leading down his stomach…to other places. His nose was a bit crooked from being broken more than once, but it didn't take away from his appearance. If anything, it made him look sexier and dangerous. His eyes were his best feature by far though. They held a vulnerability in them that made me want to crawl into his arms and try to make everything better.

He was in great shape. I guessed he had to be when he dealt with strangers who were high and desperate for their next fix on a daily basis. The muscles in his arms were well-defined, and his chest was as hard as a rock. I loved curling up in his arms. I always felt like he could protect me from anything.

"I don't want to make it worse," I said as I located my clothes.

They were next to the door, making it obvious as to how they had come off. We'd barely made it to his room before he started stripping me.

"Your parents suck. Why do they care so much about you fighting? At least they know their kid can defend herself. Personally, I'd be proud," he said as he stretched.

"They're sick of me getting kicked out of school. They said something about college and doing something with my life."

"I fought, and look at me. I'm living the high life." He grinned at me.

I rolled my eyes even though I knew he had a point. He used drugs occasionally, but he sold more than anything, and he'd made quite a lot of money doing it.

"I'm sure they'd be so proud of me if I decided dealing drugs was going to be my career choice in life. I might even get the Daughter of the Year award."

I still couldn't find my underwear, so I decided to skip them. He grinned as he watched me pull on my shorts.

"Looking for these?" he asked as he held up my underwear.

I walked over to the bed and held out my hand. "Come on, I need to hurry. Give them to me."

"Make me," he taunted.

I grumbled as I went to grab them, but he held them just out of my reach.

"Damn it, Joel."

He reached up and pulled me back onto the bed. "Maybe I don't want you to go home. Maybe I should hold your underwear for ransom, so you'll stay."

"Keep them. I'll get them another time."

I tried to sit up, but he kept me pinned against him.

"Stay for a little while longer. We can light up and have some fun."

"I can't go home stoned. That's just asking for trouble."

"But you could go home thoroughly fucked," he said as he ran his fingers down my back.

I shivered. "I could, but I need to leave."

"I'll make it quick." He started pulling my shorts down my legs.

"Joel..."

"Shh...you know you want to."

Of course I wanted to, but I was already in so much trouble.

He silenced my protests as he rolled me onto my back. His naked body was tight against mine, and I could feel just how much he wanted me. He tweaked both of my nipples with his fingers, making me moan.

Fuck it. Going home will have to wait.

"Oh fuck," I said as he nudged my opening with his dick.

He leaned down and ran his tongue across my throat and then across my breasts. I arched my back, trying to get as close to him as possible. His hand traveled down my body to my core, and he started rubbing my clit. His dick was still teasing me at my entrance. I tried to adjust my body, so he would enter.

"I thought you had to go home," he taunted.

"I do, but I thought you said you wanted to fuck me."

"Oh, I do. Grab the bedposts."

I did as he'd said, preparing myself for his entry. He didn't disappoint. He slammed into me hard enough that I had to hold on to the bedposts to keep myself from moving up the bed. I gasped out his name as he pulled out and ran his thumb along my clit.

God, I'm going to kill him for torturing me.

"Again," I said as I shifted, trying to force him to enter me.

"You like it rough, don't you, baby?" he teased.

"You know I do," I groaned.

He ran his hands over my body before grabbing my hips and thrusting into me again. Over and over, he slammed into me until I was gasping for breath. He wasn't gentle, and I hadn't expected him to be. It was just the way we were. He liked rough sex, and I was happy to oblige.

I wrapped my legs around his waist to allow him to go deeper as I met him thrust for thrust. His grip on me tightened as he came closer to his release. I couldn't hold out much longer either. I was *so* close. He continued to pound into me as he reached between us. He flicked my clit and sent me screaming into my orgasm. My legs clamped tighter around him as I came. His thrusts became harder and more erratic as he came with me.

My body went limp. Once my orgasm left me, I could see again. Joel was panting above me with his forehead resting against mine. After his breathing returned to normal, he slipped out and rolled over to his side.

"I told you I'd make it quick," he said as he grinned over at me.

"Yay for you." I stuck my tongue out at him.

He continued to grin as he leaned over, and then he kissed me. "Come on, let's get you home."

We both dressed quickly, trying to hurry. Now that I wasn't staring at Joel's naked body, the need to get home was strong. I knew I was in trouble, but I just couldn't bring myself to care at the moment. I was tired of spending all my time trying to figure out ways to get around my parents' rules.

I knew fighting didn't solve anything, but it sure as hell made me feel better. Since Joel and I had become a couple, I'd made quite a few enemies, especially from the female population, but I didn't really give a fuck. He was mine, and if people tried to come between us, I'd take care of them.

I wasn't the sweet and innocent girl I'd been before I met Joel. He'd changed me—but for the better. Before him, I'd rarely partied, and I'd never gotten into trouble. Now, I did what I wanted, and I didn't care what anyone thought of me. I had no friends of my own. I only hung out with his. It didn't bother me though. I hated girls. My solitude and bad attitude usually led to rumors that I was on drugs or helping him sell them. And both rumors were true, so they didn't bother me either because it made most people leave me alone.

But there was always some dumb skank who thought she could talk about me or try to push me around. I knew how to take care of myself. The girls who tried to start fights with me always ended up with blood dripping down their faces as they cowered on the floor.

Joel had taught me how to fight since he would bring me along to deals. He would even send me out to do them on my own if he was busy. Most people who were aware of the fact that I was helping Joel deal thought I was nuts, but I considered it a normal part of our relationship. Besides, he never sent me out on deals that were dangerous. He always handled those on his own. I would try to help him as much as possible. I knew that if I got caught, I wouldn't end up in as bad of a situation as he would since I was under eighteen.

I didn't use drugs often —with the exception of weed. While I had no problem dealing, I didn't want to end up like one of the addicts who I supplied. They were gross and pathetic. Joel smoked weed a lot, but as far as I knew, that was the only thing he did. We both knew that if he started using, his profits would disappear.

We walked down the steps from his house to where his Harley was parked outside. He was the only guy I knew who was confident enough in his badass reputation to leave his bike out on the street all night. I grabbed my helmet and put it on before climbing on the bike behind him. I wrapped my arms around him as it came to life, and we tore down the street.

I loved being on his bike more than anything else. I'd made him promise me that we would go on a road trip the summer I turned eighteen. I wanted out of this town and away from my parents. I just wanted to be free.

The ride was short but exhilarating. We arrived in front of my house faster than I would have liked. While I had been in a hurry to get home, I hadn't taken the time to mentally prepare myself for the fight that was sure to ensue. Sure enough, the front door flew open as soon as Joel parked and shut off his motorcycle. My mother stomped down the sidewalk to where we were sitting before I even had the chance to take off my helmet.

"Get. Inside. Right. Now!" she shouted.

I sighed as I pulled off my helmet. *This should be fun.* "I can explain—" I started.

She held up her hand to stop me. "I don't want to hear it. Inside the house—now."

I kissed Joel's helmet and hopped off the bike. He started it back up and left, leaving me to deal with my mother alone.

Asshole.

"Mom, let me explain," I started again, hoping that she would let me talk. "I just wanted to see him for a little bit. I planned to stay with him for only an hour or two, but then I fell asleep when we were watching a movie. I woke up and started freaking out."

"You never should have gone to him in the first place. You're grounded."

"You can't keep us apart. I love him, and he loves me!" I shouted.

"You have no idea what love even is, Alexandria! You're still a child."

"Yeah, I do. I know what I feel for him is love, and there is nothing you can do to change that."

I stomped past her, focusing on the front door in front of me. Once I made it inside, I hurried upstairs to my room. She followed, obviously not finished with me.

"You are not to leave this house for a week. You were kicked out of school for the rest of the week, and since you don't need to be there, you don't need to be anywhere."

"What does it even matter? This is the last week of school anyway. If I hadn't been suspended, I would have skipped anyway."

My mother shook her head. "I will never understand you, Alexandria. You're not my baby girl anymore, and I have no idea what happened to you. I'd blame Joel, but this attitude of yours started long before him. If things don't change, I'll—"

"You'll what? You might as well figure out what you'll do to me because this is me, and I won't change who I am to make you happy."

"You're destroying yourself, Alexandria. Look at you—you're as thin as a twig. You've dyed your beautiful blonde hair black and put red through it. You won't listen, and you have no respect for

7

your father or me." She glared at me. "And don't even get me started on those piercings in your lip and nose. They look horrible."

Currently, I was rocking a septum piercing, a piercing in my nose, and looped snakebite piercings. I really wasn't sure why she was still so angry over it. I came home with new body modifications all the time. I would think she'd be used to it by now.

"Don't forget about my tattoo. I know how much you love it," I said sarcastically.

Almost three months ago, I'd come home with a tattoo on my left arm. I wasn't eighteen yet, but Joel's friend was a tattoo artist, so he had done it for me. I'd wanted a tattoo forever, so I'd jumped at the opportunity to get one. I had drawn the design myself. It covered most of my inner arm from my elbow to my wrist. At the top was a skull that ended with partial butterfly wings. Below that was a blue rose. I loved it even though I'd ended up being grounded for a month when my mother saw it.

"I'm tired of your attitude, Alexandria. Enough is enough."

"I love you and Dad, but I'm tired of you both looking down at me. This is my life, and I'll live it however I want to. I don't have an attitude. I just can't handle how you freak out over every little thing."

My mother's nostrils flared as she tried to control her temper. She closed her eyes, and I watched as she counted to ten under her breath. Her entire body sagged the second she hit ten. It was like someone had dropped a ton of bricks on her shoulders.

"I don't know what you expect from me, Alexandria. I refuse to just sit here and watch you self-destruct."

I stared at my mother as she spoke. She looked tired, the kind of tired that came from worrying. Her blonde hair was hanging limply around her face, and there were lines around her mouth and eyes that I hadn't noticed before. Her hazel eyes that were identical to mine had fear in them. I felt a twinge of guilt for causing her any worry, but I pushed it away.

"I don't expect a damn thing from you."

CHAPTER 2

If there were a medal for sneaking out of the house without getting caught the most times, I'd be the recipient for sure. I smiled to myself as I slowly slid open my bedroom window. I glanced down to the yard below. It was illuminated by the streetlight across the road from our house. I squinted as I looked around, checking for movement of any kind.

After I was sure that it was safe, I climbed onto my window ledge. There was a large oak tree in our yard, and several of the branches were touching our house. One was positioned perfectly, so I could crawl onto it right from my window. I silently slipped onto the limb and made my way down the tree, glancing up at my window every few seconds. While I considered myself a badass escape artist, I never felt safe until I was out of our yard. I always expected my mom to appear in my window and start shouting at me.

I crossed the yard, staying in the shadows as I went. It was well after midnight, and there wasn't a soul around. Once I made it to the sidewalk, I jogged until my house was out of sight. I felt sweat on the back of my neck as I hurried along.

June was always a hot month in Ohio, but it wasn't as bad as July or August. I dreaded those months and the unbearable heat that would come with them. My pale skin hated the summer sun, so I would try to stay out of it as much as possible.

Joel was used to my escape routine, and he was waiting for me a block away. I couldn't keep the grin off my face when I saw him sitting on his motorcycle at the corner of the block. I took the helmet that he handed to me, and I pulled it over my head. His bike roared to life as I slipped on the back of it, and I wrapped my arms around his stomach. He pulled away from the curb and headed to his house.

A huge party was going on there tonight. Joel would usually have one or two parties a month at his house. I loved them. They were crazy and stupid and everything I expected from a party. Because of the amount of people that came, the parties would stay in the backyard since it was completely enclosed with a privacy fence. He was always careful of who was allowed in. Alcohol and drugs were a major part of them, and he didn't want to take a chance on someone turning him in to the police. He'd managed to stay off their radar for the most part, and neither of us wanted him to catch their attention.

Pulling up to the house, we could hear the music blaring as soon as he shut off his bike.

"Damn it. I told them to keep it down. If someone calls the cops on us—"

"I'll take care of it," I said as I pulled the helmet off my head.

Before he could stop me, I was off the bike and heading for the house. I walked inside and made my way to the back door. As soon as I opened it, I winced from the beats coming from the speakers.

"Yo! Riley! Turn the fucking music down!" I shouted as I pushed through the crowd to where he was standing.

Riley was one of Joel's closest friends. I'd met him before Joel and I became an item, and Riley and I had ended up becoming really good friends. He partied with the same crowd as us, but I'd never once seen him deal or use drugs. He drank, but that was it.

He grinned at me when he noticed me shoving my way to him. "Lexi! It's about time you showed up!"

"Turn the damn music down before someone calls the cops!"

"Oh shit, sorry." He lowered the volume to the point where my ears weren't bleeding. "Better?"

"Much."

"I was wondering if you were going to make an appearance tonight."

"Don't I always?" I asked.

"Well, Joel said you were having some parental issues, so I wasn't sure."

That was an understatement. My mom had kept me under house arrest for almost two weeks since she'd caught me coming home with Joel that afternoon. I'd felt like a prisoner in my own house, and I hadn't been handling it very well. It had seemed like my mom and I were fighting constantly because of my attitude.

"My trusty tree has yet to fail me," I teased.

Riley laughed. "You'd think your parents would wise up and cut that damn thing down."

"Let's hope they don't. I *really* don't want to jump out of a second-story window."

"Why not? It might be fun."

I rolled my eyes. "I'm sure it would be. I'm going to go find some booze. Behave yourself."

"Always do."

I weaved through the mass of bodies as I headed for the drink table. Now that I wasn't pushing through like a maniac, it was hard to move. Most of the people here towered over my five-foot-three frame. Usually, I liked being tiny—it made me feel cute—but I hated it right now.

I finally pushed through the crowd and grabbed a red cup off the table. I made a rum and Coke that had way more rum than Coke and then leaned against the table. I could see most of the party from where I was standing. I watched as people laughed, drank, and danced around me.

Off to the side, a few groups were doing something else entirely. I watched as a guy lit up a bowl and took a hit from it. I finished my drink and walked over to where he and several others were sitting. They glanced up as I approached.

"Care to share?" I asked.

"You're Joel's chick. Of course we'll share," Bowl Guy said.

He looked vaguely familiar, but I couldn't place him. He might have been a classmate of mine or someone I'd sold to for Joel. Either way, I didn't care.

I took the lighter and bowl from him. I lit the bowl and inhaled deeply, letting the smoke fill my lungs. I held it in for as long as I could before blowing it out of my nose.

I loved the smell of weed. I knew a lot of people hated it, but I found it comforting. I'd come to associate it with everything important in my life—Joel.

I took another hit before handing the bowl back. "Thanks."

"Welcome," Bowl Guy said.

He glanced behind me just as a pair of arms wrapped around my waist.

"There you are," Joel said as he nuzzled my neck.

11

"Here I am." I snuggled back into his arms, so our bodies were pressed together.

"I've been looking for you everywhere."

"I've been around. I made Riley turn his music down," I said as I felt the weed starting to relax me.

"So I heard. What are you doing over here?"

I glanced at Bowl Guy. "Making friends."

Joel laughed. "You don't need to make friends with random guys just to get high. I can take care of you."

I turned in his arms and looked up at him. "You're very good at taking care of me."

And he was. No matter what it was, Joel always took care of me and helped with whatever I needed. *Need a place to stay because my mom and I were fighting? Go to Joel. Need something to relax me? Go to Joel. Need some extra cash? Go to Joel. Need someone to hold me as I cried? Go to Joel.* Hell, he'd even helped me with my math homework more than once. He was a damn genius when it came to school shit.

"I try." He kissed me lightly. "Come on, let's go sit down and laugh at the drunk idiots."

He held my hand as we weaved through the crowd. He sat down in a chair on his back porch and pulled me down onto his lap. I settled back against his chest as we watched the party in front of us. I never understood why Joel threw parties. He would drink and party occasionally, but it was rare. Most of the time, he simply watched everyone else and kept an eye on me when I was drunk.

Riley came over a few minutes after we had sat down. I smiled as he handed me one of the drinks he was carrying. I loved that kid. He knew the way to my heart – alcohol.

"What are you two lovebirds up to?" he asked as he sat down in the chair beside us.

"Making babies," I said as I grinned at him.

"Ew…that was more than I needed to know."

I shrugged. "You should be used to us by now."

He shook his head as he stood up. "I like you both, but I think I'm going to find someone else to hang out with. Hopefully, she'll have boobs and be single."

I laughed as he walked away from us. Riley was a good guy but still a guy. He would go through a lot of girls, and very few of them had seemed to care about it. I couldn't blame them though. He was hot by anyone's standards. His blond hair was cut short at the moment, but I'd seen him grow it out until it brushed his shoulders. Either way looked good on him. His eyes were a pale blue color, and they were probably my favorite things about him. They made him look vulnerable even though he wasn't. He could lay someone out faster than I could blink when he needed to. He was protective of his friends, especially Joel, and he didn't fuck around when someone pissed him off.

"I'm glad you sneaked out. These parties are boring without you," Joel whispered in my ear.

"Yeah, right. I'm sure you'd be bored if I weren't here," I teased.

"I would. I'd be sitting here by myself with no one to talk to."

"I'm sure someone would talk to you." I thought for a moment. "Well, maybe. You do scare a lot of people away."

"I haven't scared you away yet." He kissed me behind my ear. I shivered. "And you won't. You're stuck with me."

"I don't mind—at all." He paused to kiss my ear again. "Will you stay with me tonight?"

My insides clenched at the thought of staying in his bed all night. "You know I will."

I knew my mother would probably lock me in a cage when she woke up and saw that I was gone, but I didn't care. It would be worth it as long as I got to spend the night with Joel.

"I was hoping you'd say that. I have some runs tomorrow, but I'll take you home before I leave."

When Joel said runs, he meant his drug deals. I hated the fact that he did them simply because I hated that he was constantly around addicts, but I'd come to accept it as a normal part of our lives. He was one of the most in-demand dealers in our area, so he would go on a lot of them. He'd been doing this for a long time, and he knew what he was doing, but that didn't mean I didn't worry about him all the time.

Most of his clients were casual users looking to get high once in a while. A few were hardcore addicts though, and they scared me. When people were desperate for their drug, they would do anything they could to get it. Joel had beat the shit out of people more than once when they tried to steal from him.

"I don't want to go home tomorrow. I'll help you with your runs."

"You sure? Your mom will freak if you don't go home."

I shrugged. "She'll freak anyway. I'll text her tomorrow to let her know I'm fine."

"As long as you're sure. She'll probably lock you away for the rest of the summer."

"No, she won't. I'll just leave again. I'll hide out here or something."

"She'll look here first." He pointed out.

"True. I'll figure something out. Nothing in this world will keep me away from you."

I turned to face him. The party around us faded away as my lips brushed his. We were the only two people in the entire world. I wrapped my arms around his neck as I kissed him deeply.

"I love you," I whispered.

He smiled. "I never get tired of hearing you say that."

I opened my mouth to reply, but before I could, someone said, "Joel…"

We both turned to see a girl standing next to us. I rolled my eyes when I realized who it was. Tasha was one of the chicks who I'd had words with more than once. She was Joel's age. I thought they had gone to school together or something like that. She'd been chasing Joel since right after we got together, and she'd done everything in her power to try to break us up. Her attempts had failed miserably, but I still hated her.

I couldn't help but smile when I saw how bad she looked. It was obvious that she was in need of a fix.

"Tasha," Joel acknowledged her.

"You got a second?" she asked, completely ignoring me.

"What's up?"

"I need to talk to you"—she finally glanced in my direction—"alone."

I rolled my eyes again but stayed silent. Regardless of the fact that I hated her, she was Joel's client, so I had to play nice.

"We're as alone as we're going to get. What'd you need?"

She went back to ignoring me as she stepped closer and rested her hand on his shoulder. "I need some cocaine."

I forced myself not to push her hand away from him. I didn't want her to touch him.

"How much do you need?" he asked.

"Just a little bit, but the thing is…I don't have any cash right now."

Joel's face turned hard. "I don't do charity, Tasha. You know that."

"It wouldn't be charity! I'll pay you next week, I swear. You know you can trust me."

"Not happening, Tasha. Go find someone else to bug," Joel said.

"Please! I'll do anything you want. You know, you used to let me pay you back with something other than cash." Her tone was flirty.

Joel's entire body tensed underneath me. "Not happening."

She ran her fingers down his arm as she smiled at him sweetly. "Come on, I'll let you go bareback if you want."

"I'm sitting on his fucking lap in case you haven't noticed," I said, unable to stay quiet any longer. I couldn't believe that she had the nerve to offer him sex as payment while I was two inches away from her. She reeked of desperation.

She looked down at me like I was nothing more than an annoyance to her. "So what?"

"Tasha, leave—now," Joel said, his tone cold.

"Come on, baby, you know I'm more fun than she is."

"He told you to leave." I made a shooing gesture with my hand. "Listen to him. Go."

"I'm not going anywhere."

"Fine by me," I said casually.

Joel gave me a confused look, but I only winked. Before Tasha could figure out what I was about to do, I stood and smiled sweetly at her. The next few seconds seemed to pass in slow motion as I drew back and punched her in the face. I heard a sickening crack, and I grinned as I realized that I'd just broken her nose. As soon as she went down, I was on top of her, punching any part of her that I could reach. The bitch had known better than to mess with me.

Strong arms wrapped around me, and I was pulled off of her. I kicked out, trying to free myself.

"Stop fighting me, Lexi!"

I instantly stopped struggling when I heard Joel's voice. I let him pull me away as Tasha's friends gathered around her to help her stand. Her face was covered in blood, and one of her eyes was already blackening.

I smiled in triumph as I looked at her. "I hope you'll listen next time he tells you to leave him alone."

"You're fucking crazy!" she moaned.

"Maybe I am, but maybe you should learn not to offer your vagina up to my boyfriend right in front of me, you crack whore."

"Everybody out!" Joel shouted at the crowd surrounding us. He was mad, really mad. He rarely yelled, and he *never* ended a party early.

People scrambled to the one exit in the privacy fence, pushing each other to get out. No one wanted to deal with a pissed-off Joel. Riley stood off to the side and waited until everyone was out, so he could lock the gate. I'd never in my life seen this place clear out so fast.

"You got it?" Joel asked.

"I'll make sure they're gone for sure. Go take care of Lexi," Riley said as he glanced at me. It was rare for him to be so serious.

I knew I was in trouble with both of them. *Shit.*

Joel picked me up and carried me inside his house. He walked straight to the bathroom and turned on the shower.

"What are you doing?" I asked.

He started stripping me. "Your clothes and your body are covered in blood. We need to get rid of it."

"Oh."

I hadn't even noticed until he said something. Now, I saw the blood on my knuckles and on my shirt as he tossed it onto the floor.

"Go shower. Tasha is crazy as fuck, so I'm going to go burn these. I don't want her to go to the police, and then they find these."

I was silent as he left the room with my clothes balled up under his arm. Truthfully, I wasn't too worried about Tasha turning me in to the cops, but I *was* concerned that Joel might get pulled into it somehow. I didn't want that.

I stepped into the shower and let the water wash away the blood on my skin. I felt the tension leave my body as I washed my hair. I wasn't going to worry about Tasha right now. She was too desperate for drugs to turn in the girlfriend of one of the biggest dealers in the city. If she did, no one would go near her. She wouldn't fuck herself over like that.

I shut off the water and grabbed a towel to dry off with. Joel hadn't come back inside to bring me clothes yet, so I walked to his bedroom, naked. I kept spare clothes here for the nights I would stay over or in case I needed them. I opened the dresser drawer I used and pulled out underwear and one of Joel's old shirts that I loved to sleep in.

After I had clothes on, I crawled into his bed and pulled the covers up to my chin. I always felt so safe here in his bed. It was like he could protect me from everything bad in the world. I never wanted to leave.

I heard Joel walking down the hall. He appeared in the doorway a few seconds later. He pulled his shirt over his head, and then his jeans went next. I watched him as he undressed. While I took in every part of his body, I shivered as memories of us being together flooded my brain. I wanted him, but I knew he was mad at me for what I did.

He pulled the covers back and crawled into bed beside me. I was surprised when he took me into his arms and pulled me tight against his chest.

"I thought you were mad at me."

"I am."

"Then, why are you holding me?"

"Because I'm also so fucking proud to call you my girlfriend." He kept his arms around me as I rolled over to face him.

"What do you mean?" I asked.

"You're a hard-ass, Lexi, and I fucking love it. I don't like that you got in a fight over me, but at the same time, I think it's so fucking hot that you'd do that for me."

"You seem surprised that I'd fight for you. What did you expect me to do? Let her drag you away, so you could bang her?"

Joel grinned. "You have such a way with words. No, I didn't expect you to sit quietly, but I also didn't expect you to break her nose."

"She had it coming."

"She did. I have to admit that it was a major turn-on to see you like that."

"On top of a girl?"

He laughed. "No. Don't get me wrong, it would be hot to see you with a girl but that's not what I meant. It's hot to see you get out of control like that."

He surprised me sometimes. I'd expected him to say that he was pissed at me. Instead, he was telling me that I'd given him a hard-on.

"You tend to bring my crazy out."

"I'm glad." He kissed me gently as he rolled me onto my back. "But I now have a problem only you can fix."

"And what is your problem exactly?"

"I'm still hard."

He pressed his lower body against me, showing me just how hard he was.

"I think I can help you with your problem."

CHAPTER

3

I hated mornings with a fiery passion. I had no idea who had decided that the entire world needed to wake up at ass o'clock, but that person needed to be nut-punched. Needless to say, I wasn't the nicest person in the world if woken up before noon.

Joel knew that, and he let me sleep in the next morning. When I finally managed to haul my grumpy self out of bed, it was well after noon. I changed into a pair of jeans and a tank top before stumbling into the bathroom to brush my teeth and tie my hair back. I could hear Joel moving around in the kitchen as I walked down the hallway.

He glanced up when I appeared. "Afternoon, sleepyhead."

"Ugh. Give me food," I said as I sat down at the kitchen table.

He grinned as he set a bowl of cereal down in front of me. "You're lucky I love you so much, or I wouldn't put up with your grumpy ass when you wake up."

"Shut up. I'm not grumpy."

"Whatever. Hurry up and eat, so we can head out."

I started shoveling cereal into my mouth. We did need to hurry.

Joel had a schedule of where he needed to be at certain times, so people could meet up with him. If he weren't there when he was supposed to be, we would have some seriously unhappy customers. He was never at the same place at the same time for obvious reasons. He always sent out a message to a few of his friends the night before, telling them where he would be, and they would spread the word to everyone he sold to.

I finished my cereal and washed out my bowl in the sink. Joel was already walking out the door, and I scrambled to keep up with him. We took his old Honda instead of his bike. The car was a lot less flashy, and we didn't want to attract any unwanted attention.

Joel turned up the radio as we made our way to the bad side of town. He lived in a neighborhood that was right between the good side of town and the bad side, so within minutes, we reached our first stop.

I waited in the car as Joel got out and walked over to a group of teenagers. To someone who had no idea what was going on, the scene looked normal. They were just a bunch of guys and a few girls hanging out on picnic benches at the local park, but I knew better. I grabbed the gun that Joel kept under my seat and flipped the safety off just in case I needed it.

I watched all of them closely as they spoke with Joel. I couldn't tear my eyes away as I watched the deal go down. If one of them tried to hurt him, I'd see it before they had a chance to do anything. Joel had taught me how to use a gun a few months ago when I started helping him. I hadn't used it yet, but I wasn't afraid to if he needed my help. Joel always came first. The deal was done in just a few minutes, and Joel walked back to the car.

He noticed the gun in my lap and frowned. "Why do you have that?"

"Because I wanted to be ready if you needed me. There were a bunch of them. Your back was to me, so I'd see someone sneak up behind you before you did."

His frown deepened as he took the gun from me and slipped it back under the seat. "I taught you how to use that to protect yourself, not me. I can handle myself. If something goes down, I don't want you to get involved. You're better than that, Lexi."

I shook my head. "I'm not going to just sit around if something goes down. We're in this together. As long as I'm with you, I *will* protect you. I don't care what that means for me later on."

He seemed truly bothered by my words. I couldn't believe that he would expect me to sit idly by if he needed me.

I loved him, and I'd do anything to protect him. Was he perfect? Definitely not. But then again, who was? No one in this world was perfect. We all had our faults. I hated what Joel did, but I'd come to accept it. I loved him for who he was, and I wasn't about to try to change him.

The ride was quiet as we headed to our next stop. Both of us were lost in our own thoughts. I waited in the car again as Joel took care of another deal. Only three guys were here, and I knew all of them, so I let myself relax. Joel finished up with them and headed back to the car.

He glanced at the clock once he got in. "Damn it, I'm running behind." He looked over at me. "Okay if I drop you off to do the next one for me? If it's the usual clients, I mean. They're all teenagers."

I shrugged. "Fine by me."

Doing deals didn't bother me as long as I wasn't surrounded by a ton of buyers. I had a badass reputation, and everyone around here knew it. That meant that most of the teenagers my age didn't mess around with me.

"I'll drop you off and go to the next one. I'll haul ass, so I'll hopefully be back by the time you're finished."

"Okay."

We pulled up to an elementary school. My stomach dropped. I hated doing deals at schools. It just felt wrong to me, but the playground here was big enough that it worked for us.

Joel kissed me and handed me the weed just before I stepped out of the car. I walked across the road and down the hill to where the playground was. I glanced back just as Joel pulled away, leaving me on my own.

Three teenage boys were hanging out by the chain-link fence on the opposite side of the playground. With the exception of us and a few younger kids and their parents, the place was deserted. I watched the boys closely as I approached. They were sophomores at my high school. I'd seen them hanging around a few times, but I didn't know their names.

They all looked up when I stopped in front of them.

The tallest stepped forward and smirked at me. "Joel too important for us now, so he had to send his little girlfriend to do his dirty work?"

The cocky little shit had already pissed me off. I wasn't in the mood to deal with him. I shrugged. "I guess so. If you don't like me, I'll leave, and you can go home empty-handed. It doesn't matter to me either way."

His eyes narrowed at my threat. "Calm your tits. I'm just messing with you."

"I have other places to be. Tell me what you want."

"I want an eighth, and Joey does, too." He glanced over his shoulder to one of the other boys.

"Fifty each." He raised an eyebrow at me, "It's good shit. Take it or leave it, I don't care. You know how much it costs. Don't think that you'll be able to take advantage of me because Joel isn't here."

I stepped closer to him and held out my hand. He pulled cash from his pocket and shoved it roughly into my hand. I slipped it in my pocket and grabbed two bags of weed out of my purse. I shook his hand as I passed them to him.

"Good doing business with you."

"You, too," he said, his tone full of sarcasm.

I ignored him as I turned and started walking back toward the road. I hated annoying little assholes like him. Their cocky attitude got under my skin like nothing else. If they weren't Joel's customers, I would have told their leader to go take a flying leap.

I wasn't paying attention as I walked. I was too annoyed with the guy to notice anything going on around me. I glanced up and stopped dead when I saw a car idling just a few feet away from me. My heart leaped into my throat when I saw my mom sitting behind the wheel.

How did she find me? Did she just see what happened only thirty feet away from her car?

She stepped out of her car and marched toward me, looking angrier than I'd ever seen her. I held my breath when she stopped in front of me.

"Get in the car right now, Alexandria."

"I—"

"Now!" she shouted, pulling me from my stupor.

"No! What the hell did I do now?"

Her nostrils flared. "Are you serious? I might not be young anymore, but I know what I just saw. You were selling those boys drugs! I'm not stupid."

I pretended to be shocked. "What the hell are you talking about? I'm a lot of things, but I'm not a drug dealer! I thought you knew me better than that!"

"Don't act innocent, Alexandria. You haven't been innocent for a very long time."

"I'm not acting! I have no idea what you're talking about! How did you even find me?"

"Stop lying!" she screamed "I saw Joel's car while I was out looking for you, so I followed him. I saw everything. How could you do this to your father and me? What you're doing is illegal, and you could go to *jail*!"

"You're crazy! I didn't sell those guys drugs."

"Then, why are you here?"

"I…" I needed to think fast. "Joey texted me to see if I could loan him twenty bucks. Joel had a few errands to run, so I had him drop me off here because this is where Joey said he'd be."

She laughed. "You're unbelievable. Get in the car right now, Alexandria. I'm not messing around!"

"No!" I wasn't about to get in that car. Once I did, it would be all over. She'd never let me out of the house again.

"Get in the car."

"I'm not leaving with you."

Her face twisted into an ugly snarl. "Get in the car, or I swear to God, I'll call the cops on you right now." She paused to let that sink in. "And I'm betting Joel is the one who got you into this. I'll turn him in, too."

I felt like she'd just punched me in the stomach. She was using my one weakness against me.

"You have no proof. It's your word against mine."

"I'm betting that you have drugs on you right now and so does Joel. That's all the proof they'll need."

A car pulled up several yards away from us. I glanced over to see Joel watching us with a worried expression on his face.

I turned back to my mother and gave her the cruelest smile I could muster up. "You'll have to catch me first."

I ran. I ran as fast as I could. I was by Joel's car in a matter of seconds. I jumped in and screamed at him to go. He floored it, leaving my mother in our dust.

"What the hell is going on?" he asked.

"She saw me selling to those boys. We've got to hide everything. She's going to call the cops on us."

Joel let out a string of curses that shocked even me. "This is so fucked-up!"

23

Neither of us said another word as he drove back to his house. As soon as the car stopped, we were both out of the car and running into his house. I knew where he kept everything hidden—under a loose floorboard in his bedroom. I ran to it and pried it up. I grabbed the bag he kept everything in from under the floorboard and threw it to him. He turned to leave with it, but then he stopped dead in his tracks. My mother was standing in the bedroom doorway.

"Fuck!" I growled. *How the hell did she catch up to us so quickly?*

"Give me the bag," she said calmly as she looked over at Joel.

He shook his head. "I can't. I'm sorry, but I can't let you have it."

"You've destroyed my daughter's life. Destroyed it. I don't even recognize the person she's become since she met you." My mother's voice was deathly quiet. "I haven't called the cops yet, but I will. Either give me the bag or give me my daughter. It's your choice."

Joel would be out thousands of dollars if he handed the drugs over to her. And he'd go to jail. I couldn't let him lose everything because of me.

He hung his head in defeat as he walked over to my mother.

"Wait! I'll go with you. Just leave him alone."

Joel looked back at me. "Lexi…"

"No. I won't let her destroy you over me." I stood and walked to my mother. "Do what you want to me, but leave him alone."

"You will not see this boy ever again—*ever*. If you do, I will have the cops beating on his door before you can even blink." She turned to Joel. "If you even try to contact her, it's over. Stay the hell away from my daughter."

I said nothing. There was no point in arguing with her right now. I had to get her out of his house. I followed as she turned to leave. When she tripped on one of my bras that Joel had ripped off of me at some point, I wanted to crawl in a hole and die.

She glanced down and sucked in a breath. "Why am I not surprised? Get in the car right now!"

My hands shook as I followed her. I glanced over my shoulder to look at Joel one last time. I'd never seen him look so angry or so helpless.

24

I mouthed, *I love you*, when he looked up at me.

I had no idea when I would see him again, but I knew without a doubt that I would. She couldn't keep us away from each other for long.

The car ride home was completely silent. I kept waiting for her to start screaming at me, but she never did. I wished that she would just get it over with and let me have it. I knew what Joel and I had done was wrong, but I couldn't bring myself to feel bad for it. I had been helping Joel. I didn't care what my mom thought about me.

My mom pulled her car into the garage and shut it off. The only sound was the garage door as it closed. I folded my hands in my lap as I waited for her to speak. I knew her rant was coming, and I needed to prepare myself for it.

Instead, she shocked me by opening her door and getting out.

"Where are you going?" I called after her.

She glanced back at me, and my stomach dropped as I saw her eyes filling with tears.

Damn it. I hated making her cry. Seeing that was ten times worse than her screaming at me.

"Go to your room, Alexandria. Stay there until I tell you otherwise."

I expected her to wait and make sure that I actually listened to her, but she didn't. Instead, she simply turned and walked into the house. I got out and silently made my way into the house and up to my room.

I closed my door and then lay down on my bed. I couldn't process what had just happened with my mom's reaction. First, she'd screamed at me, and then she'd flipped some kind of internal switch and shut down completely.

I wouldn't stay away from Joel. I couldn't. I had to make her see that he wasn't at fault here. It had been my decision to help him. He shouldn't have to suffer because of it. He was everything to me, and I wouldn't stop seeing him just because she'd demanded it.

An idea came to me, and my mind started spinning. Joel and I could run away together. I would be eighteen in just a few months. As long as I stayed hidden until then, there would be nothing she could do once I was a legal adult.

I pulled my phone from my pocket and sent Joel a text. I was afraid to call in case my mother was close-by.

Me: I want to run away.

Joel: That sounds like heaven right about now. I'm so sorry for what I did. If it wasn't for me, you wouldn't be in so much trouble.

Me: It wasn't your fault. I should have paid attention to my surroundings. I'm serious about running away though. We could.

Joel: Where would we go, Lexi? You're not eighteen yet, and I really don't feel like being arrested for kidnapping on top of everything else your mom could turn us in for.

Me: They'd never find us. And once I turn eighteen, there's nothing she can do about it.

Joel: No. I won't do that to you. You can't give up everything for me.

Me: Just think about it?

Joel: Not going to happen.

Me: Fine. Whatever. But she can't keep me away from you forever. I'll find a way to see you again.

Joel: I know you will, babe. I love you.

Me: I love you, too. I'm sure she's going to take my phone away soon, so don't text me anymore. I'd better go.

I deleted every single text message on my phone and stuffed it in my pocket. I didn't need her snooping through my phone and seeing something she didn't need to.

I spent the next few hours staring at my ceiling as I waited for her to come to my room. This wasn't like her at all. Usually, she would let me have it as soon as we made it home. Maybe this was a new form of punishment—making me cower in fear from anticipation alone. Normally, I didn't care when she handed out my punishment, but things were so much worse than usual.

Fear grabbed my heart as a thought hit me like a wrecking ball. *What if she is keeping me up here while she calls the cops and has Joel arrested?* I jumped from my bed, and I all but ran to the door. I wouldn't let her do that to Joel.

Just as I reached the door, it swung open. My mother and father were standing there, staring at me. This was bad. Dad worked a lot, so he was never around to yell at me. If he was home, something major was about to happen.

"Alexandria, we need to talk," my father said, his deep voice making me feel like a child.

My father was normally a calm man, but I could tell by the tone of his voice that he was upset. His green eyes were churning with an emotion I couldn't read.

I looked nothing like my father. He was tall, an inch or two over six feet, where I was barely over five feet. He had a muscular build that made him appear larger than he was. I could thank my mother for my tiny frame.

I stumbled backward until the back of my knees hit the bed. I dropped down onto it as my parents walked into my room and stood in front of me.

"Look, I know this seems messed-up, but—"

My mom held up her hand. "It doesn't seem messed-up. It *is* messed-up. I never thought I'd see the day when I watched my daughter dealing drugs. What were you thinking, Alexandria?"

"I know it's wrong, okay? I get it," I said.

"I don't think you do. You could go to *jail* if you're caught. Doesn't that scare you?"

"We're both very disappointed in you, Alexandria," my father added.

"We've been talking about what punishment is suitable for this. Obviously, you are never allowed to talk to Joel again," my mom said.

"You can't keep me away from him forever!" I said stubbornly.

My parents exchanged a look that made my stomach drop. They had a plan already, and I knew I wasn't going to like it.

"We can, and we will. You're our daughter, and it's our responsibility to protect you," my mom said.

"I don't need protection from Joel! We love each other! You should be happy that I've found someone I care about!"

"You're seventeen! You have no idea what love is," my mother stated coldly.

"We know that if we ground you, you'll just sneak out to see Joel despite your mother's threats to call the police. It's impossible to keep you away from him when you two are this close to each other."

"You're right. I won't stay away from him."

"Which is why we've decided that you can't stay here," my dad finished.

I opened my mouth to argue, but then I slammed it shut as his words registered with me.

"We don't want to do this, but you've left us with no choice," my mother said sadly.

"Do what?" I whispered, terrified to hear the answer.

"Since we can't keep you and Joel apart here, we're sending you to your grandparents' farm. You will remain there until the week before school starts."

I jumped off my bed. "There is *no* way I'm staying with them!"

My grandparents lived over three hours away in a small town in West Virginia. Truthfully, small wasn't the right word to describe where they lived. I wasn't sure if their town was even on a map. My parents used to force me to go with them to visit my grandparents every summer until I'd turned twelve. After that, I'd refused to go. I wanted nothing to do with that place. It had taken a few preteen temper tantrums to get them to let me stay home, but I'd finally managed to convince them.

While I liked my grandmother, my grandpa was a complete jackass. All he cared about was working on the farm they owned. I still cringed when I thought about how he used to make me help him in the hayfield. I'd spent hours stacking square bales, so he could load them on the trucks and store them in the barn.

"You *will* go whether you want to or not. This isn't up for debate." My mother's voice had an edge to it that made me want to crawl under my bed and hide.

"Please don't make me go. I swear, I'll listen to you guys!"

"You're going, Alexandria. Pack your bags tonight because we leave in the morning," my father said.

Tears stung my eyes as I stared at both of them. *How could they do this to me?* Going to Grandpa's farm was the worst punishment they could give me. That place was my own personal hell.

"Please leave. I need to pack." My voice was calm, but my insides were churning from the anger I felt. *I will never forgive them for this. Never.*

"Alexandria, please understand that we're not doing this to hurt you or make you miserable. We only want to protect you, and this is the only option we have left." My father's voice was full of concern, but I didn't care.

He can take his concern and shove it right up his ass.

"I need to pack."

"We'll leave you alone, but if you sneak out, I'll call the police on Joel. I'm sure he's hidden everything by now, but they'll catch him eventually," my mother said.

I turned away, unable to look at them any longer. I wanted nothing to do with either one of them. The room was silent for a minute before I heard my mother sigh. I didn't blink as she walked over to me and held out her hand. "Cellphone. Now."

I pulled it out of my pocket and dropped it into her hand without a word. She turned and walked back to my dad. They left silently, leaving the door open behind them.

I stayed where I was for a few more minutes before finally walking to the door. I slammed it shut as hard as I could, knowing the sound would travel downstairs to them. I wanted them to know how much I hated them both right now. I grabbed two bags out of my closet and filled them with clothes and other things I would need while I was away. I packed everything I could, knowing I wouldn't be back for a long time.

But there was something my parents didn't realize. I wasn't packing to go to my grandparents' farm. I was running away.

CHAPTER 4

The house was silent as I slid my window open and then tossed my bags outside. While I was worried that my parents had heard my bags hitting the ground, it didn't stop me from slipping through the window and climbing down my tree anyway. Once I was safely on the ground, I grabbed my bags and started walking toward the sidewalk. When I reached the end of the yard, I breathed a sigh of relief.

"Alexandria," a voice came from the darkness.

Unfortunately for me, my relief was short-lived.

I cried out as I spun around to see my dad stepping out of the shadows surrounding our garage.

Damn it. "Dad…"

"Don't even try to explain your way out of this one." He walked over to stand in front of me. "Give me your bags."

If my mom had caught me, I would have run. But I couldn't disobey my dad. My dad understood me a lot better than my mom ever could.

"Dad, please let me go."

"You know I can't. I understand that you love this boy—or at least, you think you do—but if you go to him, all you'll do is seal his fate. Your mother will turn him in not only for selling but also for having sex with a minor."

I sucked in a breath. "She wouldn't."

"We both know that she would. Listen to me, you've got to do this. I know it's hard, but going to your grandparents' farm is the best thing that could happen to you right now."

"I seriously doubt that. I hate it there."

"I know you do, but you need to get away for a while. Look, I'll make you a deal. If you go without a fight and come back with a little more respect, I'll talk to your mom for you. If you really love this boy, spending a summer apart won't change that. If he loves you, he'll wait. You've become a different person, Lexi, and it scares me. If you keep doing the things you're doing, you will end up in jail. Something has to change."

Tears filled my eyes. I hated disappointing my dad. My mom and I had never been close, even before Joel, but my dad was always there for me when he was home. The sad part was that he worked a lot, so he couldn't be around as much as I wanted.

"Will you at least let me say good-bye to him in person?" I whispered. "You can drive me there, so you know that I won't run."

He hesitated for a second before nodding. "Get in the car."

He didn't have to tell me twice. I ran to the car and jumped in before he could change his mind. I waited impatiently as he climbed in the car and started it. He didn't turn on the headlights as we backed out of the driveway. Instead, he waited until we were a few houses down from ours. I knew he didn't want my mom to know what we were up to.

The ride to Joel's house was quiet, but it was an easy silence, unlike the earlier car ride with my mom. Dad pulled up in front of Joel's house and shut off the car.

"Five minutes, Lexi. That's it."

I nodded as I got out. "I promise, I'll hurry."

Walking up to Joel's house felt like I was coming home. This place was my escape and my safe haven. I wasn't sure how I was going to survive without it or Joel this summer. Joel had given me the key to his house long ago, so I didn't bother to knock even though it was late. Instead, I unlocked the door and slipped inside.

The house was completely silent as I walked through it to Joel's bedroom. His door was open, so I moved quietly inside. A lamp was shining brightly on the nightstand beside the bed. I could see Joel's sleeping form underneath the covers. I hated to wake him up, but I couldn't leave without saying good-bye.

I walked to the bed and sat down on the edge, my body inches away from his. When I shook him softly and said his name, he sat straight up in bed, looking around the room as he rubbed the sleep from his eyes. His mouth dropped open when he saw me sitting there next to him.

"Lexi? What are you doing here?"

"I had to see you one last time." My voice quivered.

He rubbed his eyes. "How did you get here? If your mom finds out that you snuck out, we're both screwed."

"My dad brought me."

His eyes widened. "Huh?"

I could feel tears forming in my eyes, but I smiled at him. "They're sending me away for the summer, Joel. My dad isn't an asshole like my mom, so he let me come to say good-bye."

"You're leaving? Why?"

"They know I'll run off with you, so they're keeping me away from you. I'll be back right before school starts."

"This fucking sucks. Where are they sending you?"

"My grandparents have a farm in West Virginia. They're going to take me there."

"I'm so sorry, Lexi. This is all my fault. I never should have asked you to help me with the deals."

"It's not your fault. It's mine for being so stupid. You'd taught me to always watch my surroundings when I'm dealing, and I didn't." I sighed. "This just sucks. I'm going to be in hell for three months."

"Maybe I can come visit?" he joked.

I perked up. "Maybe! Maybe if I'm good, my grandparents will let me leave the farm or something. There's a town a few miles away from where they live. We could meet there! It's about three hours from here though."

He shrugged. "I wouldn't care if it were ten. I'm going to go crazy without you around."

"I know. Me, too. We'll be okay though, won't we?"

"Of course. Why would you even ask that?" He sounded hurt.

"Because I won't be around, and I know girls try stuff with you all the time."

I knew I sounded needy and weak, but I couldn't help it. My greatest fear was leaving him alone all summer and then coming home to see that he moved on with someone else.

He cupped my face and pulled me closer. "Read my lips, woman. I'm a lot of things, but a cheater isn't one of them. I love you, Lexi. No amount of time apart will change that. I know we're young, but it doesn't matter to me. You're mine, and I intend to keep it that way for as long as you want me. I keep waiting for the day when you'll wake up and realize that you're so much better than me."

I shoved him down on the bed and climbed on top of him. "Shut up. I'm *not* better than you. You're fucking perfect, Joel. Perfect."

My lips met his, and I forgot everything. I forgot that I had less than five minutes left with him. I forgot that I would be leaving for my own personal hell in only a few short hours. I forgot to breathe. The one thing that brought me back to the real world was the sound of my dad blowing the car horn outside.

I pulled away, gasping for breath. "I have to go."

He pulled my face back to his and kissed me softly. "I'll be here, waiting for you. I love you."

"I love you, too." I didn't even try to hold back my tears as I stood and walked away from him.

I barely remembered the walk back to the car and then the ride back to the house. The next thing I knew, I was lying in my bed again.

This hurts so damn bad. I had no idea how I was going to survive the next few months.

We left early the next morning. My dad was driving me down even though I was staying with my mom's parents. I thought Dad had volunteered to do it, so my mom and I wouldn't be forced to spend three hours in a car together.

I'd refused to speak to her this morning before we left. She'd tried to hug me, but I'd shoved her away and then made my way out the door. I just knew she had been the one who came up with this idea.

Well, fuck her. She won't win. I won't let her destroy me.

My dad tried to talk to me as he drove, but I wasn't up for conversation. After a while, he got tired of my one-word answers, and he gave up. He turned on the radio and found a country music station. I pretended to vomit, causing him to grin. He knew I hated country music. I'd rather rip out my eardrums than listen to it.

I reached into my purse and pulled out my iPod. After putting my earbuds in and turning my music up enough to drown out the car radio, I stuck my tongue out at him. I could see him chuckling at me. I loved when I could make my dad laugh. It seemed like I didn't do it enough anymore.

I pulled my earbuds out and reached over to turn off the radio. "Truce?" I asked.

He nodded. "Only if you actually talk. If you don't, I'll take your headphones away and turn the radio back on."

"Ugh, fine. What do you want to talk about?"

"I don't know. What do normal teenage girls talk to their dads about?"

"Are you saying I'm not a normal teenager?" I asked, pretending to be hurt.

"We both know you're far from normal."

I laughed. He had a point.

"Okay, I guess that's true."

"So…" He struggled to think of something to say. "Tell me about school. I know the school year is over, but tell me about last year."

I shrugged. "There's not much to tell. I go to school, sleep in class, eat lunch, and come home."

"Lexi, come on, tell me about it. It's been a while since we talked. What was your favorite class?"

"Um…art. I took two different art classes, so I could spend more time in the art room. One class focused on photography, and the other focused on drawing and actual art. Mrs. Jones really liked my photography. She even submitted some of my photos for the yearbook class to use."

"That's great! You should get a camera and start taking classes outside of school."

"That might be fun. I don't know."

"When you come home, I'll have a camera waiting on you"— he glanced over at me—"as long as your mother and I don't get any complaints about your behavior or attitude over the summer."

"Did you just bribe me to be good?" I teased.

"Yep. Nothing is below me when it comes to parenting."

I couldn't help but laugh at my dad. He was so easygoing. If it were my mom in the car with me, we both would have lost our voices from screaming by now. She'd be ranting and raving about how ashamed and disappointed she was in me. All she did was complain about how hard I was making her life.

My dad and I spent the rest of the drive talking. We didn't mention Joel or the reason we were in the car though. Instead, we talked about everything else that we could think of. Despite the fact that the miles between Joel and me were growing, I wasn't freaking out at the moment. Dad always had that effect on me. Even when I was in the worst mood imaginable, he would make me happy. I'd missed us talking like this.

We stopped in New Martinsville, the town I'd mentioned to Joel, to fill up on gas and grab something to eat. The town wasn't huge, but it did have a movie theater and shopping plazas. It was tiny compared to what I was used to, but I was pretty sure that it was the biggest town around here.

When we hit Route 7, my stomach dropped. We were almost to my grandparents' farm. My dad noticed my silence as we drove closer and closer to the farm. I was going to hate this place. I was a city girl, not some chick who liked living on a farm and seeing cows daily.

It had been a while since I was here, but the landmarks were vaguely familiar. I'd forgotten just how winding West Virginia roads were. I felt sick by the time we passed the one store on this entire road, Morris Variety Center. My stomach dropped when I realized the side road leading to my grandparents' farm was only a minute or two away from there.

I clenched my teeth to keep from cursing when we turned up the gravel road. *God, I hate this place.* I continued to stare out the window as we made our way slowly up the bumpy road.

The road was narrow and completely surrounded by trees on both sides. About a mile in, the trees cleared and opened up into one huge meadow. I knew my grandparents had cleared this land years ago to make room for their cattle and horses. My grandpa owned over three hundred acres of land, and he used all of it.

I finally caught sight of the house and the two barns as we continued up the road. The main barn was located about a mile away from the house while a smaller one sat only a few feet away. If I remembered correctly, my grandpa used the large barn to store hay for the winter. It also had a lower level that he kept open for when one of the animals got sick. The smaller barn contained grains and other things for the smaller animals—like chickens, ducks, goats, and pigs—that he kept around the house so that he could keep an eye on them. Coyotes and raccoons were bad around here.

I'm entering the world's largest petting zoo.

We rolled to a stop outside their house. I stared at it through the windshield, unable to make myself get out of the car.

"Lexi?" my dad asked.

I glanced over at him. "What?"

"I have something for you. It won't do any good out here since there's no service, but I thought you might want it. I know you keep photos on it." My dad pulled my phone out of his shirt pocket and handed it to me.

I pushed the button on it to see that he had been right. There was absolutely no service here, which meant there was no way to contact Joel. Still, I had a small piece of him with me now. My phone had hundreds of photos of us together. It would have to do—for now.

"Thank you. This means a lot."

"You're welcome, Lexi. Now, come on. Let's go see your grandparents."

I sighed in defeat as I opened the car door and stepped out. Gravel crunched under our feet as we walked to the trunk of the car and pulled out my bags. My dad carried the heavier one and left me with the lighter one as we made our way up to the porch.

My grandpa had built this house himself back when he and my grandma first got married. Even though I hated this place, I had to admit that the house was beautiful. It was a very large two-story log cabin. They had updated it some over the years, but it still looked almost the same as some of the pictures I'd seen in Grandma's photo album when I was little. I just thanked my lucky stars that it had indoor plumbing.

My dad stepped up onto the porch and knocked on the door. My grandma appeared seconds later, glancing through the blinds covering the door window. I could see the huge grin on her face just before she opened the door.

"Harold! Alexandria! It's so good to see you!" My grandmother hugged my father and then turned to me.

Her eyes widened a bit as she took in my appearance, but a second later, the shock was gone, and she was hugging me. I tried not to stiffen at the physical contact, but it was hard. I wasn't a hugger. Truthfully, I wasn't big on physical contact at all—with the exception of Joel.

My grandma looked exactly the same as how I remembered her. She'd been dyeing her hair a light brown for as long as I could remember. I could see a little gray poking through, but it wasn't enough to notice unless someone was really looking. Her eyes were a pale blue that looked kind. While she wasn't fat, she wasn't skinny either. She was right between the two. Her face had always looked kind, and it still did. She was one of those people who could make others love her just by smiling at them.

"Lily, it's nice to see you," my father said as my grandma released me.

I'd always loved my grandmother's name. When I was little, I had begged my mother to change my name to Lily. I always hated Alexandria. My dad called me Lexi, and I loved it, but my mom refused to go along with it. I thought she did it just to spite me. Then, when I'd first met Joel, he'd decided that Alexandria was too long, and like my dad, he'd started calling me Lexi. Unfortunately, the only people who called me Lexi were my dad, Joel, and a few of his close friends. To everyone else, I was still Alexandria.

"It's good to see both of you. Come on in." My grandmother motioned for us to follow her through the front door.

When I stepped inside, I couldn't help but smile. The house was exactly the same as it had been the last time I was here. The walls were made of logs, just like the outside. The floors were hardwood. A huge rug was spread out over most of the entryway. The walls were covered in pictures of my grandparents together, the farm, and my mom at different stages in her life. I glanced at one of her when she was my age, and I couldn't believe how alike we were. If my hair were still blonde, we could have been twins.

My father set my bag down by the door and followed my grandmother into the kitchen. I threw mine on top of it and trailed behind them. As soon as we walked through the doorway, I was hit with the smell of food. My stomach rumbled hungrily even though we'd eaten not even an hour before. My grandmother was a miracle worker when it came to the kitchen. I couldn't think of one thing she'd made that I hadn't inhaled.

"Something smells good," I said as I sat down beside my dad at the kitchen table.

"I made chicken and dumplings for lunch. Your mom called me last night to tell me that you would be here, and I remembered this was your favorite food when you were little. I thought I'd make it to surprise you." My grandmother smiled at me.

I was touched and surprised by her kindness even though I shouldn't have been. My grandmother was always kind to me, and I loved her. There had been more than one occasion when I felt guilty for not coming to visit her, but I'd pushed it aside. I'd missed her, but I hadn't been willing to deal with my grandfather.

"Thanks, Gram."

She beamed. "You're welcome. And I'm glad you haven't forgotten your nickname for me. It's been so long since I've seen you."

I'd started calling her Gram when I was younger, and she loved it, so it'd stuck.

"I know," I said, feeling guilty.

"Don't look so embarrassed. You're here now."

But not because I want to be. I wanted to say it out loud, but I didn't want to hurt her feelings. Instead, I smiled. "I know."

"Where's Caleb?" my father asked.

I winced at the mention of my grandfather.

"He's out with our two helpers right now. The weather has been nice these last few days, so he's trying to get the northern hayfield cut and baled."

My father seemed surprised. "He has someone helping him now?"

"Yes, he hired Kent and his son to help. Caleb even built them a small house about half a mile away from here. They've been helping for about a year now."

"Kent?"

There was an edge to my father's voice that made me look up at him. My dad was rarely bothered by anything, but he seemed annoyed at the mention of Kent. I had no idea who the man was.

Gram looked slightly uneasy. "Yes, Kent."

An awkward silence filled the room after that. I glanced back and forth between Gram and my dad, but both looked unsure of what to say next. We were saved when we heard the front door open and shut. A few seconds later, I could hear male voices coming toward us.

Gram stood and walked to the doorway. "Caleb, Harold and Alexandria made it."

"I figured as much when I saw the car outside."

My stomach dropped when I heard my grandfather's voice. It had been so long since the last time I saw him, but I was sure he would still be an asshole.

He appeared in the doorway just seconds later, followed by two men. I didn't even glance at the others as he caught me in his stare. He had aged since I last saw him. His hair was now completely gray, and more lines were running across his face, but his hazel eyes that matched mine and my mother's still looked as sharp as ever.

It was obvious that he had just come from the hayfield. His clothes were drenched in sweat, and I could see pieces of hay stuck to him. I finally pulled my eyes away from him to look at the two other men. I paid little attention to their faces, but I noticed their clothes looked the same as his – drenched and covered with hay.

"It's nice to see you, Caleb," my dad said politely.

I wanted to roll my eyes at just how polite he was. My grandfather had never been a fan of my dad's, yet Dad was always nice to him. If it were me, I would have told my grandfather to fuck off after all these years.

"Likewise," my grandfather said before he turned his attention back to me. "What the hell did you do to yourself?"

I held his gaze, unwilling to lose this staring competition we had going on. "I have no idea what you're talking about."

"Like hell you don't! Look at you—your face is covered in metal, and your hair is dyed!"

I rolled my eyes. I should have known he'd start on me as soon as he saw me. It was just how he was.

"I also have a tattoo. Want to see?" I held up my arm to show him. I couldn't help but grin as I saw anger filling his eyes.

"Lexi, enough," my father said sharply.

"You and Natasha let her do this to herself? What is wrong with you?" my grandfather asked.

"Mom and Dad didn't *let* me do anything," I spit out. I wouldn't let my grandfather start bashing my dad.

"But they certainly didn't stop you."

"Stop it! Both of you!" My grandmother's raised voice had me snapping my head over to look at her. She never yelled—ever. "Caleb, stop picking on Alexandria, and I mean it. You already ran her off once, and I won't have you do it again."

My grandfather's eyes softened as he looked at Gram. I'd forgotten just how much control she had over him. She was the only one who could reel him in when he started yelling.

"Sorry, Lily, but I don't think it's okay to have my granddaughter walking around with metal in her face."

"It doesn't matter what you think, Caleb." Gram scanned the room. "Now, let's all sit down and eat before the food gets cold."

My grandfather nodded and walked to the table. I was relieved when he sat down at the head of the table. It was as far away from me as possible.

The two men took seats across from my dad and me. I finally had the chance to look at both of them. It was obvious that they were father and son. The older of the two—Kent, I assumed—had brown hair and brown eyes. He looked about the same age as my parents, but years in the sun had taken its toll on him. His skin was deeply tanned and looked rough and worn.

His son was sitting directly across from me. He looked around my age or maybe a year or two older. He was just a younger and less weathered version of his father. His eyes were a chocolate brown, and his dark brown hair was mostly hidden by a ball cap, but some of it was sticking out from under his hat. It was the exact same color as his father's. He was also tanned from working in the sun a lot. His face had a five o'clock shadow, but other than that, it was smooth and unblemished. His nose was thin but not too thin, and his lips were full. It was impossible not to notice how attractive he was.

He glanced up and caught me staring at him. He stared right back, his eyes taking in every part of my face. I expected him to zone in on my piercings, but he didn't. Instead, he didn't even seem to be bothered by them, unlike my grandfather.

41

My grandma set a plate of food in front of him, drawing his attention away from me. "Here you go, Landon."

"Thank you, ma'am," Landon said as he smiled at her, revealing a set of perfect white teeth.

I couldn't help but notice that he had a slight twang to his voice, stronger than my grandma's.

My grandma smacked the back of his head. "I told you to call me Lily. And take off that hat at the dinner table."

Landon grinned as he pulled off his hat and hung it on the back of his chair. His hair was just shaggy enough that it curled up at the ends. I had to admit that it was a good look for him. I froze as I realized that I had been checking this guy out.

What the hell is wrong with me? I shouldn't even glance at guys, let alone stare at them.

I shook my head as Gram set my plate down in front of me.

"Here you go, Alexandria."

"Thanks." I stared down at my plate, determined not to look at Landon again.

My grandma made sure everyone had a plate before she sat down next to me, opposite my grandfather. "Who wants to say thanks?"

Shit. I'd forgotten that my grandparents said a prayer before each meal.

I could only imagine what my grandfather would do when he figured out that I didn't believe in God. He'd probably make me sleep outside on the ground.

"I will," Landon said.

I glanced up to see him looking at my grandma.

"Thank you, Landon. All right, everyone, bow your heads."

I hesitated for a split second before lowering mine. I hated doing it, but I didn't want to get in another fight with my grandpa. I'd wait until later to have that particular battle. Maybe we could strangle each other over dinner.

Landon said grace, and then we all started eating. My grandfather talked to Kent and Kent alone, ignoring the rest of us. That was fine by me. The less I had to talk to my grandfather, the better.

I glanced over at my dad to see him staring at Kent like he wanted to punch him. I raised my eyebrows but said nothing. That wasn't like my dad at all. Before my dad left, I would have to ask him who Kent was.

I turned my attention away from Dad, only to look at Landon. I was surprised to see him staring at me again. I glared at him before dropping my gaze back down to my food. I didn't want him to stare at me. I had no idea why, but I just knew that I didn't.

"Did y'all have a safe trip down?" my grandmother asked me.

"Yeah, it was pretty boring."

"Where are you from?"

I glanced up to see Landon looking at me.

"Columbiana, Ohio. It's just under three hours away from here once you make a pit stop or two."

He nodded. "I think I've heard of it before. Is it a small town, like around here?"

I snorted. "This place isn't big enough to be classified as a town. Columbiana isn't huge, but it's definitely not Bumfuck, Egypt, like this place."

"Lexi!" my dad scolded.

I shrugged. "What? It's the truth."

"Alexandria, please don't curse. It isn't very ladylike," Gram said.

I glanced over to see her frowning. "Sorry, Gram."

"It's apparent that we'll have to teach you some manners while you're staying with us," my grandfather said.

I didn't even glance at him. If I did, I knew we'd start fighting again. He was going to have to figure out that I wasn't the same little kid as before. He couldn't push me around and make me do what he told me anymore. He could kiss my ass.

No one said another word until dinner was finished. Gram collected our plates and put them in the sink to soak until she had a chance to wash them. I started to get up, but my grandpa stopped me.

"Where do you think you're going?" he asked.

"Um…up to my room."

My grandparents' house was big enough that I'd had my own room when I would come to visit. It had been my favorite part of this house—probably because my grandpa never visited me there.

"No, you're not. We have some things to discuss before your father leaves. Sit back down."

I dropped back onto my chair and turned to look at him. "Fine. I'm sitting. What do you want to talk about?"

"Your mother called and talked to Lily and me last night. She told us everything that has been going on with you, including the reason you're staying with us this summer."

"And?"

"I'm going to lay down the law while your father is here, so there is no confusion about what is expected from you. While you're here, you will help with the chores. I've made you a list that you are to follow daily. If everything is done properly, you will be allowed free time on the weekends. If not, you will have extra chores added to the list."

"And what are my chores?" I asked, already dreading the answer.

"Landon has the list, and he'll show you how to do everything tomorrow. The list isn't that hard to follow, but on top of that, you will be helping Landon with whatever he needs. His jobs vary day to day, so be prepared for whatever he needs you to do."

I glanced up at Landon to see him watching me closely. "I don't need a babysitter."

"And you're not getting one. Landon is your boss. If you don't listen to him, he will let me know."

I glanced over at my grandfather when he paused.

"If you won't listen to Landon, then you can start helping *me* every day. I think you'll prefer dealing with Landon over me."

I'd prefer to be stomped to death by a cow rather than spend the day stuck with my grandpa, but I didn't think I should tell him that.

"If you keep up with your daily chores and help us, you will have the weekends and maybe even some evenings free. If you refuse to listen to us, we will call your mother."

"What's she going to do?" I asked sarcastically. *Yell at me through the phone? Whoop-de-do.*

"She'll call the police on that piece-of-shit boyfriend of yours."

The color drained from my face. She really had told them everything.

"Since I doubt you want him to be locked up for drugs and statutory rape, I'm sure you'll find a way to push that attitude of yours to the side and do what you're told."

"I…you…" I started, but I couldn't form a sentence. *How dare he talk about my personal life while two strangers are sitting at the table with us.*

"You're dismissed. Spend the rest of the day unpacking. Lily will have dinner ready at six, so we expect you down here for that. I suggest you go to bed early because you're expected to be up at six to help Landon. Meet him outside the barn."

It was good to know that my grandfather was still an asshole.

CHAPTER 5

I refused to look at anyone as I stood and walked away from the table. *Fuck them all.* I was sure Kent and Landon were sitting there, judging me, now that my grandfather had aired all my dirty laundry right in front of them, but I didn't care. I didn't give a damn about what they thought of me.

I heard footsteps behind me, and then I felt a hand on my shoulder. I glanced back to see that it was my father.

"Want me to help you carry your bags up to your room?" he asked.

I nodded as I grabbed one bag and left the other for him. We climbed the stairs together and then walked down the hallway to my door. When I swung it open, I was surprised to see that it had been cleaned recently. I walked to the bed and set my bag down on it. The sheets and bedspread smelled fresh, like Gram had just washed them. She probably had since mom had called her last night.

"I know this is hard, Lexi, but you just have to hang in there," my father said.

"I can't stand him."

He sighed. "I know. I…I have a hard time with him, too."

"Who is Kent?"

"What do you mean?"

I could tell that he was trying to act casual.

"Don't play dumb, Dad. I saw you glaring at him."

"I have no idea what you're talking about. Listen, I need to head back. I have a flight out to California first thing in the morning."

I nodded even though he was avoiding my question. "Okay, I'll see you later."

He pulled me into his arms and hugged me tight. "I love you, Lexi. Just hang in there, and it'll be over soon."

After that, he was gone, leaving the door open. I stared at the doorway for several minutes before I decided that I needed to unpack.

I dumped my smaller duffel bag out and started sorting through the contents. I'd used this bag to pack my makeup in along with my CD collection, extra headphones, and other small items I used all the time. I'd even brought a few small posters of bands that I loved—Three Days Grace, Avenged Sevenfold, The Amity Affliction, and Slipknot. I covered the white wallpaper with my posters, trying to make the room feel more like home.

After I was satisfied with my work, I began pulling my clothes out of the bigger bag. I'd packed with the intention of running away, so almost half my wardrobe was stuffed inside. I started sorting it into piles when someone knocked on my door. I turned to see Landon standing there.

"What do you want?" I asked.

"I just thought I'd tell you to wear jeans and a light shirt tomorrow. We're going to be out in the sun for most of the day. I doubt if you have any mud boots, but if you do, wear them."

"I don't have boots." I did but not mud boots. I almost smiled as I thought about walking out in knee-high hooker boots to meet Landon tomorrow morning. The look of shock on his face would be priceless.

"I have to run to New Martinsville tonight. I can get you a pair if you want. You're going to need them."

I hesitated. I had no idea why this guy was being nice to me, but I didn't like it. People weren't nice just because. They always wanted something in return.

"Why are you being nice to me?"

He seemed surprised by my question. "I don't know. Because I can? No one's ever asked me that before."

"People aren't nice just because they can be."

He took off his hat and ran a hand through his hair. "Look, I don't know much about Columbiana, but out here in Bumfuck, Egypt, we're nice just because we want to be. It's how you're supposed to be."

I grinned. "You're not supposed to curse. It isn't very ladylike."

He snorted. "Guess it's a good thing I'm not a lady."

I studied him as I wondered if he was being nice just so he could win my trust, hoping he could find something about me to report back to my grandpa. Landon didn't look like a two-faced snake though. He looked sincere.

"All right, fine. You can get me mud boots."

"What size do you wear?"

"Seven."

He smiled. "Okay, I'll pick up a pair. I'll see you later."

He turned to leave, but I called out, "Landon?"

He glanced back. "Yeah?"

"Get me a pair with something girlie on them."

He looked at me like I'd lost my mind, but he nodded. "Um…sure."

He disappeared through the door and went back down the hall. I laughed as I pictured him in a department store, buying me yellow rubber-duck boots. I wanted to make him squirm.

The rest of the day and evening went by quickly.

Thankfully, dinner was uneventful. Landon and his dad hadn't shown up, and I had been kind of happy about that since I knew they were aware of my situation with Joel. I didn't need others judging me without knowing the whole story. My grandfather had barely looked at me, let alone spoken to me. While my grandma had seemed annoyed, I had been glad. The only time my grandfather had ever spoken to me was when he yelled at me, so I'd preferred the silence.

When dinner was finished, I showered and went to my room for the night. I made sure to set my alarm clock, so I would be up on time. All I needed was for my grandpa to come in here, yelling at me, that early in the morning.

My grandparents didn't have Internet, and there was no cell service out here, so I literally had nothing to do. I pulled my iPod out of my purse and started listening to Apocalyptica as I stared at the ceiling.

God, I'm bored. How does my grandma survive, staying in this house day after day?

49

I'd been here for only a few hours, and it was already driving me nuts. *This staying-home shit is for the birds*. I wanted to go out and have fun with Joel, like I'd always done at night.

My heart clenched as my thoughts turned to Joel. I wondered what he was doing right now. I missed him so damn much. I had no idea how I was going to deal with not being able to talk to him all summer. My only hope was that my grandparents would let me leave the farm eventually. Surely, there would be service in New Martinsville.

I picked my phone up off the nightstand and started flipping through the pictures in it. I smiled and sent out a silent thanks to my dad for letting me have my phone back. It was as close to Joel as I could get right now. I sighed as a picture of us in bed together popped up on my screen. We'd just woken up, and both of us looked like shit, but I loved it. That morning, I'd grabbed my phone off his nightstand and started snapping pictures of us together just for the hell of it. I wanted to cry over them now. It would be months before he touched me again like he had hours before that photo was taken.

I laid my phone back on the nightstand and plugged it in before turning off the lights. The last thing I remembered before I fell asleep was a single tear trickling down my cheek.

I nearly cried when I heard my alarm clock going off the next morning. I reached over and slammed my hand down on top of it, trying to make it shut up. I finally succeeded and relaxed back into bed. It seemed like I'd just closed my eyes, and I wasn't ready to get up just yet. Just as I began to drift off again, the alarm clock started back up. I groaned as I threw the covers off and stood. I shut the alarm clock off by hitting the switch instead of throwing it against the wall like I wanted to.

I shuffled to the dresser and pulled out a pair of jeans and a spaghetti-strap shirt. I peeled off my shorts and pajama top and then dressed for the day. I found a pair of socks and pulled them on, too, before walking to the bathroom.

I glanced in the mirror, and noticed that my hair looked like a tornado had gone through it. I pulled a brush through it until I finally got all the tangles out. Then, I grabbed a hair tie and pulled my hair into a messy bun on top of my head. I brushed my teeth and put on some deodorant before going downstairs. I didn't see the point of makeup when I was only going to see cows today.

I was surprised to see a pair of pink rubber boots sitting by the front door. Landon had really stuck to his word and picked them up for me.

I continued down the hall to the kitchen. My grandma was in front of the stove, frying bacon and eggs.

"That smells good," I said as I sat down at the table.

"I'm glad because it's for you." She reached for a plate and piled the food onto it. "Eat all of it, so you don't get hungry before lunchtime."

My eyes widened at the amount of food she put in front of me. "I can't eat all of this, Gram. I'll explode."

She laughed. "Eat what you can. You're too skinny. I'm going to make it my personal goal to make sure you gain a few pounds over the summer."

"I am not too skinny," I grumbled.

"What size jeans do you wear?" she asked.

"Um…threes. Why?"

She laughed. "Because you're too skinny. I'm going to make you go up at least a size before you go home."

She seemed so determined to make me gain weight that I laughed instead of getting pissed.

"Whatever you say, Gram."

I didn't even put a dent in the food she had given me. I handed a still full plate back to her and waved as I left. I walked to the front door and pulled on my pink boots before heading outside. It was still dark out, but I could see the sun trying to peek out from behind one of the hills that West Virginia was so famous for.

Landon was waiting for me by the barn doors as I approached.

He smiled when he saw me. "Good morning."

"What's so good about it?" I asked.

He laughed at my sour response. "Well, you're alive, aren't you? I consider that a good thing."

"You're weird," I stated. This guy was way too chipper in the mornings for my liking.

"And you're not a morning person. I can tell already."

"What clued you in?"

He opened his mouth, but then he clamped it shut before he could speak. Instead, he motioned for me to follow him inside the barn. We walked to one of the support beams where a chalkboard was hanging.

"These are the daily chores. Normally, my dad, your grandpa, and I all do them. We check off what we did, so someone else doesn't try to do it again. Since you're here now, I've been instructed to let you do most of them. You'll also have stuff to do that isn't on here, but those things vary from day to day."

I glanced down the list and groaned. I hated this day already. The list was several lines long, and I wanted to beat my head against the beam as I read the first few tasks.

Feed the chickens.
Water the chickens.
Gather the eggs—morning and evening.
Feed the rabbits.
Water the rabbits.
Feed the dogs.
Water the dogs.
Feed the hogs.
Water the hogs.
Let the goats out in the morning and put them back in at night.
Mow the yard.
Check the water spring to make sure it's flowing.

The list seemed to go on and on forever.

"I already gathered the eggs and let the goats out. I told Caleb that I would handle the hogs because most of them are bigger than you. Since you're so tiny, I didn't want you to get hurt when you went into the pen with them."

I glanced up at him, surprised yet again by his kindness. "Thank you."

He looked away from me. "No problem. We water everything twice a day since it's so hot in the summer. You'll water them once after lunch and then again before you head in for the night. You feed the animals when you water the second time. Just make sure that you fill their feeders completely or they'll run out by the next day. The goats are really tame, so they should go right into the pen for you at night. I'll help you though, just to make sure they listen."

"Okay, what do I have to do right now? Or am I free until before lunch?"

Landon laughed. "You're never free around here. There is always something to do. I feel kind of bad for you today though."

"Why is that?"

"Because today is shit day."

I was afraid to even ask, but I knew I had to. "What's shit day?"

"It's the day I clean all the mangers and the chicken coop out."

"Ugh. Fuck me." My day had just turned to shit—literally.

CHAPTER 6

Landon led me outside to where a four-wheeler was parked. "Come on, we'll start with the big barn. It's the easiest."

I watched as he climbed onto the four-wheeler. It had been years since I was on one, and they'd always scared me. "Go ahead. I'll just walk."

"It's almost a mile away. No offense, but you'll take forever to get there. Just get on."

"I don't want to."

He raised an eyebrow. "Why?"

I hated admitting my weaknesses to people, especially people I didn't know, but I couldn't think of another excuse as to why I didn't want to get on the four-wheeler with him.

"Look, I'm afraid of four-wheelers, okay?"

He looked at me like I'd lost my mind. "Say that again?"

"You heard me. I'm afraid of four-wheelers."

"That's what I thought you said."

We stared at each other for a few seconds before I finally broke the silence. "Why are you staring at me like that?"

"Because I'm not sure what to say. You look like a badass, but you're afraid of a four-wheeler?"

"I don't see how what I look like has to do with anything. I've been on one only a few times before with my dad, and he always went slow because he knew I was afraid."

"I didn't mean it that way. I'm sorry if I offended you. I promise to go slow on it. Now, will you please get on, so we can get the day started? I have a bunch of stuff to do today."

I crept closer to him and the four-wheeler. "You swear that you won't drive like a psycho?"

"I swear."

"Fine, but I swear, I'll stab you with something if you do." I stepped up to it and slowly climbed on. I felt awkward as I grabbed his shoulders to keep my balance.

Once I was situated, he turned back to look at me. "Ready?"

I nodded. "Yeah, just go slow."

He turned the key and pressed the button to start it. After turning on the headlights, he used the foot shifter to put it in gear. I kept my body rigid and placed my hands on my knees as he slowly pushed the gas. I had no idea why people thought these things were cool. Sure, they were safer than a motorcycle, but we weren't driving a motorcycle on uneven West Virginia hills. When I was little, my grandpa had told me too many stories about kids wrecking and dying around here. He'd scarred me for life.

Landon cut into one of the fields and started down a small hill. He hit a bump, causing the four-wheeler to tilt to one side. I squealed and threw my arms around his stomach, terrified that we were going to flip. I buried my head against his back, and then I felt us come to a stop.

"You okay?" he asked over the sound of the engine.

"Yeah. I thought we were going to wreck."

He laughed. "You'd better get used to the movement because there are holes and rocks everywhere. I promise that we won't wreck though, okay?"

I lifted my head from his back and peeked up at him. I knew I was being stupid, but I couldn't help it. I really was *that* afraid.

"Okay," I whispered. "Is it okay if I hold on to you while we're moving?"

"That's fine. Just don't squeeze me to death."

"Whoops. Sorry." I relaxed my arms just a bit. I didn't want to cut off his air supply, but I didn't want to fall off either if we hit another bump.

Landon pushed the gas again and continued down the hill. I felt stupid for clinging to him, but I felt safer this way. When he reached the bottom of the hill, he kicked it up into second gear and then third. By the time we were halfway to the barn, he had it in fifth. I almost said something, but he seemed to know what he was doing.

I couldn't help but notice how hard his stomach was. Joel worked out, but his stomach wasn't as hard as Landon's. It was obvious that Landon worked on the farm quite a lot. I felt guilty for even noticing, but it wasn't my fault. It was kind of hard *not* to notice when my hands were holding on to his abs for dear life.

Landon pulled up to the big barn and shut off the four-wheeler. I breathed a sigh of relief as I released him and scooted back. I hadn't realized how tight I was pushed against him.

"See? That wasn't so bad."

"Whatever you say," I mumbled.

Landon climbed off and then helped me throw my leg over the seat. I cursed my short legs as I fought to climb off. As soon as my feet hit the ground, Landon started walking into the barn. I followed him down to the lower level where the horse stalls, the pen, and the sick animals were.

I groaned when I looked around. This place was a lot bigger than I remembered, and we had to clean all of it.

"This sucks," I grumbled.

"It could be worse. You *could* be shoveling it in the wintertime when Caleb keeps the work horses in here constantly."

He had a point.

"Fair enough. Tell me what I need to do, so I can get this over with."

He walked to the far wall and grabbed two shovels. After handing me one, he pointed to the stall farthest from the door that led out to the field. "Start with that one, and work your way to the door. I'm going to get the tractor with the loader on it. Just dump the crap in the loader bucket, so I can take it out of here."

"What do you do with it?"

"We pile it up and use it for fertilizer when we plant the gardens."

"That's disgusting! I'm so not eating any vegetables Gram makes." I didn't even want to think about eating food that had been planted in poop.

"What do you think fertilizer is? At least ours doesn't have any chemicals in it."

He turned and walked away, leaving me to realize that I'd been eating poop-flavored food my entire life.

"I'm glad I'm not a vegan," I mumbled as I walked to the back stall.

I scooped a shovelful of "fertilizer" and walked to the door just as Landon brought the tractor around. The sun was above the hills by now, and I could see that the tractor was bright orange with the name Kubota written across the side.

He parked, so the loader was right beside the door. I dumped my shovel's contents into the loader bucket and walked back to my stall. Landon joined me and started working on the stall next to me.

The difference between him and Joel was almost comical. I was used to Joel's baggy jeans, Converse shoes, and band T-shirts, and Landon seemed to like tighter jeans and plain shirts. His mud boots made me giggle a little bit, but I stopped when I remembered that I was wearing them, too. At least mine were cute though.

Neither of us spoke for a while as we worked. I wasn't good with quiet. It drove me completely nuts.

"So, what do you do for fun around here?" I asked as I started on a new stall.

"Fun?"

"Yeah, you know, that thing you do that doesn't involve work"—I glanced at my shovel—"or playing in poop."

"I know what fun is, genius. I work here a lot, so I don't really go out like I used to. When I do, I usually go riding on the four-wheeler or muddin' in my truck."

"Muddin'?" I asked.

"You really are from the city, aren't you?"

I gave him a dirty look. "You're hilarious."

He grinned. "I know I am. Muddin' is when you take your truck or four-wheeler and find mud holes to go through—the deeper, the better."

"That doesn't sound fun at all."

"It is when you actually do it. If you're ever allowed off the farm, I'll take you sometime."

I snorted. "Yeah, like that will happen."

"Your grandpa isn't that bad of a guy once you're around him for a while. He just has high expectations for people."

"He's an asshole. Always has been, always will be. He's not happy unless he's making someone miserable."

"I disagree. I heard what he told you yesterday. If you do what you're supposed to, he'll let you have free time."

"My grandfather shouldn't have talked about why I am here or what the rules are with you and your dad in the room. It's personal."

Landon shrugged. "Hey, I don't judge. It sounds like you screwed up. So what? Everyone screws up occasionally."

"Yeah, but not everyone gets caught dealing drugs."

Landon's eyes widened a bit. "That sucks. Did you end up in jail?"

I shook my head. "No, my mom was the one who caught me. That's why I'm here. Either I come play farm girl for a summer, or she's going to turn Joel and me in for drugs."

"I'm assuming Joel is the boyfriend your grandpa mentioned last night?"

"Yeah."

I didn't comment any further than that. I was sure he was thinking about the statutory rape comment my grandpa had also mentioned.

"So, you're still with the guy?" he asked.

I glanced up to see him watching me. "Yeah, I am."

He nodded as he turned back to the stall. "I see."

"I thought you weren't going to judge me."

"I'm not. I was just curious if you were still with him."

I almost laughed as I realized what he was doing. "Is that your subtle way of asking if I have a boyfriend?"

Landon didn't look up as he said, "Nah, I was just being nosy."

I studied him as he continued to clean another stall. He really was attractive, but he was definitely not my type even if I wasn't with Joel.

"I'm going to give you a friendly piece of advice," I said.

"And what's that?"

"Don't get attached to me, Landon. I'm fucked-up, but I'm okay with that. I embrace it. I fight, I drink, and I smoke weed. I like heavy metal music and piercings. I'm the total opposite of you."

He finally stopped shoveling and turned to face me. "You're not the total opposite of me."

"How so?"

He grinned. "I drink, too."

I rolled my eyes as he turned away.

"My bad. We're soul mates."

"Nah, but don't worry, I wasn't hitting on you. Your virtue is safe with me."

I snorted. "I lost that long ago."

59

Landon burst out laughing but made no comment. He really didn't seem that bad, but I wasn't about to let my guard down around him. I was here to put my time in and then go home. After this summer, I would never see Landon again.

We finished cleaning the barn without any further conversation. Once we were done, I waited on the four-wheeler while he drove the tractor to wherever he needed to dump the fertilizer. It was hot out today, and I felt like I was on fire by the time he brought the tractor back.

"Took you long enough. I'm burning up," I said when he walked over to me.

"Sorry, I was trying to hurry." He glanced down at me. "You might want to change your shirt when we get back to the house."

"Why?"

"Because you're lily white, and your shoulders are already turning red."

I glanced down to see that he was right. "Damn it. I don't want to wear another shirt. I'm hot enough as it is. I'll just put some sunblock on."

"I hope you have something strong. If not, you're going to be hurting by tomorrow."

I scooted back as he climbed onto the four-wheeler with me. As soon as he started it up, I wrapped my arms around him. I felt a little better now that the sun was up, and I could see where we were going, but I was still nervous.

Landon and I were both sweaty from working in the barn all morning, but I didn't mind. He actually smelled kind of good when he was sweaty—not that I noticed or anything. Instead of stopping at the main barn like I'd expected, he pulled the four-wheeler into the same spot where my dad had parked his car yesterday.

"What are we doing?" I asked.

"It's time for lunch, and you need to put on sunblock."

"Oh, duh." I hadn't even realized what time it was, but now that he'd mentioned food, my stomach started growling.

He helped me climb off the four-wheeler, and then he walked beside me to the house. I was shocked when he held open the door, but he didn't seem to notice. I wasn't used to people being polite.

"I'm going to run up to my room to shower and put on sunscreen," I said as I pulled off my boots.

"Make it quick. We need to get the chicken coop done, too."

I gave him a one-fingered salute before heading up to my room. I grabbed another spaghetti-strap shirt and jeans before hurrying to the bathroom. I knew it was stupid to shower when I would get all gross and sweaty again, but I didn't care. I wasn't used to smelling bad. Hell, I wasn't used to sweating. I took the fastest shower on record and rubbed sunscreen on my shoulders and arms before dressing. Hopefully, it would keep me from burning.

By the time I made it back downstairs, Landon had finished his lunch, and he was leaning against the sink, talking to Gram. They both shut up when they saw me coming through the door. I gave Gram a questioning look, but she just smiled and shoved a plate filled with food into my hands.

I sat down and started eating the biggest lunch of my life. It was apparent that Gram wasn't kidding about making me gain weight while I was here. I ate most of my hamburger and a few fries before handing the plate back to her.

"Thanks, Gram." I kissed her cheek and then followed Landon out of the kitchen.

We shoved our feet back into our mud boots and walked outside. Landon left the four-wheeler where it was and headed for the main barn. I followed him, dreading the job in front of us. I'd had enough poop for one day.

He walked over to another orange Kubota and climbed on. "You can stand on here beside me or walk to the coop. It doesn't matter to me."

The chicken coop was only about fifty yards away from the barn, so I decided to walk rather than get on the tractor with him.

"I'll walk."

He nodded as he started the tractor and pulled it out of the barn. I stayed a few feet behind him as we made our way to the chicken coop. He pulled the tractor in so that it was close to the door, just like he'd done this morning. Once he was off the tractor, he grabbed two shovels out of the loader bucket and handed one to me.

"Come on, kid. Let's go have fun."

I laughed. "Yeah, shoveling chicken crap is equivalent to a party around here."

He winked at me, and then he opened the door and stepped inside. I followed and almost gagged at the smell. While this morning hadn't been pleasant, it was nothing compared to the smell of the chicken coop.

"Fuck, that's nasty!"

"Just wait until we start shoveling. Hurry up, so we can get this over with."

Neither of us spoke this time as we shoveled. I wasn't about to open my mouth in here. Nope. No way. I had no idea how Landon wasn't bothered by the smell. At least, he didn't seem to be, not as bad as I was. I caught him wrinkling his nose a few times as we worked.

After nearly two hours, we finally finished. I handed Landon my shovel and ran out of the chicken coop like my pants were on fire. I needed to escape that smell before I threw up. I dropped to the ground and just lay there. I was stinky, I was sweaty, and I was pretty sure I would never get that smell out of my nose.

"You gonna make it?" Landon asked from nearby.

I rolled over to see him standing above me. "I doubt it. I think I'd prefer jail at this point."

He laughed as he held out a hand to help me up. "I seriously doubt that."

"At least it wouldn't stink as bad. Ugh."

"You know, I'm kind of disappointed in you." His tone was serious, but I could see in his eyes that he was laughing at me.

"And why is that?"

"Your grandpa gave me this whole speech about keeping an eye on you because you're trouble. Then, when you get here, you look like a badass with your dyed hair, piercings, and tattoo. I'm disappointed to see that you're really just a whiny chick."

I flipped him off, and he lost his serious expression as he laughed.

"Fuck off, Cowboy."

"That wasn't very ladylike."

"Good thing I'm not a lady," I said, using his words from yesterday.

He grinned. "Come on, Alexandria. Let's go water the animals. I forgot to do it after lunch."

I shook my head. "You're a horrible teacher, forgetting your duties already."

He ignored me as we walked back to the barn.

I could already tell that I was going to like this guy. I just hoped that he wouldn't fuck me over before I left.

CHAPTER 7

Landon helped me with my chores despite the fact that I was supposed to do them on my own. I thought he'd planned to make me suffer through them on my own, but he'd taken pity on me after I dropped one of the five-gallon water buckets and soaked the front of my jeans. I hated feeling weak, but damn it, those fuckers were heavy. It made me feel even worse when I watched him pick up two of them, acting like it was nothing. I was pretty sure he could have carried two ten-gallon buckets and thought nothing of it. Hopefully, my arms would get used to the weight before too long. If my grandpa saw him helping me, we'd both get in trouble.

After we finished watering everything, we walked back toward the house.

"What now?" I asked.

"We need to go check on the cattle and do the rounds on the water springs."

"What the hell are water springs?" I asked, picturing actual metal springs covered in water.

He grinned. "Your city is showing. The water springs are what feeds the ponds out in the grazing fields. We keep an eye on two of them, especially when it gets this hot. If one starts to dry up, we have to move all the cattle into the other field."

"Oh, okay."

"Come on, we have to take the four-wheeler again."

"Yippee," I mumbled as I followed him over to where he'd parked it earlier.

He climbed on and scooted up, so I could throw my leg over. After I was situated, he started it and slowly drove down the gravel road leading to the main road. Despite the rocky road, I didn't cling to Landon like before. I was okay as long as hills weren't involved. We stopped by a gate about a mile away from the house. He hopped off and opened the gate, motioning me to pull the four-wheeler through.

I shook my head. "Not a chance, buddy."

"Come on, it's in first gear! I swear, you won't kill yourself by moving it six feet."

I debated for a second before scooting forward. *Fuck this timid Lexi.* That wasn't who I was. I grabbed the handlebars and pushed the gas, shrieking when I jerked forward. Without even thinking, I grabbed the hand brake and squeezed tightly. The four-wheeler stopped dead, and I nearly flew over the handlebars.

I looked over to see Landon holding his stomach and laughing. *Fucking asshole.* I flipped him off before releasing the brake, and I pushed the gas again, slowly this time. The four-wheeler started creeping forward. Once I was past the gate, I pulled the brake again and waited for Landon to get back on.

He appeared beside me seconds later, still grinning. "That was hilarious, City."

I ignored the nickname as I glared at him. "That wasn't funny. I could have fallen off."

"I doubt anything would have been bruised besides your pride and possibly your ass."

I said nothing as I scooted back, so he could climb back on. He took his time as we went through the field. He was careful when we came up to any bumps. Now that we were off the gravel road, I clung to him, terrified that we would roll, as we climbed the steep hills.

Jesus, West Virginia needs less fucking hill and more level ground.

We rode in silence for a few minutes before I noticed the first cow at the bottom of the hill. As soon as we reached the bottom, I saw the rest of them were all hanging around a small pond, standing in the shade.

I smiled when I saw a few baby calves running and playing in the field around us. "Aw, they're so cute!" I squealed.

I could feel Landon's shoulders shaking as he laughed silently, but he made no comment about how girlie I'd sounded. I couldn't help it. Cows were boring and huge, and they scared the ever-loving shit out of me, but the babies were cute.

We circled the field a few times as Landon checked to make sure they were all there. I expected them to run when we approached, but they simply stared at us as we drove past. Maybe they weren't so scary after all.

"They're all here," Landon said.

"Why wouldn't they be?"

"Coyotes have been thick around here lately. They got two of the calves this spring."

"Oh." I didn't know what to say to that. I felt bad for the poor little guys the coyotes had taken.

"See how close all the cows are standing to each other? Even the calves stay close to the herd."

I nodded and then realized he couldn't see me. "Yeah."

"They're always together but not this tight. And the calves are usually all over this field. I'd say the coyotes have been after them again."

Landon impressed me. For being so young, he certainly knew a lot about this stuff. To be truthful, I felt a little inadequate around him. All I knew how to do was be a smart-ass and deal drugs.

"You're good at this stuff," I said.

He glanced back at me and smiled. "Thanks, I think—unless you're making fun of me."

"Nah, I'm being sincere for once. It's cool how you know all of this farming stuff."

He shrugged. "I've been around this my whole life. It's hard not to pick up on things. We need to check the spring for this field and then head over to the next."

I was silent as we climbed the hill again and made our way down the other side. We stopped next to what I assumed was the water spring. I waited as Landon hopped off and checked to make sure things were okay.

Once he was finished, he climbed back on and continued driving. Instead of going right, back to the gate we'd come through, he went left. I clung to him as we went sideways across a hill. I had no clue how he wasn't scared shitless. It was taking everything I had to lean up, but he didn't seem bothered at all by the gravity trying to pull us down.

The ground leveled out for a bit, and I could see another gate up ahead. We pulled up to it, and Landon climbed off to open this one, too. He didn't have to tell me to pull through this time. I just did, being careful not to push the gas too hard like last time. Once I pulled through, I scooted back and waited for him. He surprised me by pushing me forward and climbing on behind me.

"What are you doing?" I asked.

"Letting you drive."

He acted like it wasn't a big deal, but my eyes widened.

"There is no way I'm driving this thing," I stated. *Nope. No way.*

I wasn't going to be responsible for wrecking the damn thing and having my grandpa rip me a new asshole.

"It's easy, and I'll help you. Come on, City, you can do it."

"Why do you keep calling me that?" I asked.

"Because Alexandria is too damn long, and because you're city through and through."

"I don't like it. I feel like you're insulting me," I grumbled.

"Fine, I'll think of a new nickname. Until then, you're City."

"Just call me Lexi."

It felt strange, telling him to call me something only a few people did, but for some reason, I felt okay with letting him in enough to do that. After all, he'd done nothing but help me.

"Lexi? Hmm, that'll do, but I'd still like to call you City. I like it when you act all pissy."

I gunned the throttle, making him fly backward. He yelped as he grabbed my waist to keep from falling off.

"Damn it. Fine. I'll call you Lexi."

"Thank you."

I waited for him to release his hold on my waist, but he didn't. I didn't say anything about it as I slowly pushed the gas and steered the four-wheeler across an obvious path through the field. I tried to ignore his hands on me, but it was impossible. They were warm and so large that the tips of his fingers touched each other as he wrapped them around my stomach. I didn't know how to explain how I felt with his hands on me, but I liked them there, and that bothered me. I didn't want another guy's hands on me. I wanted Joel's hands and Joel's alone.

"They're right up ahead," Landon said, pulling me from my thoughts.

I hadn't been paying attention, but now that I was, I noticed a few cows standing together in front of us. I kicked the four-wheeler up another gear as we approached. I'd expected to see several cows, like before, but only five or six were here.

"Why are they separated from the others?" I asked.

"Because they're pregnant. This field is a lot smaller, so we can find them quicker, and it's flat, so we don't have to worry about them having their calves on a hillside."

"Oh, I see."

"They're all okay. Just keep going straight. The spring is about a mile away."

I did as he'd told me. I carefully steered around large rocks and holes. I had to admit that driving a four-wheeler was kind of fun—at least while we were on flat ground. I wasn't sure I could handle driving on the hills.

We reached the spring, and after Landon checked it, we headed back. I drove to the gate, but then I made him drive after that. He didn't fight me on it, and I was glad. I wasn't ready to drive across the hills on the way back.

When we made it to the house, Landon parked the four-wheeler in the barn and shut it off. I climbed off on wobbly legs. He climbed off as well and started walking to the house.

"Are we done?" I asked.

"For right now. I'm going to see if Lily needs anything before I head to my house."

"You live on the property, don't you?" I asked, remembering that Gram had mentioned the helpers having a house of their own.

"Yeah. We're only about half a mile away from the main house. That way, we can help Caleb whenever he needs it."

"Where is he today?" I asked.

"He's cutting hay while my dad kicks it."

I gave him a strange look. "Your dad is kicking hay?"

He laughed. "It's a piece of equipment they use to flip the hay over, so it dries faster. We'll probably be in the hayfield most of tomorrow."

"Joy." I sighed as we walked up the porch steps.

Landon held the door open for me again, and I walked inside the house. I kicked off my boots and headed to the kitchen. For as long as I could remember, Gram was always in the kitchen. I was pretty sure she slept there. Sure enough, I saw her sitting at the kitchen table, peeling potatoes, as we walked in.

She glanced up and smiled at us. "You two hungry? I can make you something to hold you over until dinner."

"Nah, I'm good," I said.

Landon shook his head. "We finished up everything for right now, but I wanted to see if you needed anything before I went to my house."

Gram thought for a moment. "Well, I do have one job if you want to do it, but you don't have to."

"I'll take care of whatever you need, Lily," he said.

"I haven't had a chance to clean the pool this week, and I know it has to be full of leaves and bugs. Can you two do that for me?"

"Sure," Landon said as he smiled at her.

I smiled, too, knowing exactly what she was doing. Cleaning the pool wasn't work. It was a way for her to give us a task that would let us take a break.

"Do you have a bathing suit, Alexandria?" she asked.

I thought for a moment, trying to remember if I'd packed one. "I'm not sure. I'll go check."

"If not, you can just wear a shirt and shorts," she said as I turned to leave. "Landon, I washed your swim trunks the other day. They're on the shelf above the dryer."

"Thanks, Lily."

I could hear them still talking as I walked up the stairs, but I couldn't make out the words. I hurried to my room and starting digging through my drawers. Sure enough, there was my teeny-tiny black bikini that I'd packed when I planned to leave with Joel. I cursed myself for not bringing a one-piece. While I was more than comfortable with Joel seeing me in this, I wasn't comfortable with Landon and my grandma seeing it.

I sighed as I stripped down and put on the bikini. I grabbed one of Joel's old shirts that I slept in sometimes and pulled it over my head. At least I wouldn't be walking around the house half-naked. I slipped on a pair of flip-flops and made my way back downstairs. I exited through the back door and walked across the yard to where the pool was.

When I was little, I'd loved coming here just because of this pool. My grandpa might be a dick, but he always made sure that my grandma had everything she wanted. I could remember the first summer I'd come here after they put the pool in. My grandma had been so excited to show me my surprise. Apparently, she'd had him buy it just for me.

Truthfully, I was surprised that it was still here. I hadn't been back in years, but Gram must have liked it enough not to get rid of it. Or maybe she'd kept it because she hoped that I would come back to use it. I didn't think too much on that. I couldn't. I'd always felt like an ass for letting my grandfather push me away from Gram, but I'd pushed the guilt aside.

Landon was already in the pool. I could see his back as he skimmed the top of the pool.

I pulled my shirt down, trying to cover as much of my legs as I could, which was stupid since I would be taking the damn thing off in a second. I wasn't self-conscious, not at all. I just wasn't sure how I felt about some guy I didn't know seeing me in something so skimpy. No one but Joel had ever seen me in this. I'd refused to even go to the public pool in it. Instead, Joel had bought a small pool for us to use in the summer.

I cleared my throat when I reached the side of the pool, letting Landon know I was there. He turned to face me, and my breath got stuck in my lungs. I literally forgot how to exhale.

Sweet baby monkeys.

While I had admitted earlier that Landon was cute, nothing had prepared me to see him shirtless and wet in the pool. It was obvious that he'd dived under right before I came out. His hair was dripping wet, and water glistened as it ran down his chest and stomach. I knew I was standing there with my mouth hanging open, but at that moment, I didn't possess the ability to close it.

His hair was curled at the ends, even more than normal, and it gave him a boyish charm that I hadn't expected. But there was nothing boyish about his body. *Nothing.* His arms were well defined with muscle, but his abs were what had me staring. Joel was in shape. I'd always thought his body was amazing, but even I had to admit that he had nothing on Landon. His abs looked like they were made of steel, and from earlier, I knew just how hard they were.

"Lexi? You okay?"

Landon's voice pulled me out of whatever trance he'd held me in, and I snapped my mouth shut.

71

"Yeah. Why?"

"Because you've been standing there for the last five minutes."

"Oh, sorry." I felt my face heating from embarrassment. *What the hell was I doing?*

Landon was not my type. He was the furthest thing from my type. And I was with Joel. I loved Joel. I was ashamed that I'd even looked at Landon. It hadn't even been two full days since I last saw Joel, and I was staring at some other guy.

What kind of person am I?

"No worries. I've got most of the leaves cleaned out, so you can just chill in the pool if you want," he said as he watched me.

"Um…yeah, that sounds fun." I shook my head to clear it as I walked to the ladder. I kicked off my flip-flops and climbed up the short ladder. Once I was at the top, I sat down and stuck my legs in the water. After being on them all day, the water felt like heaven on my aching feet and legs. *I could sit like this all day and be happy.*

"Are you going to get in or what?"

I glanced up to see Landon watching me.

"Yeah, I was just getting used to the temperature." *And stalling*, I mentally added.

I took a deep breath before peeling off my shirt and tossing it to the ground. I stood and slipped into the water, and my eyes found Landon's. I nearly froze when I saw the way he was staring at me. He didn't stare at me the way Joel had, like he wanted to eat me alive, but there was an intensity in his eyes that had me locked in place. I knew what I looked like. Yes, I was pale, and most guys hated that, but I'd been blessed with a decent chest and a nice ass. My hips were slim though, and I hated that. They made me feel like I was a stick figure with boobs.

I dropped to my knees, so the water covered me from the neck down. Landon stared at me for another second before turning away and running the skimmer through the water. An uneasy silence filled the space between us, but I had no idea what to say to break it.

A raft was floating around the pool, but there was no way I was climbing onto that thing and exposing my body. I would just spend my time underwater, so Landon wouldn't look at me like that again.

"What's your natural hair color?" he asked suddenly.

He was still facing away from me, so I couldn't see his face. "Blonde. Why?"

He shrugged. "I was just curious. I think you'd look better blonde. The black makes you look paler than you already are."

I was quiet for a moment as I thought about his words. "I'm fucked-up inside, Landon. I'm black. I figured I might as well show it on the outside, too."

I had no idea what had made me say that, but I knew it was true.

I'd been fucked-up for a long time, and there was no use in lying to myself. I had no idea why I was the way I was. There was so much anger and hostility inside of me, and I would lash out at almost everyone. I'd felt it slowly building over the past year, but I hadn't known what to do to stop it. It wasn't like I'd had a horrible life because I hadn't. Sure, I'd fought with my mom a lot, but other than that, my life was good.

Maybe I'd taken some of Joel's anger and pain inside me when I fell in love with him. If I had, it had only been so I could protect him. Maybe, just maybe, if I could take some of his hurt away, he wouldn't feel so much pain from the life he'd lived with his dad and the one he was living now.

The realization that Joel was behind my anger was like a slap in the face. He hadn't made me this way. No, I'd done it on my own without even realizing what was happening. The drinking, the weed, the fights—they had all been outlets for the rage that seemed to fill me.

Landon stopped skimming and looked back at me. "I don't think you're fucked-up. I think you've fucked up in the past, but you're not fucked-up."

I shook my head. "Don't think the best of me. You'll only be disappointed when you figure out that you are wrong."

Before I realized what I was doing, I was climbing the ladder and then running across the yard. I didn't stop running until I made it back to my room. I stripped off my bathing suit and found a pair of jeans and a baggy shirt to change into. I collapsed on my bed and stared at the ceiling, trying to process what the hell had just happened.

I'd *never* doubted myself or my relationship with Joel—until now. It was equivalent to being hit with a ton of bricks. I tried to push the thoughts away, but they kept jumping out at me, refusing to be ignored.

Before I'd met Joel, I'd gotten drunk occasionally, but I'd never done drugs. I'd never sold drugs. I'd never been in a fight. I'd even had a few friends of my own, but I'd started to ignore them as I'd focused all of my attention on Joel. I'd become consumed by him even though I'd known he was dangerous. *Fuck, I'm dangerous now.* I could fight like a crazy bitch, and I knew how to use a gun. It was all thanks to Joel.

I ran my hands across my face, trying to wipe away all the doubt seeping into me. This was what my mother had been hoping for. She'd wanted me to start second-guessing myself and my relationship with Joel while we were apart. She'd wanted me to realize everything that was running through my mind right now.

I stood and started pacing my room. There was no way that I would let her win. I loved Joel, and I knew that he loved me back. That was all that mattered. If I was fucked-up, it was my own fault, not his. He'd never once treated me badly or made me act a certain way. He had done nothing but take care of me while making sure that I was happy. I needed to pretend like the last thirty minutes had never happened and get on with my life. I would stay here and do my time, and then I'd go home to Joel at the end of the summer and never look back.

CHAPTER 8

I didn't speak to Landon that night as he helped me do my evening chores. He seemed unsure of what to say as well, so he stayed silent, too. As soon as we were finished, I all but ran back to the house without telling him good night.

My grandpa came in about an hour before dark. He ignored me, except to tell me that he would need me in the hayfield tomorrow morning. He said the hay needed time to dry, so we'd start around ten. I was excited to sleep in until I realized I still had my morning chores to take care of.

I showered right after dinner and went straight to bed. I was exhausted, both mentally and physically. I knew I was going to have a wicked sunburn in the morning because my shoulders were already red and starting to hurt.

Just something else to look forward to.

I awoke early to the sound of my alarm clock. I winced as soon as I moved to shut the damn thing off. My shoulders felt like they were on fire. I stumbled from my bed, feeling like I'd been run over by a truck in my sleep last night.

After pulling on a pair of jeans, I pulled another spaghetti-strap shirt over my head, careful not to let the material touch my shoulders any more than it had to. I brushed my teeth and piled my hair on top of my head before walking downstairs and pulling on my mud boots. I would grab some breakfast after I was finished with my chores.

I was surprised to see Landon walking to the barn when I stepped outside. I hadn't expected to see him yet. I still felt unsure about what had happened yesterday, and I wanted to keep my distance from him. I reached the barn a few seconds after he did.

He glanced over his shoulder when he heard me approaching. "Morning, Lexi."

I was relieved that he hadn't called me City. "Morning."

"I didn't expect you to be up this early. I was going to do your chores for you."

"I'm up. I can do them," I said rudely.

I hadn't meant for it to come out that way, but we both heard the iciness in my voice.

"Okay. I'm going to go check on the cattle since we'll be busy all day today."

I was silent as he walked to the four-wheeler and started it. He drove past me without even glancing in my direction, and I was glad. I never again wanted to see that look I'd seen in his eyes yesterday. It had scared me.

I grabbed a bucket and walked to the chicken coop to gather the eggs. Even though it was barely light out, the chickens were already up and singing.

Is everyone around here a morning person? Jesus.

After gathering the eggs and avoiding a few chicken beaks, I walked out of the henhouse, cursing. One of the stupid things had managed to peck me when I was trying to get the eggs out from underneath her.

I took the eggs to the house and set them inside the door for my grandma before heading over to the goat pen. I hated goats. I always had. They smelled horrible, and they were the most stubborn animals on the planet. It took me a few minutes to shoo them out of their pen, but I finally managed it. I was bitching about goats as I walked back to the house and into the kitchen. Like yesterday, my grandma had a heaping plate of food waiting on me.

"You're going to make me fat. You know that, right?" I asked as she put the plate down in front of me.

"You're about as far away from fat as they get, Alexandria. It'll take more than one summer to make you fat."

I rolled my eyes as I dug into my eggs and hash browns. *God, Gram's cooking is the best.* I couldn't even microwave popcorn without burning it. It was obvious that the cooking gene hadn't been passed to me—or my mother, for that matter. While she was capable of making edible meals, they had been nothing like Gram's.

I finished eating and put my plate in the sink.

Gram glanced up. "Caleb won't need you until later this morning. Why don't you go rest for a while? I'll make sure to wake you up on time."

"Thanks, Gram," I said sincerely.

I could definitely use an extra hour or two of sleep. My ass was dragging.

I walked back up to my room and fell down onto my bed, not bothering to cover up. Within minutes, I was out.

I woke up to the sound of someone knocking on my door. I peeled my eyes open to see Gram standing there.

"You need to get up. Landon is waiting outside for you."

I sat up and rubbed my eyes. "Okay."

I crawled out of bed and walked downstairs with her. She watched as I slipped on my mud boots.

"Don't you have any other shoes?" she asked.

I shook my head. "Nothing that I could wear around here."

She frowned. "We'll have to take you into town to get you something. You can't wear those things all the time. You'll have hay down in them today."

"I could use a shopping day," I told her, half-kidding and half-serious. *I'd love to get out of here for a day—or six.*

"I can't take you this weekend because I have to help with a bake sale for the church on Saturday. Maybe I can see if Caleb will take you."

Not going to happen. I'd go barefoot first. "We both know that isn't a good idea, Gram. Grandpa and I don't see eye to eye."

She sighed. "I know. Your grandfather can be a stubborn man, but he means well."

I shrugged, not wanting to fight with her. We would never agree when it came to my grandfather.

"Anyway, I'll figure something out. We'll get you some shoes somehow," she said.

I nodded as I turned and walked out the door. Landon was sitting in a truck parked in the driveway. There was a flatbed trailer hooked up to the truck.

Ugh, I hate that trailer. I knew from when I was younger that every time I saw it, it meant I was going to be miserable that day.

I walked to the truck and opened the passenger side door. As soon as I was in, Landon started down the driveway. We were both quiet as we bounced along. We stopped by yet another gate, and I waited as Landon got out and opened it. He was back in the truck seconds later. He didn't bother to close the gate after we passed through and continued down the road.

After a few minutes of driving along the narrow road, we came to a clearing. I groaned out loud. I'd forgotten just how big this field was. It had been years since I last saw it.

"Don't groan. We haven't even started yet," Landon said as he glanced over at me.

"Is this day over yet?"

"Nope." He hesitated before continuing, "Look, I didn't mean to upset you yesterday. I'm really sorry."

I blinked, trying to clear the tears that were suddenly clouding my vision. I had no idea why I wanted to cry. "It's no big deal. Don't worry about it."

"Well, I am worried about it. You could use a friend, Lexi, and I'd like to be that friend—at least for the summer anyway."

I turned to look at him. "I don't need friends."

He gave me a barely there grin. "I think you do, City. You just don't realize it."

We both stared at each other, neither of us sure what to say.

I didn't need a friend. I didn't *want* one. I was just fine on my own.

"We better get to work." He reached behind the seat and pulled out two pairs of gloves. "Let's stack them first. Then, we'll pull the truck around and load them."

I nodded, unable to speak. My mind was traveling at warp speed, and I needed to focus all my attention on shutting it off. I grabbed a pair of gloves from him and stepped out of the truck. It was barely after ten, but the sun was already beating down on us, hot and unforgiving.

I walked a few feet to where the first square bale was. It felt like it weighed a hundred pounds as I picked it up and carried it to the next closest one. Landon walked farther down the field and grabbed two bales to add to my pile.

Show-off.

I grabbed another and carried it back as well. Once we had enough in this pile, we moved on to make another one, and on and on it went. The only positive thing was that this was busywork. It kept my thoughts away as I concentrated on stacking the bales together. As I worked, I listened to the sound of the tractors on the other side of the field, letting the dull roar fill my ears.

Time seemed to pass in slow motion as we worked. I kept glancing at my phone, expecting an hour or two to have passed, but in reality, it had only been ten minutes. Sweat trickled down my face, and my shoulders were on fire. I cursed myself for not putting on sunblock again. I was going to be fried by the time I made it back to the house.

"I think we have enough for a load. Finish stacking these while I go get the truck." Landon started walking back to where he'd parked the truck earlier.

I watched him walk away, unable to keep my eyes off of him.

What is wrong with me? I would rip this boy to shreds and never look back if he kept hanging around me. It was what I did. I destroyed everything I touched.

I pulled my eyes away from him long enough to walk to the next bale. Just as I reached for it, I heard my phone make a noise in my pocket. Confused, I pulled it out to see a text had popped up on the screen. My eyes widened when I noticed that I had one bar of service. *Holy shit!*

The text was from Joel, and it had been sent sometime late last night.

Joel: I mis u bby. My bed cold. Com her.

I raised an eyebrow. It was obvious that he'd been drinking when he sent it. I pulled my gloves off and typed back a quick response, praying it would send.

*Me: I miss you, too. God, it's hell here. I have no
cell service either. I'm on a hill, so apparently, I'm
high enough to get it right now. I wish you were
here. I just want to come home to you.*

I sent that and waited for a reply. I sighed when nothing came
through.

*Me: I'll probably lose service again, but I wanted to
tell you that I love you. I'm hoping that they'll let
me go into town soon. If they do, I'll find some way
to let you know when and where. Love you.*

I waited again, praying that he would respond, but he never
did. I sighed in defeat and shoved my phone back in my pocket
when I saw Landon driving the truck toward me. I waited as he
pulled up next to me and shut the truck off.

"You hand them to me, and I'll stack them until they get too
high for you to throw up. Then, we'll switch."

I nodded as I grabbed a bale and handed it to him. He started
stacking the truck first, shoving the bales in tightly after I handed
them to him. Once we had this stack loaded, he pulled up to the
next. He filled the back of the truck up and then started on the
trailer. I watched in fascination as he twisted and turned the bales,
so they fit perfectly into rows. We filled up the bottom of the
trailer and then started another row. Halfway down the field, I
couldn't throw the bales up high enough.

"Give me your hand, and I'll help you up," Landon said as he
reached down.

I grabbed his hand, and he pulled me up like I weighed
nothing. After explaining to me how to stack the rest of the bales,
he jumped down and started throwing them up to me.

I was in awe of him. There was no use in denying it. This guy
was strong, and it wasn't from going to the gym. It was from
working out in the hot sun day after day.

We finished loading the bales. I looked down at the ground,
gulping as I did so. It was so damn far away. I had no clue how I
was supposed to get down, and I sure as hell wasn't going to ride
up here on the way back to the house.

"You can get down now," Landon said as he tied two ropes to the frame of the trailer.

"Um…how?" I asked.

"Just climb down the bales."

He'd made it sound like the simplest thing in the world, but it wasn't. I wasn't good at this farm stuff, unlike him. He'd probably just jump down if he were stuck up here.

"There is no way I'm going to climb down," I said.

"Come on. I'm standing below you in case you fall." He stared up at me expectantly.

"Promise you won't let me fall to my death?" I asked.

He rolled his eyes. "I swear."

I turned and slowly climbed over the bales in the back. My palms were sweating so bad that I nearly lost my grip before I even started. I pulled my gloves off and threw them down to the ground before trying again.

"You're good. Now, just climb down. I always stack the bales so that they're easy to climb down."

"Easy for you," I muttered as I further lowered my body down the bales. My foot found a spot to stand on as I reached for the strings on another bale. I smiled. I had this.

The next thing I knew, my hand was slipping off the rope, and I went falling backward. I didn't even have time to scream before I hit something hard. I waited for the pain, but besides my sunburned shoulders, there was none. I opened my eyes and stared up at Landon. He'd caught me.

"Holy shit, City. Clumsy much?"

My mouth opened and closed, but no words came out. My heart was beating so fast that I thought it might beat out of my chest. I hated it. I hated feeling scared.

He cradled me in his arms for a second longer before setting me down on the ground. "You okay?"

I nodded. "Yeah, thank you. That scared the crap out of me."

"Remind me to bring a ladder for you next time," he joked.

"Shut up." I flipped him off, grabbed my gloves off the ground, and walked back to the front of the truck.

As soon as we were both in, he started the truck and headed back down the road. I stuck my head out the window, trying to cool off, as he drove. If I'd thought I was hot yesterday, I was wrong. It hadn't even come close to how I felt today. Landon tapped his fingers on the steering wheel as we approached the barn.

"Stop that. It's annoying," I grumbled.

He shot a grin my way as he continued to tap away. "Deal with it."

I ignored him as he pulled up to the barn and slowly backed into it. Once the trailer was partially inside, he shut the truck off.

"Come on, City. Let's get this over with."

It took us almost two hours to get the truck and trailer unloaded and the hay stacked in the barn, but we did it. I dropped to my knees in the grass and threw my gloves down beside me.

God bless it. My shoulders were on fire. *I* was on fire. My happy ass wasn't cut out for the farm life.

I tried to lift my arm to push my bangs away from my face, but I couldn't do it. Both of my arms were shaking, and they felt like jelly. I was pretty sure that if I tried to stand up right now, my legs wouldn't hold my weight. So, I just went with gravity and fell the rest of the way down onto the grass.

"You gonna make it, City?"

I raised one hand in the air to flip him off again. "Stop calling me that."

I looked up to see him standing above me with a worried look on his face.

"Your shoulders look like shit."

"They feel like someone took a blowtorch to them."

"Did you put sunblock on them today?" he asked.

I shook my head. "I forgot."

"You're an idiot. Get up."

"I don't wanna," I whined.

Nothing short of a promise from my grandma that I could go home would make me get up.

"Get your skinny ass up, and come with me," Landon said, sounding annoyed.

"Fuck off."

I heard him grumbling under his breath. Then, I was suddenly scooped up. I squealed, shocked by the sudden movement.

I shoved at his chest. "Put me down!"

"Nope. I tried to be nice about it, but you're being stubborn as usual."

He started walking away from the barn but in the opposite direction of the house.

"Where are we going?" I asked.

"My place. It's closer to here than the main house, and I have something that will help you."

"I'm fine, Landon. Seriously, put me down."

For one, I hated being carried around like a little kid, and two, I couldn't even imagine how he was holding me after unloading the hay. My arms were barely functioning.

He ignored me as he cut down a hill. I grumbled as he carried me, but I didn't fight anymore. I didn't have it in me. A few minutes later, we approached the front of a single-story house. With the exception of that, it looked similar to my grandparent's house. Landon didn't stop until we were inside. He set me down and motioned for me to follow him. It wasn't like I had much of a choice now that I was here. I followed him into a bathroom. I took a seat on the edge of the tub as he rummaged through a medicine cabinet.

"What are you looking for?" I asked.

"Aloe vera. It works like a charm on sunburns." He pulled a container of green goo out.

"Ew…that looks nasty."

"It'll help. Trust me."

I reached for the goo, scrunching my nose. I hoped it smelled better than it looked. I opened it and squeezed some on my fingers. I had to admit that it did smell pretty good. I rubbed some of it on the tops of my shoulders and sighed in relief. Its effects were almost instant. My shoulders already felt cooler than they had a second ago.

"Holy crap. Thank you," I said as I handed the container back to him.

"You're welcome. Turn around, and I'll put it on where you can't reach on your back."

I studied him for a moment before turning away. "I think you're probably the nicest person I've ever met."

He snorted. "I doubt that."

I shook my head. "No, you really are."

"Thanks, I guess. I used to be an asshole back in high school, but I finally figured out that it wasn't going to get me anywhere.

83

We're only on this earth for a while. Might as well make the best of it."

"How old are you, Landon?"

"Nineteen. Why do you ask?"

"Because you don't act like you're nineteen."

I shivered when I felt his hand against my back as he put the goo on me.

"I grew up fast." He paused. "I'm going to move your shirt straps. Is that okay?"

I nodded, but my stomach dropped. "Sure."

I didn't move a muscle as I felt his fingers slip under my bra strap and my shirt strap before he pushed them down my arms. It felt intimate to me, too intimate.

"Why do you say that?" I asked, trying to distract myself.

"Say what?"

His voice was deeper than before, and it sent shivers down my spine.

Why does he get to me like this?

"That you grew up fast," I said.

I jumped when I felt him rubbing the goo on me.

"I already told you I was an asshole through most of high school. I thought I owned the whole damn world. Boy, was I wrong. My mom got sick, really sick, at the beginning of my junior year. She was fine one day, and the next, she was in a hospital bed, barely hanging on."

I swallowed hard. "God, Landon, I'm so sorry."

"Don't be. You didn't give her cancer. She was gone within two weeks. Just...gone. It hurt so damn much to watch the one person who loved me regardless of what I did wither away."

He was still rubbing my back, but I wasn't sure if he was even aware of it. I closed my eyes as tears filled them.

The pain was evident in his voice as he continued to speak, "After that, I straightened up, and I stopped acting like a jackass. I figured out just how hard the world could fuck you. I wasn't invincible like I'd thought I was."

"You're pretty damn close to it." I turned to see him staring at me.

"Why do you say that?"

"Over the past two days, I've watched you lift things that no human should be able to lift. I'm starting to think you're Superman."

He smiled, but his eyes were still sad. "I'm not Superman, not even close. I'm just trying to be the guy my mom always told me I could be."

Damn if this doesn't hurt. I didn't understand why I cared that he was hurting, but I did. Maybe it was because I knew deep down that Landon was one of the good guys.

"I think she'd be proud of you, especially for putting up with me." I said, trying to lighten the mood.

"You're not so bad. I think you have a lot of shit going on in your head and a chip on your shoulder, but you're not a bad person. Under all the piercings and hair and shit, I think you're a kind person. You just took the wrong road."

My breath caught as he lifted his hand and ran it down my cheek.

"There's something in your eyes begging to get out, but you keep it locked up. You've got to let it out, City. Just let it go."

I jumped to my feet, and his hand dropped back down to his side.

"We finished?"

He nodded as he looked away. "Yeah, we're good. Let me get you one of my shirts to wear while we're out in the field. You need to keep the sun off of you for a while."

He was gone after that, only to return a minute later with a shirt in his hand. He left me alone to change. I peeled my shirt off and threw it in a hamper next to the door before pulling his over my head.

My stomach was in knots, and my heart was racing. *What just happened? Why am I feeling like this all of a sudden?* I didn't want anything to do with Landon. I had Joel, and that was all that mattered.

I took a deep breath before opening the door and walking back out to meet Landon.

Whatever was happening, I wouldn't let it.

CHAPTER
9

The rest of the week went much like the first two days. We spent Wednesday, Thursday, and Friday out in the hayfield, loading hay and then stacking it in the barn. I stopped complaining and just went with it. There was no point in whining. All that did was annoy myself and probably Landon, too—not that he ever said so.

Joel had never texted me back, not even once, and I had service the entire time we were in the field. I tried not to let it bother me, but it did. It was like he didn't even care that I was gone. All of the doubt I'd felt before seeing him the night I left came back with a vengeance. I kept picturing him with other women.

And then, there was Landon. He was constantly around, and my eyes were always on him. It was like they had a mind of their own. He'd never mentioned that day in his bathroom, and neither had I. I didn't even want to think about it. I tried to keep my distance as much as possible.

"Alexandria, I know I told you I'd take you to town to get stuff, but I don't think I can for another week or two. I've got a bunch of stuff going on all next week and the one after," my grandma said as we were eating lunch Friday afternoon.

Landon and I had just finished up with the hay, and I could barely move, let alone think about a shopping trip.

I shrugged. "I'm getting used to wearing the mud boots all the time. It's not a big deal."

She sighed. "Yes, it is. You need boots and clothes. You can't keep wearing the same clothes all the time. They're going get worn out."

"I have my license. I could go by myself," I suggested.

My grandfather sent a glare my way. "You're not going anywhere by yourself. You'd probably steal my car and take off."

"I would not," I grumbled even though the thought had crossed my mind. I needed to see Joel. I had to know why he wasn't answering me.

"No." His voice told me that I wasn't going to change his mind.

"I could take her tonight after the chores are done," Landon spoke up.

My head snapped up to see him looking at my grandfather. After the last few days of me ignoring him, I had no idea why he was offering.

"You don't have to do that, Landon. You've worked your ass off this week in the hay. Take the weekend off, and go have some fun."

"With all due respect, sir, she's worked just as hard as I have this week, and she hasn't caused any trouble. I could take her to New Martinsville and watch her."

I looked at my grandfather to see him staring back at me. Hope rose in my chest when I saw that he was debating. I looked away as I pretended to act like I didn't care.

"Alexandria, if I let you go with him and he tells me that you did *anything* wrong, you will not leave this farm for the rest of the summer."

I nodded. "I won't try anything, I swear."

It kind of sucked that he didn't trust me at all. Sure, I wasn't here for a vacation, but I'd been on my best behavior since I arrived. He could at least give me a chance.

"Landon, if you're willing to put up with her, she's your responsibility. If she does anything wrong, it's on you," my grandfather said.

Landon glanced at me. "I know. I don't think she'll cause me any trouble."

He was right. I wouldn't do anything that would get him into trouble, not after he'd helped me so much.

"All right then. Landon, you're in charge of her."

I couldn't help but grin. *I'm free!* At least, I would be free in a few hours.

I glanced up to see Landon smiling at me. I owed him big time, and he knew it. I had no idea why he was helping me escape my prison sentence, but I truly appreciated it.

The rest of the day seemed to drag by now that I had something to look forward to. I went out a little bit early to finish my chores, and then I hurried to the house, so I could shower and change. After I showered, I blow-dried and straightened my hair, and then I applied my usual makeup. I hadn't bothered with my hair or makeup since I'd arrived here, so it felt good to look like a girl again.

I walked back to my room and pulled on my favorite pair of Converse shoes, black skinny jeans, and a band T-shirt. *God, it feels so good to be me again.* I started digging through my purse to find my wallet. I sighed when I saw how much money was inside. Hopefully, New Martinsville had a clothing store for broke people like me.

I glanced at the clock in my room before walking down the stairs. Landon had told me that he'd pick me up outside right at six. I had a few minutes to wait, so I walked into the kitchen to talk to Gram.

She glanced up and smiled when she saw me. "Hey, sweetie. You look great."

"Thanks. I feel a lot better. I feel like me again."

"You're always you, regardless of what you wear or how you do your hair." My grandma smiled at me. "I have something for you."

I raised an eyebrow but said nothing as she walked to her purse. My eyes widened when I saw her pull out a wad of cash.

"Take this with you, and get what you need." She grinned at me. "And have some fun while you're out. Get something to eat, watch a movie, whatever you want. You've been doing great here, and we're both proud of you even if Caleb won't admit it."

"Thanks, Gram. I'll bring back what I don't use, I promise." I took the cash and shoved it into my purse.

"Don't even worry about it. Go enjoy yourself with Landon. Just make sure you're home before your grandfather wakes up."

I laughed. "I doubt Landon and I will be pulling an all-nighter."

It was Gram's turn to raise her eyebrows, but she said nothing else. I had no idea what that look was supposed to mean, and I didn't think I really wanted to know. I walked out of the kitchen and out the door. I saw Landon sitting in a really big silver truck. I wasn't even sure how the hell I was going to get in it.

I opened the door to see him grinning at me. "Hey."

"Hey. Need help?" he asked as he watched me eyeball the seat.

"Nah, I've got it." I grabbed the door handle and the seat as I scrambled up into the truck. "Good Lord, this thing is huge."

Landon laughed. "My mom and dad bought it for me a couple of years ago. I saved up until I could afford a lift kit, and then my friend Johnny and I put it on."

I shook my head. "You're a strange one, Cowboy."

"Nah. It's a guy thing. We all like big toys with powerful engines."

I rolled my eyes. "Whatever you say."

We were both silent as he started the truck and drove away from the house. I still felt awkward about the other day, and I didn't want him to bring it up.

"Where do you want to go first?" Landon asked as he pulled out onto the main road.

"Um…wherever I can get some clothes for cheap. Gram gave me some cash so that we could get something to eat or whatever while we're out, too."

"Cool. There's this awesome Mexican place if you want to eat there."

"Mexican sounds pretty good right about now."

"Great. We'll stop by Walmart, so you can get some clothes, and then we can go to this small shoe store that sells really sturdy boots."

I nodded. "Okay."

We were almost to New Martinsville before either of us spoke again. I was too busy trying not to get sick from the winding roads.

"Why are you being so quiet?" he asked.

I shrugged. "I don't know. I'm just tired."

It was the truth—kind of. I also was trying to avoid conversation in hopes that things wouldn't get awkward again.

"Whatever. Even when you're tired, you never shut up."

I stuck my tongue out at him. "Are you trying to tell me that I talk too much?"

"Nah. If you talked too much, I'd just put duct tape over your mouth."

"At least you're honest," I grumbled.

"Seriously though, are you sure nothing is wrong?"

"I'm sure," I said as we pulled into the Walmart parking lot.

I opened the door and jumped down as soon as he parked.

God, this truck needs to come with a ladder for short people like me.

Landon was right behind me as I weaved around people in the parking lot. Once we were inside, I grabbed a shopping cart and started walking toward the clothes.

I glanced back to see that Landon was still following me. "You can go shop or whatever it is guys do in stores."

"I don't need anything."

"Well, go look."

He laughed. "Are you trying to get rid of me?"

"I am." I needed to get a few sports bras, and I did *not* want him around when I was looking through them.

"Not going to happen. My luck, you'll run out the front door and hitchhike all the way home."

"I'm not going to run off, I swear. Please just go."

"Nope."

"Ugh. Fine, whatever." *He can just stand in the bra section with me and look like an ass. See if I care.*

I ignored him as I started searching for new jeans. I found a few pairs and threw them in the cart, not bothering to try them on. I headed for the shirts next and found a few tank tops and T-shirts to wear. The whole time, Landon stayed right with me.

I didn't look back at him as I walked over to the bras. I needed a few sports bras to wear while I was working. My boobs were always in the way when I was trying to do my chores. I walked through the first aisle, ignoring the pretty bras, and headed straight for the sports bras. I stopped in front of them and started looking for my size. I found a couple and pulled them off the rack. Turning to Landon, I grinned. I wanted to embarrass him.

"Which color do you like?" I asked, pretending to care what he said.

The smile slipped from my face when I saw his expression. His eyes darkened as he stared at me, and I stood there, frozen.

"I like them all." His voice was gruff as he looked away from me.

I turned and threw them in the cart, refusing to look back at him. Landon needed to take my advice and stay far away from me. Nothing could come of us, and he needed to realize that. I hurried to the front of the store and got in line. It seemed like forever before it was finally my turn to check out. As soon as the lady finished ringing me up, I paid and all but ran from the store and Landon, which was stupid since he had to unlock the truck.

I tapped my foot impatiently until he finally caught up and unlocked the door for me. I ignored him as he helped me throw my bags in the backseat. After pushing my cart to the cart drop-off, I walked back to the truck.

Landon was waiting on the passenger side. "I figured you might need some help getting in since you're vertically challenged and all."

He grinned at me, and I relaxed when I saw his eyes were no longer darkened.

"Thanks." I smiled. "And really? Vertically challenged? Like I haven't heard that one before."

My heart stopped when he grabbed my bottom and helped me climb into the truck. His hand lingered there until I was up on the seat. I had no idea what to think about him touching me like that or the way it made my body tingle.

Landon closed my door and walked to his side of the truck. I stayed silent as he got in and backed out of the parking spot.

"The boot place is right down the road. We'll get you a pair and then grab some food. I'm starving."

He seemed to be ignoring what had just happened, so I decided I would do the same.

I rolled my eyes at myself. I was being ridiculous. Landon had helped me, and I was turning something innocent into something that wasn't. I needed to get over myself.

It only took a few minutes to get to the shoe store. I let Landon lead the way as we walked inside. He took me straight to an aisle of work boots.

"I'd get something steel-toed, just in case. You never know what we're going to get into."

I nodded as I grabbed a pair and tried them on. They felt heavy, but they were a lot better than those stupid rubber boots I'd been wearing every day. I shoved them back in the box and walked to the front of the store. The cashier gave me a strange look, but she said nothing as she rang me up. I couldn't blame her. I stuck out like crazy around here. Apparently, no one in West Virginia had ever heard of hair dye or piercings.

The Mexican restaurant was packed when we arrived. After waiting a few minutes for a table, the hostess led us back to a booth. I picked up the menu and started looking through it. Our waitress appeared a few seconds later.

"Landon! I haven't seen you in a while!" she said as she gave him the brightest smile I'd ever seen. If she kept smiling like that, I might need sunglasses.

"Hey, Shelly. How have you been?" His voice was polite, but I could tell that he was annoyed.

"I'm good. Just working and stuff. I tried calling you a few times, but you never called me back."

I smirked at him over my menu. He'd ignored her, and now, he had to pretend to be nice. The nice guy in him wouldn't let him do anything else.

"Sorry. I've just been busy lately."

I didn't miss the look he gave me.

Shelly glanced over at me. "Who's this?"

I almost laughed at the jealousy in her voice. "I'm City."

Landon snorted but said nothing.

"City?" Shelly asked. "That's an…interesting name."

"Landon picked it out."

I watched as she tried to hide her confusion. *I really shouldn't get this much enjoyment out of tormenting Landon's friend or whatever she is, but I am.*

"Can I get a sweet tea?" Landon finally asked.

"Um…yeah, sure." She turned to me. "What do you want?"

"Coke is fine."

"Great. I'll be back in a few minutes with your drinks." She walked away, glancing at Landon over her shoulder as she went.

"Shoot me now," Landon said.

"Old girlfriend?" I asked.

He shook his head. "She wishes. I've tried to be nice about it, but she won't leave me alone."

"So, tell her that. Don't torture the poor girl."

"I know. I just don't want to hurt her feelings. I was hoping she'd take the hint when I didn't call her back."

"She likes you, so that means that she will only see what she wants to see. You've got to be blunt."

"I don't know."

"Trust me on this. I'm a girl. I know how our brains work."

"You seem to know what you want out of a relationship. Are you sure it's everything you're thinking it is? Or are you like Shelly?"

"What do you mean?" I asked, confused by the sudden change in topic.

"You said girls see what they want unless the guy spells it out for them. Is that how you are? Are you seeing things differently than your boyfriend?"

"I…" I started but stopped. I had no clue how to respond to that. "Fuck off, Landon."

He smirked. "I didn't mean to piss you off. I just wondered if you'd thought about that."

"I know exactly where I stand when it comes to Joel and my relationship with him."

At least, I'd thought so until I came here. After a week of silence from him, I was starting to wonder though. Surely, he'd read my messages, so I didn't know why he wasn't responding.

"Then, why does it look like I just kicked you in the stomach?" Landon asked.

"I have no idea what you're talking about."

"Tell me something."

"Okay…"

"What were you like before you got with him? Did you look like this? Were you such a hard-ass?"

I shrugged. "I've been with Joel for a while. I've spent most of that time growing up and realizing who I want to be. Did I look or act like this before him? No, but that doesn't mean he made me do it."

"Were you selling drugs before him? Or using them?"

I raised an eyebrow. "Who said I was using them?"

"Using and selling go hand in hand. We both know it."

"I don't use anything heavy. And no, I didn't sell or use before him."

"I didn't think so. Just think about what you just said—you've changed everything about yourself since you got with him."

"Look, Joel is a good guy. Does he have faults? Sure. We all do. But I love him, faults and all. He takes care of me, and he makes me feel loved."

This conversation was going in a direction that I didn't even want to think about.

"Are you guys ready to order?" Shelly asked as she appeared beside us.

I could have kissed her for interrupting us.

Landon and I both placed our orders, and Shelly left. I stared at the table, unable to look him in the eye.

How dare he try to put doubt in my mind.

I barely knew him, and he had no right to screw with my emotions like this. I was still *me*. I'd never changed who I was.

"Look, City, I'm really sorry if I upset you. I didn't mean to, I swear. I just…I like you. I think you're a good person under all the attitude. I don't want you to screw up your whole life for a drug dealer who might possibly be using you."

"You don't even know me, Landon."

"But I'd like to. Every time I try to talk to you, you shut me out. You're allowed to have guy friends, Lexi."

"I do have guy friends. Maybe I just don't want to be friends with you."

He sighed. "Look, let's just pretend the past fifteen minutes didn't happen, okay?"

"Fine by me."

The only problem was that I couldn't ignore the fact that Landon had been right—at least on part of what he'd said. I'd changed myself when I started hanging around Joel. It scared me to think that I might not be who I'd thought I was and that maybe my relationship with Joel wasn't what I'd thought it was either.

CHAPTER 10

I was afraid that the rest of our dinner would be awkward, but it wasn't. Landon wouldn't let things stay awkward. After he picked on me for a few minutes, I finally relaxed and started joking with him. Landon was easy to talk to when things didn't get too deep.

I almost choked on my drink when I realized that I considered Landon a friend. I couldn't remember the last friend I'd made who wasn't friends with Joel first. Regardless of the way my thoughts were spinning, I knew I liked Landon. There was just something about him that wouldn't let me ignore him.

"Do you want to go home? Or should we do something else?" Landon asked when we were walking to his truck.

"Do you really have to ask that?"

"Good point. What do you want to do?"

I shrugged. "I don't know. Gram said there was a movie theater here. We could watch a movie or something."

"I haven't been to the movies in months. Sounds like a plan."

The theater was located in a plaza only a few minutes away from the restaurant. I hadn't expected a huge theater like we had back home, and I didn't get one.

"What do you want to watch?" Landon asked as we stared at the movie listings.

"Um…let's watch the zombie one."

He laughed. "Why did I even ask? Of course the emo chick wants to watch people get eaten."

I stuck my tongue out as we walked to the counter to buy our tickets. Landon tried to pay for both of us, but I refused. I didn't want him to think of this as a date. Both of us passed on the popcorn since we'd already eaten, but we did grab drinks.

The theater was as small on the inside as I'd expected, but it was clean. We walked to our theater and climbed to the top row of seats. I was surprised to see that only a few other people were here.

"Where is everyone?" I asked.

"This is how it usually is. We're not a big city."

"Oh."

I sipped my drink as the lights dimmed, and the previews started playing. With only a few other people, the theater felt intimate. I didn't like that feeling. I shook my head and turned my attention away from the fact that Landon was only inches away from me in the dark room as I looked back to the screen. I needed to stop worrying about Landon.

I relaxed back into my seat as the previews disappeared, and the movie started. I loved zombie movies, and I couldn't wait to spend the next two hours of my life watching zombies eat people.

Ten minutes later, I was cowering in my seat. Dear God, I hadn't expected this when I decided to watch this movie. The effects were amazing, and it seemed like someone was dying every two seconds.

"You okay?" Landon whispered in my ear.

I jumped—again. "Yeah, I'm great," I mumbled, unwilling to admit that I was terrified.

"Sure you are. Come here." He raised the armrest between us and pulled me tight against him.

My body went rigid at the contact. "I'm fine."

"Relax, okay? I'm not going to try to do dirty things to you in the back of a movie theater." He paused for a second. "Unless you want me to."

"Shut up and watch the movie."

I could feel his body shaking with laughter, but I ignored it. I was too busy over-processing the fact that he had his arm around me with his body tight against mine.

I shouldn't be here. I shouldn't let any guy, except for Joel, touch me.

"Please relax. You're like a board," Landon whispered into my ear again.

I shivered as I felt his breath tickle my ear, but I forced my body to relax. Landon settled back into his seat and pulled me tighter against him. Again. I tried to pay attention to the movie playing in front of me, but all I could focus on was the way his body felt against mine and how good he smelled.

I almost pulled away when I realized how much I was enjoying being wrapped in his arms, but I didn't. It felt too good. I decided to enjoy it for right now. I could worry about my guilt later. I knew Landon well enough to know that he wouldn't try anything with me.

For the rest of the movie, I cowered in his arms. When something scared me, I hid my face in his side, like a two-year-old. I couldn't help it. He made me feel safe and protected.

When the movie was over, I moved away from Landon and stretched my arms above my head. "That was fun."

He laughed. "I definitely liked it, but I never expected you to be scared of zombies. I always pictured you as the type to fight them."

"I usually don't get freaked-out, but that was a pure gore fest." I shuddered.

"Come on, let's get out of here."

We stood and walked out of the theater. We threw our drinks away once we reached the lobby. It was dark when we walked outside, and I kept glancing over my shoulder, expecting a zombie to jump out and attack me.

"You're a dork," Landon said as he walked up beside me and threw his arm over my shoulders.

"I am not. I'm just making sure no one is sneaking up on us," I lied.

"Sure you are."

"I am! I swear."

"The only things you're looking for are zombies. Don't worry, I'll protect you."

"You'd probably trip me and make a run for it," I grumbled.

"Nah, I like you too much for that."

I didn't reply to that. I wasn't sure if we were still joking or if he was trying to be sweet.

We reached his truck, and he released me, so he could unlock the doors. I hurried up into the cab before he decided to help me again. I heard him chuckle as he closed my door, and then he walked around to his side.

I stared out the window as he pulled out of the lot and headed back toward home. The night had passed by too fast. It had been fun to escape for a while.

"What are you thinking about?" Landon asked.

"I just hate to go home. Tonight was fun, but it's back to prison now."

He was quiet for a minute. "I don't have to take you home just yet, if you don't want to go."

I turned to look at him. "Where else is there to go? It's late, and everything is closed."

"We're in the country, City. We make our own fun."

"Okay…"

"I do need to stop by my house real fast though."

"Fine by me as long as I don't have to go home."

"It'll just take a second. I need to pick up something."

"Where are we going after we stop at your place?"

"Nowhere."

I raised an eyebrow but said nothing. If he wanted to get all mysterious on me, then more power to him. I didn't care what we did as long as it didn't require me to go home.

I closed my eyes and leaned back into the seat. I'd been up since sunrise, and I was exhausted at this point, but no matter how tired I was, I didn't want to go home. I must have fallen asleep because the next thing I knew, I woke up to see Landon getting back into the truck.

"Where are we?" I asked, still half-asleep.

"My house. You can nap for a few before we get to where I'm taking us."

"Okay," I mumbled as my eyes slid shut again.

I went in and out of consciousness as I felt the truck going back down the gravel road, and then it bumped along the uneven pavement of the main road. After a few minutes, I felt the truck turn onto a side road. I opened my eyes to look around as we bounced across the potholes. I was surprised when we stopped in the middle of a field.

"We're here," Landon said as he opened his door.

"Where is here exactly?" I asked.

"It's a spot where I come to think sometimes. Come on."

I opened my door and went to the back of the truck where he was lowering the tailgate. He jumped into the bed and grabbed a wadded-up blanket. After spreading it out, he helped me climb up to join him.

He kicked off his boots and sat down. "Sit down with me."

"Sure," I said as I settled down next to him.

"I brought us a present." He reached through the cab window into the backseat and pulled out a bottle of Jack Daniel's.

"Sweet!" I said as I grabbed it from him. I took a drink, and I winced as it burned its way down my throat. "Shit. I forgot how strong it is."

He laughed as he watched me take another sip. "Easy there, City. I don't want you throwing up in my truck."

"I can hold my liquor. Thanks."

"I'm sure you can." He took the bottle from me, had a drink, and then passed it back to me.

"What are we doing here?" I took another drink.

"I just like to come out here to get away sometimes. It's peaceful, and it has a killer view."

"Yeah, I'm loving the view. Nothing like staring at a field."

He laughed. "Look up, City."

I glanced up and saw what he was talking about. There wasn't any light for miles. The sky above us was filled with stars, and the moon was the biggest I'd ever seen. "Wow. It's beautiful."

"Not what you're used to?"

"Nope. There are too many lights where I live, so we can't see the sky this well." I took another drink before lying down on the blanket to get a better look.

"We could have stayed on the farm and had the same view, but I figured you wanted to get away altogether." He lay down beside me.

"Thank you."

"You're welcome, City."

We were both silent as we passed the bottle back and forth and stared at the stars above us. It was nice to just…be. I didn't have to pretend not to care about anything or act like a hard-ass out here. I was just being me. I was surprised that I felt safe enough to be myself around Landon. I wasn't sure what it was about him, but he made me *feel*. Or maybe it was just the whiskey running through me. Either way, I felt content and even happy.

"Tell me about yourself, Cowboy."

"Not much to tell. I grew up in Hundred, which is about twenty minutes from here. We lived in the same house from the time I was born until Caleb hired my dad and me. Once Caleb built our house on his farm, my dad and I moved in and sold the old one."

"How come my grandpa hired you guys?" I asked.

"He's known my dad since he was a kid. When we needed extra money, my dad used to help Caleb occasionally. Dad took time off from the construction company when Mom got sick. When he finally went back, they laid a bunch of guys off, and he was one of them. Caleb heard about it and offered us both jobs."

"That was nice of him." I couldn't hide the surprise in my voice.

My grandpa never did anything nice for anyone, except for Gram.

He laughed. "You sound surprised."

"I just can't see my grandpa being nice to anyone."

"He's not that bad once you get to know him." He hesitated for a second. "When my dad was a teenager, he used to help him all the time."

"And…" I could tell from his tone that there was more to the story.

"My dad dated your mom through most of high school."

"Oh! I didn't see that one coming. I guess that explains why my dad didn't like him much at dinner."

"Yeah, I think the feeling is mutual. Your mom ran off to college and met your dad. She broke up with my dad over the phone."

I winced. "Ouch. That's cold, even for her."

Landon shrugged, causing his shoulder to bump mine. "It was a long time ago. My dad met my mom not long after, so it all worked out for the best."

I took the whiskey from him and took a drink. "I guess so."

I closed my eyes and relaxed. The whiskey was making my brain foggy. I also blamed it for the way my body kept creeping closer and closer to Landon's.

His fingers wrapped around mine as he grabbed the bottle. I opened my eyes to watch him as he took another drink.

"I think I drank too much already," he said.

I shrugged. "Oh well, we can hang out here until you sober up." My tongue felt thick when I spoke. Apparently, I'd drunk too much as well.

"Works for me."

"Tell me more about yourself."

"Um...I played football in high school, but our team sucked. I've had only one girlfriend, and my middle name is James."

"Mine is Lynn. And you've had only one girlfriend? I find that hard to believe."

"Why?"

"Because you're...you."

"Want to elaborate on that?"

I glanced over at him and grinned. "You're sweet. There are very few guys out there as sweet as you. And you're kind of attractive. You have the whole cowboy vibe going on, and you make it hot."

"So, I'm a hot cowboy?" He laughed. "Never heard that one before."

"I'm sure you have. Maybe not the cowboy part, but you have to know you're attractive. You're not my type, and even I noticed it."

"I've never really paid much attention to girls. No one has ever really caught my eye before."

"You sure you're not gay?" I joked. The whiskey was making me talk more than I normally did.

"No, definitely not gay." He grinned at me. "You're kind of hot, too, even if you're not my normal type either."

I reached across him and grabbed the bottle before taking a big gulp. Funny, it didn't even burn anymore. "Thanks, I think."

"It was definitely a compliment. I noticed how pretty you were the moment I saw you."

I took another drink so that I wouldn't have to reply. I had no idea what to say to that. Landon was a good guy, and I didn't want to hurt him. He deserved better than that.

"Landon..."

"Don't say anything, Lexi."

I sighed. "I don't want to lead you on, Landon. You're a good guy, and I am...me. I'm not a nice person, and you deserve someone a hell of a lot better than me."

"You are a good person. You try to hide it, but you are. And I think I can decide who I deserve."

"I'm with Joel. You know that."

"I do, but I also know that he hasn't even attempted to contact you. I saw you checking your phone every two seconds while we were working out in the field. I don't mean to be an ass, but maybe you're not as important to him as you thought you were."

"You think I haven't thought about that a million times since I got here?" I whispered as tears filled my eyes almost instantly.

"Shit, City. I didn't mean to make you cry."

"I know."

"Come here."

He pulled me into his arms, and I didn't even struggle.

"You're something special, City, and if he doesn't realize that, too bad for him."

"See? You just proved that I'm right. You're such a sweet guy."

"My thoughts are anything but sweet when I'm holding you like this. That day on the four-wheeler, I could barely stand to hold you like that and not kiss you."

"Don't say stuff like that. Please," I whispered as I rested my head against his chest.

"I can't help it. You make me want things that I know I can't have." He put his fingers under my chin and forced me to look up at him. "I want to kiss you more than anything right now."

"You can't, Landon."

"Yes, I can."

Before I could stop him, his lips were on mine. Shocked, I let him kiss me. Where Joel had always been rough, Landon's kiss was soft and sweet. I found myself kissing him back even though my mind was screaming for me to stop. He ran his tongue across my bottom lip, and I gasped in shock. He took advantage of my parted lips and slipped his tongue inside. I moaned, unable to stop myself.

This feels so good...too good. I'm cheating on Joel right now. It shouldn't feel this good. It should feel wrong.

He rolled us over until he was on top of me. I moaned again as I felt his hard body pressed up against mine. I wrapped my arms around his neck, pulling him closer.

"You taste like candy and whiskey," he whispered before kissing a path from my lips to my neck.

I grabbed his face and pulled his lips back to mine. God, my body was on fire. I moaned again when I felt his knee pushing my legs apart. He ran his hand down my stomach to my leg and rested it there. I could feel him through his pants as he rested his lower body against mine.

He pulled away, gasping for breath. "Damn it, City. You're going to make me lose my mind."

Reality crashed over me instantly. "Oh my God, I kissed you!"

"No, I kissed you. You just kissed me back."

"Get off of me, please. This isn't right."

I'd kissed another man. I'd cheated. Shame washed over me like a bucket of cold water. *How could I let this happen?*

Landon leaned down and pressed another kiss to my lips before rolling off. "Don't look at me like I'm some horrible person, City."

"You're not the horrible one. I am."

"No, you're not. I know you feel something for me even if you try to ignore it."

"Landon, I have a boyfriend. I don't care if I feel something for you or not. It doesn't matter. I'm a lot of things, but a cheater isn't one of them." I winced when I remembered that Joel had said the exact same thing to me the night I told him I was leaving.

Landon leaned over me, his face inches from mine. "I'm telling you right now that I'm not going to give up on you. I want you to be mine, City, and before the summer is over, you will be. I've never wanted someone the way I want you."

My heart started racing as I let his words sink in. What he wanted was impossible, and I was going to break him.

"I'm sorry, Landon," I whispered.

"Don't tell me that. I'm not letting you go."

There was a determination in his eyes that scared me and excited me all at once. Some small sick part of me didn't want him to give up. It wanted him to chase me until I gave in.

CHAPTER 11

He drove me home without either of us saying a single word. I looked back at him when I closed the truck door. The same determination I'd seen earlier was still in his eyes. I shook my head as I walked up the steps and unlocked the door.

The house was silent as I headed up to my room. I dropped down onto my bed without bothering to change into my pajamas. The whiskey was still clouding my mind, but Landon's kisses had sobered me up a lot. Tonight had started out so well, only to end in disaster. I'd done something horrible, and no matter how hard I wished I could take it back, I couldn't. I'd kissed someone other than Joel.

Before I realized what I was doing, my feet were on the floor, and I was sneaking down the stairs to where my grandparents' landline phone was. I needed to hear Joel's voice. I needed to know he still cared. I was careful not to make a sound as I crept into the kitchen where the phone was. I left the lights off and felt my way around the table until I reached the phone on the opposite wall. I picked it up and dialed quickly, hoping that he would answer.

I nearly cried when his voice mail picked up. "Damn it, Joel. I need to talk to you. Why haven't you returned my texts? Where are you? Don't call me back at this number. It's my grandparents' number. I…I love you. I need to know we're okay."

I hung up and leaned against the counter. *Damn him for not answering when I need him the most.* I balled my hands into fists, trying to control the rage coursing through my veins. I'd given up everything for him. I would have gone to jail for him, and he couldn't even be bothered to talk to me.

And here I was, drowning in guilt. I sighed as my shoulders sagged in defeat. I needed to see him. There had to be a way.

I groaned and rolled over as someone knocked on my bedroom door. It seemed like I'd just fallen asleep only moments ago.

"Alexandria, it's time to get up. You need to get ready for church."

"Fuck," I moaned as I rolled over to look at the door. "Go ahead without me, Gram."

There was silence for a moment before my door swung open. "Come on, dear, you need to get up."

"I'm not going," I said calmly. I didn't want to fight with Gram, but there was no way I was going to church. I wasn't about to walk into that building and pretend to worship a god I didn't believe in.

"Why not?" she asked, confused.

I sighed. "Gram, I don't believe in God."

Her eyes widened. "Don't you dare say that, Alexandria. God loves you, and you should love him back."

This was not the way I'd wanted to wake up—at all. "I'm sorry. I really am, but I'm not going to change my mind." I rolled back over, hoping that she would leave it at that. I loved Gram more than anything, and I hated to disappoint her. I wasn't sure what I would do if she started yelling at me.

I felt my bed dip as she sat down on the corner. "I know you've gone through some tough stuff lately, but you should never turn your back on God. I won't force you to go, but I want you to think long and hard on your decision. You've done wonderfully this past week. I know you'll find yourself again and put all the bad things behind you. God can help you do that."

I stayed silent, unwilling to acknowledge her words. I heard her sigh as she stood and left my room. As soon as she was gone, I closed my eyes and fell back into the peaceful oblivion of sleep.

I awoke sometime later and rolled out of bed. My head was hurting, but it wasn't bad enough to keep me from the shower that I desperately needed. I hurried to the bathroom, before my bladder exploded. After taking care of that problem, I grabbed a towel and hopped into the shower.

Images from the previous night flashed through my mind as I rinsed my hair. What I'd done was wrong on so many levels. And the worst part was that I'd enjoyed kissing Landon. I'd enjoyed it so much that I hadn't even tried to stop him. Instead, I'd pulled him closer.

I shook my head as I shut off the water and then grabbed my towel. I needed to stay far, far away from Landon. What had happened last night couldn't happen again. It didn't matter that I was attracted to him. I was with Joel, and I loved him with every beat of my heart. I needed to get away from this farm and find out what the hell was going on with him. I just hoped that I wouldn't find him with someone else.

I glanced around the bathroom and groaned when I realized I'd forgotten my clothes in my hurry to pee. At least my room was right across the hall, and no one was home right now. I wrapped my towel around me and opened the bathroom door. As soon as I stepped out into the hallway, I ran headfirst into a very hard chest. I shrieked as I looked up to see Landon staring at me in shock. His eyes scanned my body, and the shock turned into something else—lust.

"What are you doing here?" I squeaked as I pulled my towel tighter around me.

"I, uh…I came to talk to you about last night. I knocked, but no one answered, and the door was unlocked, so I let myself in."

"There's nothing to say about last night, Landon. You need to go."

"I wanted to apologize for what happened. I shouldn't have kissed you like that."

"It's fine. Just go, please." I was not going to have *this* conversation while in a towel.

He sighed. "I never meant for that to happen. I wanted the first time I kissed you to be different. I wanted you to be free, so you wouldn't feel the guilt you felt last night."

"Landon, I'm in a towel. Leave!"

He grinned. "But, at the same time, I can't feel as much remorse as I should when you're standing in front of me like this."

I tried to walk around him, but he blocked me with his arm.

"Landon, my grandparents will be home soon. Please leave before you get me in trouble."

"They're at the church cookout, so don't worry." He lifted his hand and ran it down my cheek. "I'm not going to try anything with you again, I promise—at least, not until you want me to."

"That's not going to happen," I stated firmly.

I needed to get to my room—now. The lust in his eyes was making me dizzy, and it was making me want things that were wrong.

"I'll wait until you're ready," he said as he smiled at me. "I'll leave you alone. I already did all the chores, so you don't have to worry about them."

I watched as he turned and walked down the stairs. I didn't breathe until I heard the front door open and close. I rushed to my room and grabbed a pair of jeans and a shirt. After throwing them on, I ran from the room and down the stairs. I stopped by the door and grabbed the extra set of keys that my grandparents kept there. I prayed that they had taken my grandfather's truck instead of Gram's car because I couldn't drive a standard.

Luck was with me when I opened the garage door. My gram's Escort was sitting there, promising me the freedom that I was desperately craving. I had to get to Joel and find out what was going on before I lost control of everything. The only reason I'd even noticed Landon was because Joel had completely disappeared from my life. That was the only explanation I could come up with. I'd been with Joel for so long, and never once had I even looked at another guy the way I looked at Landon.

I hurried to the driver's side and threw open the door. Just as I started to get in, a voice spoke from behind me.

"What are you doing?"

I turned to see Landon standing behind the car. I cursed as I slid into the driver's seat. "I'm leaving. I'll be back."

"Are you going to him?" he asked.

I nodded. "I have to know what's going on."

"You know there will be hell to pay for this."

"I know. I'll take whatever punishment my parents or my grandparents hand out."

"I'm coming with you." He walked to the passenger's side and opened the door.

"No, you're not."

"Yes, I am. If you fight me, I'll take the keys from you."

I glared at him. "This is bullshit."

"Deal with it. I'm not letting you drive that far by yourself. And you don't know what you're walking into."

He'd backed me into a corner, and he knew it. I ignored him as I started the car and backed out of the garage.

"You're going to be in trouble, too," I said.

"I don't care. I have a bad feeling, and I'm not letting you go by yourself."

We were both silent as I drove down the gravel road to Route 7. As I flew around the turns, he tried to talk to me occasionally, but I ignored him. I didn't relax until we crossed the bridge over the Ohio River and back into my home state. I had no idea what time my grandparents would be home, but once they figured out that Gram's car was missing, I was sure that my phone would start blowing up.

Sure enough, about an hour later, my phone started ringing. I picked it up to see that it was my mom. I ignored the call and then silenced my phone. I couldn't deal with them until I knew what was going on with Joel.

Landon stayed silent for the rest of the drive. My palms started to sweat when I saw the exit leading to Columbiana. Just like Landon, I had a bad feeling. We got off the interstate, and I took the back way into town, careful not to pass even remotely close to my house. It was dusk by the time we made it to Joel's house. My stomach dropped when I saw the cars parked around his house. He was having one of his parties.

"This is it," I told Landon as I searched for a parking spot.

I finally found one almost a block away. I stepped out of the car and hurried back up the road to Joel's house with Landon right behind me. Just as I'd expected, the front door was unlocked. We walked through the house to the back door and stepped into the chaos that was Joel's party. I scanned the crowd, searching for him. I blended in with the crowd, not wanting anyone to alert him of my arrival. Something told me that I needed to surprise him. It was obvious that he was still here, having the time of his life, while I was stuck in West Virginia.

I passed Riley and some chick sitting at a picnic table, wrapped around each other like they were glued together. I rolled my eyes and continued through the crowd.

"Jesus, this is nuts," Landon said as he glanced around. It was obvious that he was out of place here.

I ignored him as I continued my search. Everyone was either drunk or stoned out of their minds, and several people had separated from the crowd for some alone time. Once I reached the other side of the mass of bodies, I stopped dead, unable to process what I was seeing. Landon nearly knocked me down as he ran into me. I barely noticed. I was too busy staring at Joel. He was sitting in a chair next to the sound system with Tasha straddling him—topless.

"No," I whispered.

My world crashed around me as I watched his hands cup her bottom to pull her tighter against him.

"City? What's wrong?" Landon followed my gaze and cursed under his breath. "Come on, let's get you out of here."

I shook my head as I started walking toward Joel. I heard Landon calling my name, but it didn't even register with me as I reached Joel and Tasha. I pulled her off of him and punched her in the face before turning my attention to Joel. His eyes were glazed. It was obvious that he was on something—something strong.

Joel's eyes widened in surprise a split second before my fist collided with his nose. Everyone froze as I leaped onto him and started hitting every part of him that I could reach.

"You son of a bitch!" I screamed. "I gave you fucking everything, and you do this to me!"

I was crying by the time Landon was able to pull me off of Joel. I curled up into him, unable to breathe. I'd never felt pain like I was feeling right now.

Joel staggered to his feet, blood dripping from his nose and busted lip. "Lexi, what are you doing here?"

"Fuck you!" I shouted. "I knew something was up when you didn't text me or call me back!"

His eyes were still glazed, but I could tell that my beating had pulled him from a drug-induced haze. "What are you talking about? Some asshole stole my phone last week."

"Bullshit! You're fucking lying. You've lied about everything. How could you, Joel? And with her?" Tears streamed down my face as I struggled to get away from Landon. All I wanted was to hit Joel again.

"I swear, I didn't know you were trying to get a hold of me. I'm so sorry that you thought I abandoned you."

"Even if you're telling the truth, how do you explain Tasha?" I screamed as I looked around for her. I wanted to kill her.

His eyes filled with regret. "I fucked up, Lexi. I was lonely, and she kept coming on to me. I snorted cocaine tonight, and she knew it."

"I hate you. I hate you so much," I whispered as I fell back against Landon. "Stay away from me. I never want to see you again."

"Please, Lexi…"

I ignored Joel. "Get me out of here, Landon."

Landon nodded as he turned me, and we started walking through the crowd. They parted easily for us this time. I let Landon lead me because my eyes were too swollen to see properly.

"Lexi, wait!" Joel shouted as he followed us.

I refused to look back. I never wanted to see him again.

Landon led me through Joel's house and out the front door. He picked me up and carried me back to where I'd parked Gram's car. I could hear feet pounding on the pavement behind us. Landon put me down and took the keys out of my pocket to unlock the door just as Joel reached us.

"Lexi, please don't go. I'm so sorry."

"Go back to your whore, Joel. She's what you wanted all along, so you should be happy."

"I don't want her, Lexi. I want you. I love you."

"Don't. You don't get to say that to me anymore," I spit out.

"Go back to your house, buddy. She doesn't want anything to do with you," Landon said as he stepped in front of me, blocking me from Joel.

"Who the fuck are you?" Joel growled.

"It doesn't matter who I am. Leave her alone," he said, his Southern accent more noticeable from his barely controlled anger.

"Fuck you, asshole. She's mine."

"Last warning—leave her alone, or I'm going to kick your ass." Landon's tone was cold, and I knew he wasn't messing around.

I had no doubt that he could beat Joel if they fought. He was stronger, and Joel was half out of his mind from the cocaine.

"Mind your own fucking business. This is between Lexi and me."

Landon shrugged. "Suit yourself."

Before I could say a word, Landon stepped away from me and threw a punch at Joel. Landon knocked Joel back a few steps, but he caught himself before he fell. He came at Landon and tackled him to the ground. I screamed when he hit Landon in the stomach. That was the first and only punch he got in. After that, Landon flipped Joel over and beat the shit out of him. I screamed for them to stop, but neither heard me as they struggled.

"Landon! STOP! You're going to kill him!" I screamed.

Landon stopped mid-punch and looked at me. There was a rage in his eyes that made me take a step back. He rose and walked slowly to me as Joel rolled over.

"I'm sorry, City. I didn't mean to scare you."

I simply nodded, staring at the blood covering his knuckles.

Riley came running down the street, and he stopped dead when he saw us. "Jesus Christ. What the fuck happened, Lexi?"

"Get him home and take care of him, Riley. I never want to see him again. Don't let him try to find me."

Riley helped Joel to his feet, and I turned and opened the car door.

"Lexi, I love you," Joel whispered.

I squeezed my eyes shut as I sat down on the passenger seat. Landon made sure I was okay before closing my door and walking to the driver's side. He got in and started the car. I watched Joel lean on Riley as they walked back to the house. I knew it was the last time I would ever see him again. Landon pulled away from the curb and headed back the way we'd come. I didn't speak, except to give him directions.

We stopped at a gas station and filled up. Landon went inside to wash his hands and get us something to drink, but I refused the water he tried to hand me. I didn't want it. I didn't want anything. Everything I'd thought mattered was a lie. Joel didn't love me. He'd never loved me. He had used me, and that stung like a bitch.

My tears started flowing again once we hit the interstate. "I'm so stupid."

"No, you're not. You cared about him, Lexi. That doesn't make you stupid. It makes you human."

"I gave him every part of myself," I whispered.

I would never recover from this—never. Joel had ripped my heart out of my chest. He had been the one person in this world who I trusted completely, and he hadn't even cared about me.

CHAPTER 12

When we made it back to the farm, my grandfather's rage didn't even faze me. I stood there, not saying a word, while he screamed at me. I wasn't really here. I was trapped in my own head, too filled with anger and heartbreak to care about what was happening around me. I only snapped out of it when he started shouting at Landon.

"No, don't yell at him. This isn't his fault. He didn't decide to steal Gram's car. I did. He only came with me to keep an eye on me."

"Where did you go?" my grandfather demanded.

"To hell," I said simply.

He stared at me for a moment before turning to Landon. "Where did you two go?"

I winced at the hostility he directed at Landon, but Landon didn't seem bothered by it.

"She went back to her boyfriend."

I didn't think my grandfather could get any angrier, but I was wrong.

His face turned red. "What happened? Why does it look like your knuckles went through a shredder, Landon?"

Landon hesitated, looking at me. I knew he was asking for permission to tell my grandparents. I shrugged. It didn't matter. He could tell them. They already knew I was a fuck-up, so he might as well let them know the extent of it.

"Lexi found her boyfriend with another girl."

My grandma's eyes widened.

"She beat the crap out of him, and we left his house. He followed and refused to leave her alone, so I stepped in."

"Lexi, are you okay?" Gram whispered. It was the first time she'd ever used my nickname.

"No," I answered truthfully. "I'm going upstairs. I can't handle anymore tonight. Do what you want to me tomorrow, but please leave me alone tonight."

My grandfather looked like he wanted to say more, but Gram gave him a look.

He sighed and motioned toward the stairs. "Go. I need to call your parents and let them know you're safe."

I turned and walked away. I couldn't even remember walking up to my room, but somehow, I ended up in my bed. Now that I was alone, I let my tears fall again. I was ashamed at how stupid I'd been. Joel had fooled me completely. I would have done anything he asked—anything.

I jumped when I felt arms wrap around me. I looked behind me to see Landon. "What are you doing here?"

"I thought you might want some company," he said as he pulled me against him.

"You shouldn't be in here. You're in enough trouble already because of me."

"Your grandma knows I'm here. She knows I won't do anything."

I nodded, satisfied with his answer. I didn't want him to suffer my grandpa's wrath because of me, but if Gram was okay with Landon being here, then so was I. Right now, I really didn't want to be alone despite what I'd told my grandparents.

"Want to talk about it?" he whispered.

I shook my head. "There's nothing to talk about."

"Well, if you change your mind, I'm here."

"I know. Landon?"

"Yeah?"

"Thanks for beating the shit out of him for me."

He chuckled. "I enjoyed it, trust me. I never want to see you hurt like that again."

"Don't worry. I'll never get that close to someone again." My words had a bitter edge to them.

Landon was gone when I woke up the next morning. I remembered falling asleep in his arms, so he must have snuck out while I had been sleeping. I stared up at the ceiling, unable to get out of bed. I knew I was being pathetic, but I didn't care. My whole world had come crashing down around me last night. I deserved to lay here and have a pity party.

Of course, that wasn't in the cards for me. The second I thought the words *pity party*, my door swung open, and Landon walked in. He'd been gone for a while. His hair was still wet from a shower, and he had on clean clothes.

"Morning, sunshine." He walked to the bed and threw the covers off of me.

I groaned and rolled onto my stomach as I pulled my pillow over my head. "Go away."

"Nope. It's time to get up. We have stuff to do."

"You've got to be kidding me."

"Not happening. Now, get up."

I pulled the pillow off my head and threw it in his general direction. I didn't even come close to hitting him. Instead, I heard it drop to the floor. I didn't have it in me to look and see if it had done any damage. All I wanted to do all day was lie in bed and mope.

I yelped as I felt myself being lifted from the bed. "What are you doing?"

"If you won't get up on your own, I'll help you. Now, go shower, so we can get shit done," Landon said as he set me down.

"Landon, leave me alone. Please."

He shook his head. "Not a chance. Grab your clothes, and go shower. If you don't, *I'll* go through your underwear drawer and find something for you."

I glared at him as I walked over to my dresser and jerked open a drawer. I pulled out a bra and underwear before stomping to my closet to grab an outfit. "You're an ass."

"You'll thank me later. I'm not going to let you think about him today."

"Too late for that," I grumbled as I walked to the bathroom.

I took my time in the shower. I wasn't ready to face this day. I wasn't sure if I would ever be ready. I finally shut off the water and dried off before dressing. Landon was waiting out in the hall

119

for me. I ignored him as I walked down the steps and pulled on my new boots.

"Don't you want to eat first?" Landon asked as he stopped next to me.

I opened the door and walked out without glancing over my shoulder. "Not hungry."

Landon sighed as he followed me out the door. "Head to the barn. We've got to fix a fence today."

I walked over to the barn. The four-wheeler was sitting in the doorway with a bucket of nails, fence stretchers, and a hammer in the rack on the front of it. I didn't even care that we were going to spend the entire day out in the field, baking in the sun. I just wanted to get everything done, so I could go back to the house and mope some more.

Landon walked past me and climbed onto the four-wheeler. I hopped up behind him as he started it. He glanced back at me once before pulling away from the barn and driving toward the driveway. I wrapped my arms around him once we started to go across the field. I hated to admit it, but he made me feel safe— even more so after last night. But feeling safe was as far as I was going to let my feelings go when it came to him. After what Joel had done to me, I didn't think I would ever be able to trust any guy again.

He drove farther than last time, passing the water spring and continuing into the woods. The path was narrow, and we had to duck more than once to avoid getting hit in the face with a tree limb. Finally, the trees opened up to another clearing.

We climbed a hill, and Landon parked the four-wheeler at the very top. We were high up on the hill, and I could see for miles around us. I couldn't deny that West Virginia was beautiful. No matter where I looked, there was nothing but green trees and hill after hill. I hopped off the four-wheeler and waited as Landon climbed off after me.

He pointed to where the fence line was. "We need to redo a few lines of fence over there. The deer have been jumping through it, and it's too loose. I can tighten most of it, but I'll have to replace a few places."

I nodded as I grabbed the bucket with fence staples, and I started walking to the fence. I heard Landon grabbing everything else before following me. We stopped once we made it to the first spot where the barbed wire was hanging loosely.

"What do you need me to do?" I asked, almost wincing at the sound of my own voice. There had been no emotion in it at all. It was like I was dead inside.

"I'm going to have you pull it tight while I use the hammer to tighten the staples."

I nodded as I watched him grab the stretchers and pull the fence through.

"Just hold it tight like this while I nail."

I took the stretchers from him and held it tightly as he grabbed the hammer and nailed the fence staple back to the post. We continued working together for the next hour or so with me holding the fence as he nailed.

Once we had all of it fixed, he grabbed a roll of barbed wire and started stringing it out along the fence line to replace some of it. Just as he set the line down and started walking back to me, my phone beeped.

My heart stopped with that one little beep. *Why did I bring it with me today?* I knew why—it was second nature to have it with me. I just never expected someone to text me. My hands were shaking as I pulled it from my pocket and unlocked it. My heart started working double-time when I saw the message was from Riley.

> *Riley: Can you call me when you get a chance? I know you're upset, but it wasn't what it looked like. Tasha has been after him for a long time, and she took advantage of him last night. He loves you, Lexi. He'd never hurt you like that. He's freaking out. He wants to drive to WV to find you, but I won't let him.*

I took a deep breath as I reread the message a few times. I wanted to believe Riley. Every cell in my body was screaming at me to text him back and tell him to let Joel know that I still loved him and that things would be okay, but I couldn't. No matter how hard I tried to push it away, the image of Joel and Tasha together last night kept flashing before my eyes. I would never be able to let it go. I would never be able to trust him again. I couldn't live my life that way.

Tears streamed down my face as I typed out my reply.

> *Me: Please keep him away from me, Riley. I can't handle seeing him ever again. Regardless of how she ended up on his lap, she was still there. I can't go back from that. What if he's been cheating on me the entire time? I'll never trust him again.*

I started to put my phone back in my pocket, but he replied back almost instantly.

> *Riley: Please don't do this to him, Lexi. Please. He loves you.*

> *Me: I'm sorry that you're in the middle of this, but I can't go back. I'll never be able to forgive him for what he did to me. Please don't contact me again.*

I shut off my phone and tucked it back into my pocket. I could barely see through the tears filling my eyes. I wiped them away as they streamed down my face. *God, this hurts.* I never thought I would ever be strong enough to tell Joel to stay away from me, but I had been. I'd felt a little piece of myself die as I had done it, but I'd stayed strong.

Landon's arms were around me suddenly, and I clung to him as I cried. He pulled me down to the ground with him, and I curled up in his lap as I cried. I felt guilt mix with my pain as I let him hold me, but I didn't care. I needed someone to hold me right now. I wasn't cheating on Joel by letting Landon touch me. There was no Joel anymore. It was just me. I only wished that things had ended differently between Joel and me. Now, Landon would never get that chance he had been waiting on. I was damaged, and I would only hurt him.

"Please don't cry, City. I can't stand to see you like this," he whispered in my ear as he rocked me back and forth.

I hiccupped. "I'm sorry. It just hurts so badly. I was so stupid."

"I told you last night—you're not stupid. You're human. We care too much, and sometimes, that blinds us from the truth."

"He ruined me completely. I'll never trust anyone again," I whispered into his chest as my sobs quieted.

"He didn't ruin you. It hurts right now, and I know you feel like you have no one, but you have me. I won't hurt you, I swear."

"I can't be what you want, Landon. I'm so sorry, but I can't."

"I don't want you to be anything. Don't even worry about me right now. Just focus on healing and moving on, okay? I'm your friend and nothing more."

I wrapped my arms around him and hugged him tightly. "Thank you for everything."

He hugged me back. "You're welcome, City. If you need to talk, I'm here."

We sat like that for a while, both of us unwilling to move. I made a vow to myself then and there that I would never hurt Landon. He was too good of a person to be destroyed by me. I was going to put him in the friend zone and keep him there.

After my breakdown, fixing the holes in the fence took us much longer than Landon had expected.

Several hours later, we were ready to return to the farm. He flipped the headlights on, and we drove home in near darkness. I clung to his back, unwilling to let him go. I felt guilty for using him, but I couldn't seem to stop myself. He'd said that he was my friend, and right now, I needed a friend more than anything.

When we pulled up to the barn, my stomach dropped. "Oh my God, this can't be happening."

Landon looked over to see what I was talking about. Joel's car was parked in the driveway in front of the house. We watched as he stepped out and started walking over to us. He stopped a few feet away from the four-wheeler, and I winced when I saw just how bad his face looked. Landon really had beat the shit out of him.

"Lexi…"

123

A shiver ran through my body at the sound of Joel's voice. It took every ounce of willpower I had not to jump off of the four-wheeler and run into his arms. Instead, I stayed put and tightened my grip on Landon.

"What are you doing here, Joel?" I asked, my voice cold.

"I came to find you. We need to talk about last night."

"I have nothing to say to you, Joel. You wasted your time coming here."

"I'm not leaving without talking to you"—he glanced at Landon—"alone."

"If you think I'm going to leave you alone with her after what happened, you're out of your damn mind," Landon said angrily.

"Listen, buddy, I don't know who you are, and if you want the truth, I really don't give a flying fuck. This is between me and Lex, and you need to butt out," Joel said as he glared at Landon.

"Don't talk to him like that, Joel. He's been here for me while you've been out partying and fucking Tasha," I spit out.

Joel looked between Landon and me. His eyes dropped to where I was still holding Landon. "I'm sure he's been a real nice guy to you. Maybe I should be asking you about what you've been doing this summer."

Landon's body tensed under my grip.

"Don't you dare accuse me of cheating, you ass! I've *never* slept around on you. I actually cared enough about you to stay away from Landon or any other guy!"

Joel's shoulders dropped in defeat. "I know you wouldn't cheat on me, Lexi. I'm sorry. I just…I don't know what to do here. What you saw last night wasn't what it looked like. I was messed-up, and she knew it."

Unable to stop myself, I pulled away from Landon and climbed off the four-wheeler. I stomped over to where Joel was standing and slapped him. "You're a fucking asshole, Joel! Regardless of whether or not you were fucked-up, you were still with her! Have you been with her the entire time we've been together?"

I heard Landon climb off the four-wheeler, and he came to stand behind me. He rested his hand against my lower back to let me know that he was there.

"What? No, of course not! I've never cheated on you, Lexi!"

"I don't believe you. As far as I know, you probably fucked her once I left your house each night! That would have been awesome for you, wouldn't it? Fuck me, and then fuck her, too!" I shouted as Landon's fingers dug into my side. I wasn't sure if it was because of what I'd just said or because he was preparing to hold me back in case I went after Joel.

"Lexi, I swear to God, I haven't been with anyone since we've been together." Joel stepped forward until he was only inches away from me. "I love you, Lexi. It has always been you. I've been waiting for you to finish school, so we could leave Columbiana together and start over. I know my…job isn't the best in the world, and I'm working on it. I swear, I am. I want us to be together more than anything."

"It's too late, Joel. I'll never forgive you for what you did," I said as I pushed him back.

Landon released me and stepped away from us. He knew I needed to get this rage out, or I would explode.

"You're fucking worthless, Joel. Go back to your drugs and your whores. Live your life however you want because I'm no longer a part of it."

"You're mine, Lexi. I'm not giving up on us!" Joel shouted.

"It doesn't matter what you want. I'm not yours, not anymore. Now, get in your car and leave before I hit you again."

"Hit me! Kick me in the balls for all I care! Whatever makes you feel better. I'll do anything to make you forgive me. Please give me another chance!"

"Leave!" I shouted as I stepped forward and shoved him again.

He caught my hands and pulled me against him. Before I could stop him, he crushed his mouth down on mine. My body hummed at the contact, begging me to forgive him. I let myself go for just a minute, and I kissed him back. He moaned into my mouth as I kissed him, thinking that I was forgiving him. But I wasn't. Instead, I was using the kiss as a final good-bye.

I broke the kiss and stepped away.

He smiled down at me. "Lexi, I—"

I took another step back. "Good-bye, Joel. Don't contact me again, or I swear to God, I'll call the cops on your ass. I won't stop my mother from pressing charges against you."

His face fell. "Don't do this to me, to us. Please."

"Good-bye." I turned and walked past Landon. "Please make sure that he leaves."

He nodded as he glared at Joel. I continued walking until I was inside the barn. I stopped once I made it to the back room where my grandpa kept all the grains. I sat down on a stack of feed bags and let myself cry. I could hear shouting outside for a few minutes, and then I heard a car door slam shut. I breathed a sigh of relief when I heard Joel's car start and then pull away.

Landon found me a few minutes later. He didn't say anything as he sat down beside me and let me cry. I leaned into his side as he wrapped his arm around me. When my tears finally dried, I pulled away and looked up at him.

He frowned and wiped the tearstains from my cheeks. "Don't cry, City. He isn't worth it."

I stared up at him, taking in just how different he was from Joel. They were complete opposites in every way imaginable, inside and out. Joel had a darkness to him where Landon was all light.

"I'm done crying over him. He's caused me enough tears to last a lifetime. I just want to forget about him and get on with my life."

Landon smiled, but it was weak. I knew he hated to see me like this.

"Good. Now, come on. I'm sure Lily has food ready."

I laughed. "When doesn't she have food ready? I swear, I'll be huge by the time I leave this farm."

"I doubt that. Besides, you're beautiful, fat or skinny." He leaned down and pressed a kiss to my forehead. "Let's go."

I smiled as I stood and followed him out of the barn. I refused to look down the driveway, afraid that I would see Joel standing there. My heart ached when I realized that I still loved him despite everything. But the anger and heartbreak I felt were enough to push away any thoughts of going after him. I was better than that. I would move on. I would survive.

One Month Later

I hated the summer heat, but I was getting used to it. It was only a week into July, but it was ten times hotter than June had been. I barely noticed it anymore. While I worked outside, I always zoned in on what I was doing and shoved away everything else, including the heat. My grandfather would watch me closely when I worked around him, but I never gave him a reason to yell at me again.

I hadn't turned on my phone in over a month. I'd felt like I was missing a part of my body by not having it on or with me, but I'd dealt with it. Turning it on would only lead to more tears, and I'd cried enough. It was time to move on and get my life back on track.

When I'd first come here, I had dreaded the summer. Now that I wasn't with Joel, I was dreading the day when I would have to return home. I still had a month and a half before I would have to go back for school, and I was savoring every day. I didn't want to go back. I was afraid that I would run into Joel or someone would start shit with me at school. Now that I wasn't under Joel's protection, I was sure that I would be targeted a lot more by the girls at my school.

I'd spent the last month learning how to forget about Joel. It still hurt to think about him, but I was slowly healing and moving on. The longer I spent without him, the more I realized just how much he'd changed me. No, he hadn't been the one who changed me. That was on me. I'd become a different person because I thought that was who I was supposed to be to make him happy, but no more. I decided to accept myself for who I was and let the anger go. It was almost as hard as not thinking about Joel, but I was doing it. Maybe by the time I made it home, I would be healed.

"Let's do something fun tonight," Landon said as he closed the barn door. Then, he started walking to the house with me.

Over the past month, I'd started to open up to him more. He never mentioned our kiss or the day after, but I knew when he was thinking about it. I would catch him staring at me when he thought I wasn't paying attention, and he was always careful not to touch me any more than he had to. I had put him in the friend zone, and I was trying my hardest to keep him there.

Since we were both ignoring our attraction for each other and focusing on being friends, we'd become even closer. Landon was my best friend now, not that I'd had one before. I would tell him everything that bothered me. I'd talked about Joel and the things I'd done for him. My stomach had turned when I told Landon about dealing drugs for Joel. Now that I was thinking clearly, I understood just how fucked-up it had been to do that. I was realizing just how fucked-up several things in my life had been.

"Like what?" I asked.

"I want to take you muddin' tonight. I think you'll have fun. These storms we've been having lately have left a lot of mud holes."

"I don't know."

"Oh, come on. You have to try it at least once. You don't have to drive the four-wheeler or anything, I swear."

I studied him for a moment. He took off his hat to wipe the sweat off his brow. His hair had gotten long enough now that it hung in his eyes when his hat wasn't on. I still loved how it curled at the ends. It made him look so cute and sweet.

"All right, I'm in," I said.

"Cool. Let's eat dinner, and then I'll come pick you up on my dad's four-wheeler. We can't ride on the property, or your grandpa will kill me, but I know of a spot close-by."

I nodded as I stepped up onto the porch. "See you in a few."

I walked into the kitchen where Gram was setting the table. After washing my hands, I dropped into my chair. Landon and I had spent most of the day moving the cattle from one field to the other, and I was exhausted after chasing them. For such big animals, they could move fast when they wanted to.

"Did you get the cattle moved?" Gram asked as she put a plate in front of me.

"Yeah, finally. A few of the calves gave us some trouble, but we finally got them."

"Caleb will be happy. He kept saying that the grass was getting short in the field he had them in."

I nodded. "It was. The other field is almost overgrown, so we won't have to worry about them for a while."

"Good. So, what are you up to tonight?"

Ever since that night with Joel, Gram would constantly try to get me to do things besides sit in my room all night.

"I'm going out with Landon. We're going muddin' on his dad's four-wheeler."

I thought her face might split in two from the grin she was giving me.

"That's great!"

"We'll see. I'm not sure if I'll like it or not. Plus, four-wheelers still make me nervous."

"You have nothing to be nervous about. Landon will watch out for you."

"I know. They still make me nervous though."

"So, how are things between you and Landon?" Her tone was light, but her eyes were sharp as she waited for me to answer.

"Um…good. Why?"

"I just wondered…well, never mind. It's none of my business."

"Gram, what are you trying to say?"

She smiled. "I see the way that boy looks at you. I was just curious as to whether or not you noticed."

I stared down at my plate to avoid looking at her. "I've noticed."

"But you don't feel the same way?"

"I…ugh. I like him, and we've ended up being really good friends, but I'm not interested in being with anyone. I couldn't handle feeling the way I felt when Joel broke me ever again."

"Oh, Alexandria, you can't let what happened control you. Landon is nothing like Joel."

"I know that, but I'm not ready to get hurt again. Besides, I'll be leaving next month. There's no point in starting something that can never go anywhere."

"Life is a funny thing. You never know what's going to happen. My honest opinion is that if you like Landon, don't let anything hold you back. You're a good girl, and you deserve to be happy. Don't let the past control you."

I pushed my plate away and stood up. "I'm going to go shower before he shows up. I smell like a cow."

I hurried from the room before she could say anything else. I didn't want to think about Landon that way. I wanted a friend who I could depend on and nothing more. I couldn't handle anything else. I just had to keep ignoring how I felt about him. I could do that for a little while longer.

I got ready and then headed back downstairs. Just as I was pulling on my boots, I heard a four-wheeler approaching the house. I took a deep breath, pushing the conversation with my grandmother away, and I stepped outside. Landon looked like a country god. He was sitting there with his cowboy boots, blue jeans, and his plain shirt that was tight enough to see every muscle he had. I focused on the ground instead of him as I walked over.

"Hey! You ready?" he asked.

I glanced up to see him smiling at me. "Yeah, I guess. I'm still nervous."

"Don't be. You're going to have fun, I promise."

He scooted forward, so I could climb on behind him. Gram's words were still running through my head, making me feel awkward and unsure, as I wrapped my arms around his stomach. He turned the four-wheeler around and tore down the driveway, going faster than he ever had before. Apparently, Landon was all about getting me to loosen up tonight if his speed was any indication. We reached the main road in minutes, and he turned left toward Hundred. I knew it was against the law to ride a four-wheeler on the main road, but I doubted if anyone cared around here.

We stayed on Route 7 for a few miles before turning onto another road. Truthfully, it was more of a four-wheeler path than an actual road. Tree limbs brushed against us from both sides as Landon drove down the trail. We arrived at the edge of a clearing, and I noticed two other four-wheelers with a guy on each of them. Landon pulled up next to them and shut the four-wheeler off.

"What's up, guys?" he asked.

Both guys were staring at me. I tried not to notice as I relaxed my grip on Landon.

"Not much. I just got here a minute ago," one of them said.

He was huge, even sitting down. His hair was cut short enough that it looked like he'd shaved it off. The other guy was smaller. He was more around Landon's size. He had a blond ponytail hanging out of the back of a baseball cap. Both guys were good-looking. Apparently, farm looked good on these guys.

"I figured we could ride for a few hours until it's too dark to see," Landon said.

"Sounds good. I drove out a few minutes before Jackson got here. It's a swamp." The smaller guy glanced over at me. "I'm Will, and this giant over here is Jackson."

"Alexandria," I said as I smiled at him.

"That's a long-ass name," Jackson said as he smiled over at me.

"You can call me Lexi if you want."

He nodded as he turned back to Landon. "Let's go."

All three of them started their four-wheelers at once, and then we all tore down the field. I clung to Landon as the four-wheeler went over small mud holes and ruts. We made it halfway across the field before they stopped again. I winced when I saw the mud hole in front of us. It really was a swamp from all the rain.

"We're going through that?" I asked.

"Yeah. That's the point of muddin'—you get muddy," Landon joked.

"What if we get stuck? It looks deep."

He shrugged. "If we do, one of these guys will pull us out."

"Good thing I wore my mud boots," I grumbled.

Landon laughed as Will turned his four-wheeler around and headed back the way we'd come.

"Mud boots aren't going to help you today." Landon said.

"Where is he going?" I asked as I watched Will.

"He's going to get a running start before he goes in, so he doesn't get stuck. Just watch."

I watched as Will turned and headed back toward us, going way faster than before. I held my breath as he came up on the mud hole. He didn't slow as he began to plow through it. Mud flew everywhere as his wheels spun. I shrieked when some of it landed on us, but Landon just laughed. Will almost got stuck in the middle, but he finally got enough traction to get the rest of the way through. I couldn't help but laugh as he exited on the other side. The boy was covered in mud from head to toe. He drove back around the mud hole and stopped between Jackson and us.

"That was fun. Watch the center. It's really mushy," Will said.

"My turn," Jackson said.

He took off down the field like Will had. Jackson flew back down the field to us, and then he dived into the mud. He got stuck almost instantly, and I could hear him cussing as he gunned the throttle. He finally broke free and gave it hell as he tried to make it the rest of the way. When he reached the other side, he looked as muddy as Will.

"You ready?" Landon asked as he glanced over his shoulder at me.

"I guess." I wasn't used to stuff like this, and it made me nervous.

No one played in the mud for a good time back home. We would get drunk and high. This was a whole different world from what I was used to.

"Hold on to me tight. I don't want you to fall off in the middle of the pit," Landon said as he drove across the field.

I wrapped my arms around him as tightly as I could. I tried not to notice how my breasts crushed against his hard back or how my legs wound around his, pushing my core against his backside. Suddenly, the night felt too hot.

Landon turned the four-wheeler around and tore down the field. I held my breath as we approached the mud. He didn't slow down when we reached it. We dived in, slowing down drastically as the mud tried to hold on to us. The jolt from slowing down so fast would have knocked me off if I hadn't been clinging to him like a monkey. Landon gunned the engine and plowed through it. We slid to the left and then the right, but we didn't get stuck. Mud flew everywhere, covering my boots and legs.

When we reached the center, the water flew with the mud, and I was soaked from head to toe. I hid my face in Landon's back, trying to keep it from getting covered, and then we made it to the other side finally. I glanced over Landon's shoulder as we drove back to Will and Jackson. They both laughed at me before turning back down the field. I watched with my mouth hanging open as they hit the mud at the same time. I could barely see Will on the other side of Jackson. The mud and water flying through the air was too thick.

"So, what do you think?" Landon asked as he looked back at me.

I laughed when I saw his face. He was completely covered in mud.

"I think you need a bath."

"You don't look much better," he pointed out.

I glanced down to see that there wasn't an inch of me that wasn't covered in mud, and I laughed again. "Good point. It was…it was fun and different. I never thought I'd be playing in the mud for fun."

"Want to drive next time?" he asked, his eyes sparkling with mischief.

"I don't think so. I feel safer riding back here," I told him truthfully.

"Me, too. Besides, I like when you hold on to me like that. Let's go again."

I stayed silent as he took off down the field again.

We spent the rest of the evening going through the mud over and over again. Jackson got stuck once. Will tied a rope to both four-wheelers and pulled Jackson until he could get traction.

By the time we called it quits, there wasn't an inch of us or the four-wheelers not covered in mud. It was going to take me an hour to get the mud out of my hair. Gram would probably shoot me when she saw my clothes. I'd probably have to strip down to my undies on the porch.

We talked with the guys for a few minutes after we finished. I learned that they had both graduated the same year as Landon. After high school, instead of going away to college, they'd both stuck around to help their parents out on their own family farms. That surprised me. My mom and dad were always pushing me to go to college, but their parents hadn't seemed worried about it. They had been fine with their children sticking around here to help out since they would eventually take over the farms. The guys waved good night, and then they started their four-wheelers and headed home.

Landon turned to me. "You want to head home?"

"Not yet—unless you do."

"It's fine. What do you want to do? We can't exactly go anywhere looking like this."

I looked up to the sky above us. "I just want to look at the stars again."

He climbed off the four-wheeler and held out his hand to help me. "We can lie in the field. I don't have anything to lie on, but I doubt if you're worried about getting dirty."

"Yeah, I think it's a little late for that," I said as we walked between the four-wheeler and the mud hole.

I grinned as a thought struck me. Without warning, I shoved Landon hard, and he fell into the mud hole. He grabbed my hand at the last second, and I went tumbling in with him.

"What was that for?" he shouted as he laughed.

"I felt like it," I said as I tried to stand.

Landon grabbed me and pulled me back so that I was sitting in the gooey mud. "Where do you think you're going?"

"Me falling in wasn't part of my plan. I'm trying to escape."

"Well, too bad."

He grabbed a handful of mud and threw it at me. It hit me in the chest and fell down into my lap. I picked it back up and tossed it at him. When it landed on top of his head, I laughed so hard that I almost started crying.

We continued to throw mud balls at each other, and I shrieked while he laughed. By the time we crawled back onto solid ground, we both had mud falling off of us in chunks. I felt gross as I rolled onto my back and stared up at the stars above us. Landon collapsed next to me. Neither of us spoke. We just enjoyed each other's company.

A cloud blocked the moon, throwing us into almost complete darkness.

I couldn't deny that tonight had been fun despite my uncertainty. I never should have thought otherwise. I always had fun when I was with Landon. He was the one who had cheered me up time and time again when I would get depressed from thinking about Joel.

"Thanks for tonight," I said, breaking the silence.

"You're welcome. I thought you could use some fun."

"I definitely needed it."

I closed my eyes and let my body relax. The only sounds were the crickets and Landon breathing beside me. It was heaven out here. The longer we stayed, the less I wanted to go back to the farm.

"What are you thinking about?" Landon asked quietly.

"Just how peaceful it is out here. I like it."

"Do I make you feel peaceful?"

His question caught me off guard. "Yeah, I guess you do."

I'd never really thought about it, but he did make me feel peaceful. I hadn't felt that way in a very long time.

"I'm glad that I can make you feel something."

The cloud finally moved past the moon, and I could see again as I turned on my side to face him. I hadn't missed the hidden meaning in his words.

"You make me feel a lot of things, Landon, but it doesn't matter. I'll be leaving at the end of next month, and we'll probably never see each other again."

"What do I make you feel?" he asked, ignoring the rest of my words.

"Does it matter?" I asked as I rolled back onto my back.

"It does to me. If you care about me the way I care about you, why do you keep pushing me away?"

"Because nothing good can come from it. Besides, you deserve someone a lot better than me."

"I think you should let me decide what I do and don't deserve, City."

I opened my mouth to respond, but he silenced me by rolling over and pressing a kiss to my lips. I didn't fight him as his tongue slipped into my mouth and tangled with mine. I didn't have it in me to fight it. It felt too good. *He* felt too good, so I was going to enjoy this moment for a minute before I had to face reality again.

My arms wrapped around his neck and pulled him closer to me. He was on his side next to me, but he rolled the rest of the way over so that his body was hovering over mine. My body felt stiff as the mud dried to my skin, but I ignored it as we continued to kiss. I didn't want it to end.

He pulled back, causing me to grumble. "See, City? Things are so much easier when you stop worrying about stuff."

"Things are never easy," I whispered.

"Stop stressing over us, and just let things…go. Whatever is meant to happen will happen."

"I'm so afraid of getting hurt again. I don't ever want to feel the way I felt after what Joel did to me."

I felt Landon's body stiffen above me.

"City, I would *never* do that to you. I've never given you a reason not to trust me, have I?"

"No, but that doesn't mean that you won't hurt me."

He lifted his hand to run it down my face. "I'll never hurt you, I promise. Will you give me a chance? I know you're still trying to get over him since it's only been a month, but I swear, I'm nothing like him."

"I…I don't know. I can't answer that right now. I still love him, Landon. I'm slowly letting what I had with him go, but he's still under my skin. I thought he was it for me."

"I told you before that I could wait, and I meant that, but I'm not going to just sit around and wait for you to make up your mind."

"What do you mean?" I asked, confused.

He grinned down at me. "Prepare yourself to be blown away by my charm. I'm going to do everything I can to win you over."

"Landon…"

He pressed two fingers against my lips. "Shush. Nothing you say will stop me from trying."

I stayed silent as he pressed another kiss to my lips. He released me and stood. He held out his hand to help me up from the ground. Both of us were silent as we walked to the four-wheeler and climbed on. I rested my head against his muddy back as he drove us back to the farm.

I had a lot to think about. I knew that something good could come from being with Landon, but I was still scared. I didn't want to get hurt again, but being around him just felt right. I'd noticed that from the very beginning. Even then, I'd forced myself to ignore my attraction to him because I was with Joel. Now, I was free, and I was even closer to Landon than before. I liked spending time with him, and I liked it when he'd kissed me. It was soft and innocent and something I'd never had with Joel.

Instead of taking me back to my grandparents' house, he went to his house.

"Why did you bring me here?" I asked.

"Because I figured you'd want to shower and wash your clothes before you went home. Your grandma will have a heart attack if she sees you like this."

"Oh, okay. I don't have any extra clothes with me though."

He shrugged as we climbed off the four-wheeler together. "You can wear mine until yours are dry."

I kicked off my boots by the door and walked inside.

He pointed toward the bathroom. "I'll get you some clothes. Help yourself to whatever you need. I don't have any chick shampoo though. Sorry."

"No biggie. I'll survive."

I walked to the bathroom and shut the door. I stripped off my muddy clothes and put them on top of the hamper. I couldn't help but laugh when I noticed that even my bra and underwear were soaked. Once I had the water adjusted, I slipped into the shower stall and closed the door. The hot water was just what I needed. I stood under it for a minute before grabbing a bottle of Axe shampoo and running it through my hair.

Once I had all the mud scrubbed off of my body, I shut the water off and dried myself with a towel. I stepped out of the shower to see that Landon had left a pair of sweats and one of his shirts for me to put on. My dirty clothes were gone. I hadn't even heard him come in. At least the shower was surrounded by frosted glass, so I didn't have to panic over whether or not he'd seen me naked.

I pulled his clothes on and laughed at how big they were on me. I had to roll the pant legs up several times, so I wouldn't trip on them. His shirt looked like a dress on me, but there wasn't much I could do about that. I couldn't help but sniff his shirt. I loved the way he smelled. I opened the bathroom door and stepped out into the hallway. I turned to my left, but that led into the kitchen. I went right instead and made my way past the bathroom and into the living room.

"Landon?" I called softly, not wanting to wake up his dad.

Landon appeared around the corner and motioned for me to follow him. We walked into his bedroom. I tried not to stare at him when I noticed that his jeans and shirt were gone. Other than a pair of shorts, he had nothing on. I couldn't help but glance up at his naked chest, taking in just how fit he was.

"I'm going to go shower. Make yourself at home in here, but don't go through the rest of the house. If my dad sees you like this, he'll flip."

I nodded as I sat down on the end of his bed. "Got it."

He turned and walked out of the room without another word. I stared around his room as I waited for him to come back. Looking at his country music posters and the pictures of him and his friends in football uniforms, I realized that we were two totally different people. He was the golden boy while I was the problem child.

I lay back across the foot of the bed and stared up at the ceiling. I had no idea what I was doing when it came to Landon. If I were smart, I'd sneak out of the house while he was in the shower. Of course, I rarely did the smart thing. Part of me wanted to tackle him to the bed the minute he walked back into the room while the other part wanted to curl up in a ball and hide from him. I wasn't sure which part would win.

Landon returned to his room a few minutes later, looking relieved when he saw that I was still on his bed. "I figured you would sneak out."

"Nah. I'm tired, and it's a long-ass walk back to the main house."

He laughed as he sat down next to me. "Lazy ass."

"Always." My eyes closed as I felt exhaustion take over.

The next thing I knew, he was lifting me and placing me back down on his bed, so I wasn't lying across it anymore. I snuggled down into the blankets after he covered me up. I needed to go home, and I would—right after I took a nap.

I was too hot. I tried to move to throw off the covers, but an arm wrapped around me had me trapped. I glanced behind me to see Landon sound asleep. He was pressed up tight against me, and I could feel his thickness pressed against my ass. I wiggled, trying to free myself, and he moaned. I sucked in a breath as he pushed his hips tighter into me.

His hand drifted up and started rubbing circles across my hip. My shirt had come up sometime during the night, and the feeling of his fingers against my bare skin made me snuggle back into him further. Despite how good it felt, I needed to move off this bed. I still had no idea whether or not I was ready to be something more with Landon, and waking up in bed with him was not how I'd wanted to start our relationship.

I tried to squirm away, but his arm wrapped completely around me again. I shivered as he ran his fingers up and down my stomach. If his breathing wasn't still even, I would have sworn he was trying to get a free pass to feel me up. His hand crept higher until it was cupping one of my breasts. My breathing became shallow as his thumb ran across my nipple. I shoved him away roughly and jumped out of the bed.

His eyes sprang open, and he stared up at me. "City, what's wrong?"

"I…nothing. I just didn't know where I was and got scared," I lied.

If it were any other guy but Landon, I would have let him have it. But I knew Landon better. I knew he wouldn't push me like that. I turned and walked out of the room and to the bathroom. I stood with my hands on the sink and stared at myself in the mirror. I wasn't ready for sex with anyone. I wasn't sure if I would ever be ready again. But damn it, my body was humming, and there was an ache between my legs from where he'd touched my body.

My head was a mess. *Why can't I just let Joel go and take a chance with Landon?* I knew he was nothing like Joel, but I was still terrified to let myself feel again. Joel had completely destroyed my trust in men, and I hated him for that. He'd ruined me and left Landon with someone who was terrified of him when it came to something more than friendship.

I smacked the sink before opening the door and returning to Landon's room. He was sitting on his bed, running his hands through his hair. I watched him silently as I waited for him to look up and notice me. He stood and pulled off his shorts, leaving him in only his boxers. My eyes widened in surprise, but I didn't utter a word. I stared at his body and wondered what the hell was wrong with me.

He grabbed a shirt off the bed and pulled it over his head before grabbing a pair of jeans and putting them on as well. He turned to face me and stopped dead when he noticed me. A grin tilted up the corners of his mouth as we stared at each other.

"How long have you been standing there?" he asked.

I felt my cheeks warm. "Uh…just for a few minutes."

He laughed. "Were you hoping to see me naked?"

"What? No! I just—"

"I'm only kidding, City. Don't freak out on me." He walked across the room and took my hand to lead me back to the bed. "Come sit down with me. I want to talk to you."

"About what?" I asked as we sat down.

"Look, I know we talked last night, but you're still acting so damn skittish around me. I want you to understand that I'm not trying to pressure you into anything. You know me better than that. Do I want you? Hell yes. But I know everything that has happened to you with Joel, and I would never expect you to jump right into a relationship with me, no questions asked."

"I don't want you to think that I'm just leading you on. I'm not. I'm just afraid to start a new relationship with someone. I care a lot about you."

"Then, give me a chance, please. We'll go slow."

I studied him closely. I could see the truth in his eyes. *This man won't hurt me. He won't use me like Joel did.*

"We'll go slow," I said. My stomach felt like it was going to fall out as I said those words, but I meant them.

I had to let go of Joel and move on. I was pretty sure that I wasn't going to find anyone that was as sweet and caring as Landon.

Landon pulled me into his arms and hugged me tightly. I snuggled down into his arms. It felt right to be in them, and like always, I felt safe as he held me. I decided right there that I would stop worrying and let things go wherever they were supposed to go.

"I'd like to start going slow by taking you somewhere today."

I pulled away to look up at him. "Where?"

"You'll see. Go get dressed. Your clothes are in the dryer."

"Okay..." I stood and walked into the hallway.

I'd seen the washer and dryer in a small room next to the bathroom last night. I walked in and pulled my clothes out before continuing on to the bathroom. I changed quickly and dug through the cabinet until I found a brush. I brushed my hair and tied it back into a ponytail before grabbing the toothbrush Landon had obviously left for me out of the package.

A few minutes later, I reemerged from the bathroom to see Landon standing in the hallway by the front door. The armor around my heart shattered when he gave me the biggest smile ever. This boy was crazy about me. There was no hiding it. I just hoped that he wouldn't hurt me or that I wouldn't push him away.

"Let me brush my teeth, and then we'll head out. Don't look in the bag by the door," he said as he walked past me and into the bathroom.

I stared at the bag he'd mentioned, trying not to cheat. He came back a minute later and picked it up before I could.

"All right, let's go."

We walked out onto the porch, and he waited as I slipped on my mud boots. I giggled as I stared at the mud covering every inch of them. He held my hand as we walked to the four-wheeler. He picked me up and sat me on it before climbing on himself. He threw the bag on the front and then started the four-wheeler. I wrapped my arms around him as he drove up a hill next to his house. I'd never been this far out on this side of the farm, so I had no idea where we were going.

I rested my forehead against his back as we climbed the hill and started down the other side.

God, he smells good. I inhaled deeply, breathing him in.

Neither of us spoke until we came to a stop. I looked over his shoulder, and my mouth dropped open.

"I never even knew this was here," I told him as I stared out at the pond.

Truthfully, it was much larger than an average pond. It was roughly a quarter of a mile wide and long. Ducks and even a few geese swam around on the pretty blue water.

"We use these fields in late fall once the cattle eat everything in the other two. Then, once winter hits, we take them back to the fields closer to the house, so we can feed them hay."

"You're so good at all of this. I mean, I do my chores and stuff, but I have no real knowledge of this stuff. You live and breathe it."

He jumped off the four-wheeler and grabbed the bag off the front. I followed him as he walked to a spot next to the water. He set the bag down and opened it. I watched as he pulled out a thin blanket and spread it out on the ground.

"Most folks laugh at people like me for being too backwoods. But you know what? I like it. No, we don't have crazy fast Internet or cell service, but we all know each other around here, and I couldn't tell you the last time someone got in trouble with the law around here. Plus, I'd probably go nuts if all I had to look at was concrete all day. Farming isn't easy, but it's a way of life. If the world came crashing down around us, I know I could survive off the land and take care of myself."

"If the world ever ends, you can bet your ass I'll be hiding out here with you," I joked before glancing at the blanket on the ground. "Are we having a picnic?"

He grinned. "We are. I thought it would be nice to just get away for a few hours."

"I probably should have called Gram to let her know where I am. She's worried, I'm sure."

"I called her earlier this morning while you were sleeping. She knows you're with me."

"Oh, okay."

Only Landon would be able to call my gram early in the morning to let her know that I was with him and not get in trouble. I guessed that was just another sign that he really was trustworthy.

"Come sit down. I brought food," Landon said as he dropped down onto the blanket.

I stepped forward and sat down next to him. I started laughing as he pulled our *food* out of the bag.

"Really? I don't think snack cakes and Reese's Cups classify as actual food."

"I can't cook to save my life, so deal with it. Besides, I love this stuff."

"You have a sweet tooth? I never would have guessed that by looking at you," I said, not thinking about my words until it was too late.

"Why? How do I look?" he asked.

I could see laughter in his eyes as I squirmed under his stare.

"We've already had this conversation once. You're hot, Cowboy, and you know it."

He chuckled as he handed me a snack cake. "That's probably the nicest thing you've ever said to me."

I ate my cake while watching the ducks play in the water only a few feet away from us. The wind blew softly, causing the surface of the water to ripple gently. *This was peace right here. This entire farm was peace.*

Dread filled me as I realized that my time here would be over soon. I had no idea how I would deal with leaving the farm and Landon behind to go back to the only home I'd ever known. I didn't want to leave this place. I didn't want to go anywhere near where Joel was. Home would be a reminder of him.

I looked over at Landon as he shoved two Reese's Cups in his mouth at once. I wanted to stay with him. We were just starting to trust each other, and I wasn't ready to let him go.

I looked back to the water as I tried to clear my mind. *Maybe I could come here on the weekends or something. Yeah, that would work.* Even if nothing came of Landon and me, I still wanted to stay at the farm sometimes. This place just made me happy. Even Grandpa wasn't as bad as I'd thought he was. We weren't going to hold hands and sing songs together anytime soon, but we'd been decent to each other since my epic screw-up.

Landon reached over and pulled me tight against him. I snuggled into his chest as I stared out across the water. We spent the next hour just talking and getting to know each other better. Now that we weren't both trying to ignore what was between us, things were easier. There was no tension.

Every few minutes, he would tilt my chin up, so he could kiss me softly. I melted into him each time, unable to stop myself. Things hadn't felt this right in a while. I was going to cherish it while I could.

Even when we ran out of words, our lips never stopped moving. Our kisses grew deeper as we lay on the blanket. Landon balanced his weight on his elbows, so he wouldn't crush me. He kissed a trail from my mouth to my neck and then up to my ear. My heart was pounding so loud that I was sure he could hear it. His hands roamed across my stomach but never went higher or lower. He respected me enough not to try for something more.

When it was almost dark, he took me back to my grandparents' house. After a long kiss good night, I walked inside as he drove away. I felt light and happy as I nearly skipped through the house and up to my room. I grabbed pajamas and walked into the bathroom. I sang loudly as I showered, not caring if anyone heard me. I'd spent the entire day with Landon and I couldn't be happier if I'd tried.

Gram was sitting on the end of my bed when I walked back into my room. She smiled as soon as she saw me.

"Hey, Gram. What's up?" I asked.

"Oh, nothing. I was just curious about why you're in such a good mood. I heard you singing clear downstairs."

I grinned at her. "Nothing in particular. I'm just happy today."

"So, it had nothing to do with the fact that you spent the entire day with Landon or the fact that I happened to look out of the kitchen window right as he kissed you?"

I blushed at the thought of my grandma watching me kiss a boy. "It might have something to do with that."

"Oh, Alexandria, you don't have to hide anything from me. I've known this was coming for a while."

"How did you know that?"

"I watch people. It was hard to miss the way you two looked at each other when you thought no one was looking."

"We're taking things slow. I'm terrified that I'll get hurt again."

"I've known Landon since he was just a baby. He's a good boy, Alexandria. You're both so different from each other, too. I think that you'll help even out each other. Just go with your gut, and see what happens."

"What about when I leave at the end of the summer?"

She smiled at me. "We'll figure that out when the time comes. For now, just enjoy each other. I want to see you happy again, and this is the happiest I've seen you since you got here."

I hugged Gram tightly. "Thank you."

"For what?" she asked, confused.

"For not giving up on me. I know I was a mess when I got here, but you treated me the way you always have."

"Like I said before, you're a good girl. You just got confused." She stood and walked to my door. "Good night."

"Night, Gram," I called out before she shut the door.

I tossed and turned for a few minutes, missing the feel of Landon next to me, before finally falling asleep.

CHAPTER
15

July passed quickly, and before I knew it, it was the second week of August. The past few weeks had been the happiest time that I could remember in a long time. After spending so much time with Landon, I realized that I'd never been truly happy with Joel. My happiness had always been darkened with fear over whether or not he would cheat on me with one of the junkies and that he would get arrested and I'd never see him again.

Being with Landon was completely different. The only fear I felt was over the fact that I'd be leaving him in only two-and-a-half weeks. Other than that, things were perfect between us. We would spend most of the day working, and then we'd do something fun in the evenings. A lot of the time, we'd go swimming in Gram's pool, or we'd watch a movie at his house. I loved snuggling up with him on the couch.

My grandpa and Landon's dad knew we were together, but they never mentioned it. Gram said that his dad was happy about it. My grandpa was just relieved that I was acting like a normal human being again. I ignored that when she told me. I was too happy to let my grandfather's sarcasm bring me down.

Landon and I kissed a lot, but he never pushed for more. I knew he was being respectful of me, but it'd been over two months since I had sex, and our kisses were starting to drive me mad. I wanted more. I was ready. I just wasn't sure how to ask for it. I was afraid that Landon would turn me down.

I finally decided to take a chance and see what happened.

On Saturday evening, we went to New Martinsville. We watched a movie and had dinner together. I claimed that I needed something from the local drugstore, so I had an excuse to go in and buy condoms. I seriously doubted if Landon had any, and even though I was on the pill, I didn't want to take any chances. I'd had unprotected sex with Joel more times than I could count, and now, I was worried that I might have caught something since it had been obvious that he hadn't been one-hundred percent faithful to me. I wouldn't feel safe until I saw my family doctor after I made it home.

I'd dressed extra sexy, hoping to get Landon in the mood. I wore my favorite miniskirt and a plain black tank top that showed off both my stomach and a fair amount of cleavage. On my feet were my favorite knee-high black leather boots. I received more than one dirty look while we were in New Martinsville, but I ignored them. Landon couldn't keep his eyes off of me the entire night, so I figured the stares were worth it.

Landon seemed like he could barely control himself around me tonight. He would help me into the truck every chance he got, and his hands would linger on my bare legs longer than necessary.

I rode in the center of the bench seat in his truck on the way home with my hand running up and down his thigh.

"Do you want to come back to my house to watch another movie? Or do you want me to take you back to your house?" he asked, his voice gruff, as he drove up the driveway.

"Let's hang out at your house for a while. Your dad left this morning with Grandpa to go fishing, so we'll have the place to ourselves."

He only nodded as he steered the truck toward his house. As soon as we came to a stop, I grabbed my purse that had the condoms in it and hopped out. I followed him up the steps and waited as he unlocked the door. I walked past him as he held the door open for me. The minute the door closed behind us, he grabbed me and pulled my body tight against his. His mouth crashed down on mine, and I opened up to allow his tongue entry. My arms wrapped around his neck, and my fingers latched on to his hair. He picked me up, and I wrapped my legs around him.

"Damn it, City," he gasped as he pulled away. "You've been driving me crazy all night."

"That was the point," I said.

I jerked his head down, so I could kiss him again. I nibbled on his bottom lip, and he groaned.

"You're making it really hard not to lose control," he whispered against my lips, his breathing heavy.

I untangled my body from his and took his hand to lead him back to his bedroom. My heart was pounding out of my chest as we walked. My body was tight with tension as I wondered whether or not he would turn me down. I knew his body wanted me, but I wasn't sure where his mind was.

As soon as we made it to his room, I shoved him down onto his bed and pounced on top of him. I didn't give him a chance to speak as I kissed him hard. My body was begging for more. I wanted him tonight more than I'd ever wanted anything in my life. I kissed him one last time before sitting up. He watched me with glazed eyes as I grabbed my tank top and pulled it over my head. I felt his body stiffen.

"What are you doing, City?" he asked.

I reached around behind me and unclasped my bra. "I want you, Cowboy—tonight."

His eyes dropped down to my naked breasts, and he swallowed roughly. "Are you sure? We can wait until—"

I pressed my finger to his lips, silencing him. "I've waited long enough. If you want me, take me."

A shiver ran down his body as he stared up at me. I saw it in his eyes the minute he decided. His brown eyes turned black with hunger. He flipped me over and climbed on top of me, kissing his way from my mouth to my chest. I whimpered as he wrapped his lips around my nipple and sucked.

"God, City, I want you so bad."

"I'm yours," I whispered.

And I'd meant it. I was his, totally and completely. I'd spent enough time moping over Joel. I had Landon right in front of me, and I wasn't going to waste any more time.

He switched to my other nipple as his hand explored my body. He stopped at my hip bone and started rubbing circles. His fingers felt like heaven as they caressed me. He stood and pulled his shirt off before tossing it to the side. I sat up on my knees and grabbed his jeans to pull him closer. My gaze never leaving his, I unbuttoned his jeans and unzipped them. I pulled them down over his hips and down his legs, and then he kicked them off.

I ran my fingers down his chest and stomach, enjoying the fact that he shuddered at my touch. My tongue snaked out to run across first one nipple and then the other before I kissed a trail down his stomach. His breathing became erratic as I slipped my fingers into his boxers and tugged them down. They dropped to the floor, and I stared at a completely naked Landon.

My eyes dropped to his shaft. He was bigger than Joel. I reached out and ran my fingers across his hips before wrapping them around his shaft. His sharp intake of breath told me everything I needed to know. I ran my hand up and down his dick over and over again until his legs were trembling. I stared up at his face as I leaned forward and took him into my mouth. His hips bucked as he thrust forward into my mouth.

"Oh fuck, City," he groaned.

I sucked and ran my tongue along his shaft. His fingers found my hair and tugged gently, wanting me to go faster. He tightened his grip as I obliged. A minute later, he pulled away and cupped himself as he came.

The throbbing between my legs was almost unbearable as I watched him come. I needed him now.

Then, he turned and walked out of the room, and I nearly cried.

Did I do something wrong? Am I moving too fast? Terror gripped my heart as I stared at the empty doorway.

He returned a few seconds later with a towel in his hand. He gave me a sheepish grin. "Sorry, I needed to clean up."

Relief washed through me as I realized that I hadn't scared him away. He threw the towel to the floor and picked me up off the bed. He stood me up and unfastened the clasp on my skirt. It dropped to the floor, leaving me in only my black thong and knee-high boots. I knew I probably looked like a hooker, but I didn't care.

"Damn, City. Those boots are killin' me," he whispered as he knelt in front of me.

I watched as he unzipped one and then the other. I lifted my legs one at a time to let him pull them off of me. Next, he reached up, grabbed the thin strings of my thong, and pulled it down my legs. I stepped out and waited, completely naked, to see what he would do next.

He stood and picked me up again, only to lay me gently on his bed. "You're the most beautiful girl I've ever seen."

He climbed into the bed with me and started to kiss my jaw and my neck. I turned my head to the side to give him better access. I gasped as he ran his thumb over my nipple. My body was hypersensitive, and every touch was almost unbearable.

"Landon, I need…" I whispered, my breath ragged.

"What do you need, baby?" he asked just before his tongue replaced his thumb.

"Oh God! I need to come. Please," I cried.

"I'll take care of you."

He kissed his way down my stomach. I nearly came off the bed when he ran his tongue across the inside of my thigh. He pushed my legs farther apart and kissed me where I needed him the most. His tongue thrust out, and I screamed at the sensation. My body came up off the bed as he sucked my clit into his mouth. I grabbed his head and held him in place as I came. His mouth never once slowed as I shouted his name over and over again. My body was on fire.

When I finally came back down to earth, he climbed on top of me and positioned himself at my entrance. "Are you sure, City?"

"I've never been more sure of anything in my life," I said as I stared up into his beautiful eyes.

My heart nearly stopped when I saw the love shining in them. *Dear God, this man loves me. Me.*

"Protection!" I blurted out.

His face fell. "I don't have anything, City."

"I do."

He gave me a questioning look.

"I, uh…I bought condoms tonight. They're in my purse."

He grinned as he leaned over and grabbed my purse off the floor where I'd dropped it when he carried me to his room. He grabbed the box of condoms out of it and took one out. I watched as he ripped it open with his teeth and slid it on. He positioned himself again and thrust into me quickly. He waited to give me time to adjust to his size before pulling out and thrusting back in again.

"You okay?" he asked.

"I'm more than okay," I said.

He leaned down and kissed me. Sex had never been this way with Joel, not even in the beginning. He had never been gentle with me like this. The only time he'd ever stopped to ask me if I was okay was when he'd taken my virginity.

Landon started thrusting, keeping up a slow but steady rhythm.

"Go faster," I said as my hips rose to meet his.

He did as I'd asked, moving in and out of me faster and harder. I wrapped my legs around him, allowing him to go deeper.

"You feel like heaven, City," he grunted as he continued to pound into me.

I didn't bother to reply. I was too busy matching him thrust for thrust. I never wanted this to end. I positioned myself so that he hit my sweet spot each time he entered me. I clawed at his back and groaned as his thrusts became erratic. I knew he was close.

"Come with me, City," he groaned into my mouth before he kissed me.

I felt him let go, and so did I.

We lay together for a few minutes, both of us trying to remember how to breathe. Landon peppered my face and neck with kisses before finally standing up. He pulled the condom off and threw it away before climbing back into bed with me, still naked.

He wrapped his arms around me and kissed me softly. "That was incredible."

I stretched before snuggling into his side. "I agree."

We fell asleep that way—naked and clinging to each other.

Landon was it for me, and I knew it. I felt safe and loved whenever I was with him.

I awoke in the middle of the night, my body throbbing and needy. I raised my head up to see Landon sound asleep on his back, a peaceful look on his face. I smiled as I leaned forward and nibbled on his ear. I knew he'd be happy with the way he was about to be woken up.

I kissed my way from his ear to his neck and then down his chest. He moaned in his sleep but didn't wake up. I cupped his shaft in my hand and started squeezing gently. He moaned again as his eyes opened.

"Hey," he whispered, his voice thick with sleep.

"Hey yourself," I said as I continued to squeeze and stroke him.

"This is a really good way to wake up," he mumbled.

"That was the plan," I told him as he grew thick in my hand.

I could already tell that I was going to become addicted to being with him like this. I reached across him and grabbed a condom from the box. He watched me with hooded eyes as I opened it and rolled it on.

"You got to play last time. Now, it's my turn."

"I'm all yours, City," he whispered as he watched me climb on top of him.

I bit my lip to keep from moaning as he filled me. He didn't try to hide his own moan as I rose up and slammed back down onto him roughly.

"Jesus, City."

I smiled as I rolled my hips and tightened my internal muscles. While I loved how gentle he'd been with me earlier, I loved rough sex. I raised my body up again and slammed back down onto him.

"Ah!" he groaned as he grabbed my hips.

After that, he met me with a hard upward thrust each time I came down on him. I leaned forward and ran my tongue across one nipple and then the other. My fingers dug into the hard muscles of his stomach. I couldn't help but admire his body. Every part of him was hard and chiseled as if he were made from stone. I wanted to explore every inch of him.

He was gripping my hips so hard that I was sure I would have bruises in the morning, but I didn't care. The room was filled with our groans and the sound of our bodies coming together as we slammed into each other over and over again. I went down onto him one final time and came. He followed right behind me. Completely spent, I dropped down onto his chest.

Once we were both breathing normally again, he gently grabbed my chin and lifted my head so that I was staring into his eyes.

"You're incredible, City. You're the most incredible woman I've ever met. I...I love you. I know it probably scares the hell out of you to hear me say that, but I do."

Unsure of what to say, I froze. "I...uh..."

"Don't worry. I don't expect you to say it back—at least, not right now. I just wanted you to know."

"I care a lot about you, Landon. You make me feel things that I've never felt before. I know I'm safe and loved when I'm around you, and that means more than you know. Just…just give me some time, okay?"

He nodded as he pushed my hair away from my face and tucked it behind my ear. "I'll wait. I don't care how long it takes. I'll wait for you to love me back."

I kissed him softly, trying to tell him everything I couldn't say.

I should have known that my world would come crashing down around me soon. Things had been too perfect, but I never would have guessed how it would actually happen.

CHAPTER 16

I was locking the barn door when strong arms wrapped around my waist. I grinned as Landon pulled me back against his body and nibbled on my ear. It had been like this for the past two days. Even though we'd spent both days together, working around the farm, he couldn't seem to get enough of me—or keep his hands off of me. I loved it. He made me feel wanted, and that was the most amazing feeling in the entire world. Every time I would look into his eyes, I could feel my heart healing just a little bit more. He was slowly erasing the pain that Joel had caused me.

"I missed you," he whispered.

He turned me to face him and started kissing along my jaw. I sighed as I wrapped my arms around him. *This was heaven.*

"You were only gone for half an hour."

"Still too long in my opinion."

I smiled as I slipped from his grip. He took my hand in his, and we walked back to my grandparents' house. From the very beginning, I'd known that Landon was sweet, but I never would have guessed he could be like this. I regretted the time I'd spent moping over Joel and pushing Landon away. I'd wasted so much time, and summer would be over soon. I still had no idea what would happen once I went home, but I knew Landon and I needed to talk about it. I thought neither of us had brought it up yet because we didn't want to think about it.

"I'm starving. I hope Lily has something to eat," Landon said.

"It's Gram. She *always* has food ready. I think she's afraid that we'll starve," I joked.

We walked inside and kicked off our boots. Landon followed me as I walked into the kitchen. Gram was sitting at the kitchen table, staring down at it. I was surprised to see her like that. She never sat still. She was always cooking or cleaning. When she wasn't doing one of those, she would be washing clothes or gardening. Before this moment, I couldn't think of a time when I'd seen her just sitting.

"Hey, Gram," I said.

Landon and I took two of the seats at the table. She glanced up and smiled at us, but it was forced. Something was wrong.

"Are you okay?" I asked cautiously.

"What? Oh, yes, I'm fine. I was just about to start dinner."

Landon and I glanced at each other, unsure of what to say. Gram always had dinner ready by the time we finished our chores.

"Are you sure you're okay, Lily?" Landon asked, concern filling his voice. He knew something was wrong, too.

She looked between us before her eyes landed on me. Of all the emotions I expected to see on her face, pity wasn't one of them, but it was the one shining through.

"I need to talk to Alexandria, Landon. Can you give us a minute?" she asked.

"Uh…sure. I'll be outside."

He started to stand, but I held up my hand to stop him.

"Gram, whatever is going on, you can say it in front of Landon."

She hesitated before nodding. "All right then. I just…I don't know how to say this."

"Say what?" I asked.

"Your mother called earlier while you were outside. She had some news that she wanted to share with you."

"What kind of news?"

She sighed. "Oh, Alexandria. I'm so sorry that I'm the one who has to break the news to you. Your mother called because she wanted to tell you that something happened to Joel."

I raised an eyebrow. "This is about Joel? How would she know anything about him?"

"He's…he's gone. He was reported missing yesterday, and they found him this morning. Your mother's friend was one of the responding officers. I guess the police have been watching him for a while because she instantly recognized him. She called to let your mom know what happened because of your relationship with him. She wanted to make sure that you were okay."

"What do you mean, he's gone? I don't understand." My voice didn't sound right. It was too low, too deep. I couldn't process what she was telling me.

"He's dead, sweetheart. I'm so sorry."

"He can't be dead!" I shouted. "He's Joel! Everyone knows that he's untouchable!"

"I'm so sorry," she repeated. "Your mom said that it looked like a drug deal had gone bad. They found him behind one of the dumpsters at the park. He was shot."

The world seemed to tilt, and I lowered my head to the table. *Joel is gone. Joel is dead. This can't be happening.* I was angry with him, but I still cared about him. A small part of me still loved him. A sob escaped as I lost control. With my head still on the table, I hid my face in my arms as the tears took over. My body shook as I tried to process what was happening.

"Shh…" Landon whispered as he wrapped his arms around me and pulled me into his chest.

I clung to him as I continued to cry.

"This can't be happening," I managed to get out between sobs.

"I'm here. Just let it out," Landon said softly.

I knew it had to hurt him to watch me cry over another man, but I couldn't stop myself. Joel had been my whole world for so long. No one spoke until my sobs finally quieted.

I looked up at Gram. "When did it happen?"

She seemed unsure as to whether or not she should tell me any more. "He was reported missing yesterday morning. They think it happened sometime the night before."

He'd been dead for over a day, and I hadn't known.

How could I have not known something like that? I should have felt it.

I pulled away from Landon and stood up. "I…I need to be alone right now."

Before either of them could reply, I turned and walked upstairs to my room. I shut the door behind me before walking over to my bed. I lay down on the bed and curled into myself. *This hurts so bad.* I shut my eyes, trying to block out the pain, but all I could see was Joel. He had been such a hard-ass when we were around others, but with me, he'd always been laughing and joking. His smile had been like the sun to me.

I should have been there with him. He'd always yelled at me for having my gun ready, but I had done it to protect him. If I had been with him when he needed me, I could have stopped whoever it was from shooting him. If I had stayed with him, he would still be alive right now.

I sucked in a breath as another thought hit me. If it happened the night before last, that meant that I'd been with Landon when it happened. *Oh God.* Fresh tears slipped down my cheeks as I tried to process that. I had been having sex with Landon while Joel died alone with some druggie.

My eyes drifted to the nightstand where my cell phone was sitting. Before I could think about what I was doing, I grabbed it and took off running. I stopped long enough to pull on my shoes before continuing outside. I ran to the barn and threw open the doors. The four-wheeler was sitting where Landon had parked it earlier with the key still in it. I jumped on and started it. After backing out of the barn, I tore down the driveway. My mind shut off as I drove to the gate leading to the hayfield.

I almost expected someone to follow me, but no one did. I was grateful as I unlocked the gate and then drove the four-wheeler through it. I was careful as I drove through the trees and into the field. As soon as I made it, I shut it off and pulled my phone from my pocket. Once I powered it on, it started dinging to alert me that I had new text messages. I waited until it stopped before opening my messages. The first one was from Riley. It had been sent only an hour before.

> *Riley: I need you to call me, Lexi. Something happened. It's Joel. He's gone, Lex. He's gone. Please call me when you get this.*

Tears clouded my vision as I backed out of his message and stared at the rest. My phone showed that I had over twenty texts from Joel's number. Either he'd lied to me about losing his phone or he'd purchased a new one. I held my breath as I clicked on his name and scrolled to the oldest one.

> *Joel: I'm so sorry, baby.*

Joel: Please call me. I was fucked-up and didn't realize what I was doing.

Joel: Lexi, you're my world. Please call me.

Joel: I want to make this right.

Joel: I know I hurt you. I'm so sorry. I can't tell you that enough times.

Joel: Please, baby, I can't take this. I can't function, knowing how much you hate me. Call me.

Joel: Lexi, call me. I'm not giving up on us. You mean too much to me. I can't just let you go.

Joel: I know I fucked up, but this is cruel. Call me.

Joel: I love you.

Joel: I get it. You're not going to respond, but you will be home in a few weeks. I will make this right.

Joel: I miss you so much. You're my everything, and I fucked it up. I've never loved someone the way I love you.

There were several more like those. Finally, I reached the last one. It had been sent three days ago.

Joel: Lexi, I fucked up. I know it, and you know it. I want you to know that I haven't touched alcohol or drugs, not even weed, since that night. I'm trying to change, so I can be the man you need me to be. I'm going to stop selling as soon as I get a little more cash saved up. Then, I'll find a real job and make you proud. I've never loved someone the way I love you. You're the most precious thing in this world, and I know that if you give me another chance, I can make all of this better. You're my everything, baby. I love you so much. I'll see you soon.

I dropped my phone and watched as it bounced off the four-wheeler and onto the ground. He'd never given up on us while I was off having fun and falling for Landon. Joel had planned to make things right with me. He had planned to stop selling and change his ways. He'd wanted to give up a life that he excelled at just to make me happy.

Tears streamed down my face as I lay back on the four-wheeler and stared up at the sky. *How can I have any tears left at this point?* I couldn't stop thinking about how I'd been with Landon while Joel was dying. *What kind of person does that make me?*

Landon found me after dark. The moon was exceptionally bright tonight, making it easy to see him. I didn't pay him much attention as I was still staring up at the sky, unable to move. My mind wasn't working anymore, and neither was my body. I watched as he grabbed my cell phone off the ground and shoved it into his pocket. He scooped me up into his arms and climbed onto the four-wheeler. He held me against his chest as he started it and drove us back to my grandparents' house.

I never said a word as he carried me up to my room and tucked me into bed. I continued to stay silent when he climbed into bed with me and wrapped his arms around me.

"I'm so sorry, City. I'm here for you," he whispered into my ear.

I grinned as Joel kissed my forehead.

"You're so beautiful, Lexi."

"I'm sure you say that to all the girls," I said, only half-joking.

We'd been a couple for almost a month, and it still didn't feel real. I couldn't believe that I'd snagged Joel. Every chick in this town wanted him, but he'd picked me. That didn't mean that I didn't feel jealous when I watched other girls throw themselves at him. Ever since he'd told me he wanted to be with me exclusively, he'd pushed them away every time. I couldn't help but feel smug about that.

I sighed as he leaned in and kissed me gently. His kisses felt like sunshine to me. I loved them.

"Stay with me tonight," he whispered against my lips.

"I can't. My mom will freak out if I don't come home."

She had blown a gasket when I told her that I was officially with Joel. I knew she didn't approve, but I didn't care. She thought I was out with a few girls from school tonight. That was a lie, of course. I'd never made plans with anyone besides Joel. If she knew I was here with him right now, she would beat the door down to get to me. She, like everyone else in this town, knew of his reputation as a badass and a drug dealer.

"Please...I can't wait any longer, Lexi. I need you," Joel said, his eyes pleading with me.

My stomach churned at his words. I knew what he wanted—sex. I wanted it, too, but I was scared. I'd never been with anyone like that, and I'd heard stories from other girls at school about how much it hurt.

"I...I don't know," I whispered.

"Do you trust me?" he asked as he cupped my face.

"Of course! I'm just afraid."

He smiled before kissing me again. "There's nothing to be afraid of, Lexi."

"I'm a virgin!" I blurted out. "I'm afraid that it's going to hurt."

His eyes widened for a split second before he masked his surprise. "It'll hurt, but I promise, I'll be gentle. Trust me."

He took my hand and led me through his house to his bedroom. I was terrified and excited at the same time. I'd wanted him like this since the first time we met, but I'd been scared that the pain would be too much.

What if I'm not good at it and he decides that he doesn't want me?

As soon as we reached his bedroom, he grabbed me and pulled my body tight against his. His lips found mine, and then he plunged his tongue into my mouth. I moaned, loving the feel of his body against mine. I could feel just how much he wanted me as his hardness pressed against me.

I gasped as he pulled back far enough to pick me up and toss me onto his bed. He pulled his shirt off and tossed it aside before

*climbing on top of me and kissing me again. Fire shot through my
veins as his hands started roaming underneath my shirt.*

How could I have been nervous? This is heaven.

*He sat up and pulled me up with him. After tugging my shirt
off, he tossed it to the floor and pushed me back down onto the bed.
Now that my shirt was gone, he explored more of my body. His
hands roamed across my stomach before moving up. His fingers
skimmed across the top of my bra, making me jump. No one had
ever touched me like this.*

*"You're beautiful, Lexi," he murmured. His lips settled on
where his fingers had been seconds before.*

*"Keep touching me," I said as he kissed up my chest to my
neck.*

He chuckled softly. "I can do that."

*I froze for a second as he lifted himself up on one arm. He
reached between us and unsnapped the front clasp on my bra. He
pushed my bra away and ran a finger between my breasts.*

*"You've never done anything with a guy before?" he asked
softly.*

*I shook my head. "No, you're the only one who has ever seen
me like this."*

He smiled. "I like that—a lot."

*My body jerked when he leaned down and ran his tongue
across one of my nipples. "Ah!"*

"You like that?" he asked.

"Yes," I managed to gasp out as he repeated the action.

"Let's spend tonight finding out what else you like."

*I closed my eyes as he kissed a trail from my breasts to the top
of my shorts. When he reached them, I felt him unbuttoning them. I
opened my eyes to watch as he slowly tugged them down my legs.
Once they were gone, he grabbed my underwear and pulled them
down, too. I watched him as he hungrily stared down at my body.
No one had ever seen me like this. I suddenly felt self-conscious.*

What if I'm not good enough?

*Without even realizing what I was doing, I crossed my arms
over my chest to hide my breasts.*

*He grinned as he tugged my arms away. "Don't act shy now,
Lexi."*

"I'm sorry. I just…this is new to me."

"I know. Don't worry, I'll show you everything you need to know."

He stood and kicked off his jeans. I couldn't take my eyes off of him as he slid his boxers off. I felt my cheeks warm as I stared at that *part of him.*

He laughed as he climbed back onto the bed with me. "You're adorable."

I frowned. "That's not something a girl wants to hear when she's in a guy's bed."

"I meant it as a compliment. Your innocence and shyness is adorable. I love it."

He kissed me after that, and no more words were spoken. I dropped my head back as he kissed my neck. His fingers tweaked my nipples as he nibbled his way down my body. I moaned when he kissed my hip bone. He ran his hand down my leg to my knee and then back up.

"You're so soft," he whispered as he kissed lower. He stopped right above where my body was throbbing with need. "You trust me, right?"

"I do." And I did.

He smiled as he pushed my legs apart and lowered his head. I shouted as his mouth covered my clit. I'd never felt anything like this. I was sure that my body was going to explode with need as his tongue darted out and made circling motions around my clit. His fingers found my opening, and he slowly slid one inside me. His mouth never slowed as he thrust first one finger and then two, in and out. I lost control of my body as stars exploded behind my eyelids.

"Oh my God, Joel!" I shouted as my fingernails dug into his shoulders.

"Let it out, baby," he said, his voice strained.

When I finally came back down to earth, Joel was watching me.

His eyes were almost black with lust. "That was so hot, Lexi. Jesus, I'm about to explode."

I stayed silent as he scooted up the bed and reached over into his nightstand. He pulled a condom from the drawer and ripped it open. After putting the condom on, he turned his attention back to me. I wrapped my arms around him as he moved until he was hovering over me.

"Are you ready, baby?"

I nodded, but my body tensed.

He felt it. "Lexi, you have to relax, or this is going to hurt."

"I'm sorry," I whispered, trying to relax.

"It's fine." He leaned down and started kissing me passionately.

I moaned as I kissed him back. I felt him nudge my opening, but I was too busy kissing him to care.

He broke our kiss for a split second. "Here we go, baby."

Before I could speak, his lips covered mine again. His mouth muffled my cry of pain as he slid into me. Tears leaked from my eyes.

"I'm sorry, Lexi. Are you okay?" he asked, concern filling his voice.

"I will be. Just give me a second."

He nodded as I waited for the pain to fade.

"I think I'm okay now," I said once the pain eased.

"If it hurts, tell me, and I'll stop."

I said nothing as he pulled out and thrust back into me again. My pain was replaced by pleasure as I felt him moving inside me.

"Oh!" I gasped out. "That feels good."

"I'm just getting started," he mumbled just before he kissed me. "Wrap your legs around me."

I did as he'd said, allowing him to go deeper. My hips rose to meet him each time that he thrust into me. I couldn't stop the moans escaping me as he built me up, higher and higher.

I will never forget this night for as long as I live.

"Babe, I'm about to explode. I can't hold back," Joel said, his voice rough.

"Then, don't."

He kissed me once before pulling back and slamming into me with enough force that I was pushed up the bed a few inches. He continued pounding into me roughly until I felt his body shudder with his release. I followed right behind him, clinging to him with my arms and legs.

He pulled out and dropped to the bed. I smiled as he pulled me into his arms and kissed me.

"That was incredible, babe."

"I have no experience here, but I thought it was pretty good, too," I joked.

He laughed. "I promise, I'll give you tons more experience. I'm not going anywhere anytime soon."

"Glad to hear it," I mumbled into his chest before sleep overtook me.

I woke up crying. Of course I would dream about our first time together. Even after all this time, it had been a night that I could never forget. I'd known then that I was falling for Joel. The things he'd made me feel that night were seared into my brain. I couldn't believe that he was really gone.

This has to be just another dream...a nightmare.

But it wasn't, and I had to deal with it.

I rolled onto my side to see that Landon had fallen asleep next to me. More guilt crippled me as I realized that I was with him again, and Joel was gone. Landon shouldn't be here. I shouldn't find comfort in the fact that he was here. That wasn't fair to Joel.

I slipped silently from the bed and walked downstairs to the living room. I curled up on the couch and waited for sleep to take me. I hoped that there wouldn't be any more dreams this time.

CHAPTER 17

The next few days seemed to pass in a blur.

My mom had arrived at my grandparents' farm two days after I learned about Joel's death. She'd tried calling numerous times, but I'd refused to talk to her. I'd refused to talk to anyone, even Landon. He'd stayed by my side constantly, trying to get me to open up, but I hadn't wanted to. I'd wanted to hide within myself and deal with the fact that Joel was really gone. I wasn't sure if Gram had called my mom or if she'd decided to come on her own, but it didn't really matter.

My mom helped me pack my stuff and load it into the back of her car. Gram cried as we said our good-byes, and even my grandfather hugged me.

"Please let me come with you. I want to help you," Landon said.

"I don't want you to help me," I said quietly.

"You're hurting right now, City. Let me take care of you. I want to be with you."

It almost killed me to say the next words, but I did anyway. I couldn't be with him now. I couldn't be with him ever. Joel was gone, and that was the only thing that I could focus on.

"I don't want you, Landon, and I sure as hell don't want you there when I go home. You don't belong there. Good-bye."

I watched as pain filled his eyes.

"City…"

I ignored him as I climbed into the car, and my mother pulled away. I looked back once to see Landon still standing in the exact same spot. I closed my eyes as I fought the tears trying to fall. It had been the right thing to do. He could move on, and I could…I could mourn Joel.

Mom spent most of the car ride alternating between telling me what she knew and asking if I was okay. We both knew that I wasn't, so I didn't bother to answer her each time she asked. Over the past two days, details of Joel's death had emerged. The most shocking was the fact that Joel had been working with the police over the last few months. That was how they'd recognized him so fast.

The police were aware of who he had gone to meet that night. He hadn't been selling. He had been buying. He'd been wearing a wire, but something had happened, and it had malfunctioned, so the cops hadn't known what was going on. When they had tracked down the man Joel met that night, he'd opened fire on them. He had been killed. I couldn't bring myself to care since they were ninety-nine percent sure that he had killed Joel. I hoped the fucker was rotting in hell right now.

Joel had died from a gunshot to the chest. My mother said that he'd died instantly. She was sure of it. He hadn't suffered. That should have brought me comfort, but it didn't. He was gone, and that was all that mattered.

The rest of the ride home was silent. When we finally arrived, my mother helped me bring my bags upstairs. Joel's funeral was tomorrow, so she laid out a black dress for me to wear. I appreciated it. I wasn't sure if I was capable of doing it on my own. Getting dressed had seemed to be hard enough, and that had been when I threw on whatever my hands had landed on.

Mom tried to get me to eat, but I refused. She finally gave up and left me alone for the night.

Even though I curled up in my bed before eight o'clock, I didn't fall asleep until well after midnight. Memories of Joel and I together kept running through my head. When I finally did pass out, I had nightmares, one right after another. I woke up drenched in sweat. I managed to drag myself from the bed to shower and get dressed. I barely remembered any of it. It was like my mind had shut down.

I'd been so angry with Joel for hurting me that I didn't realize just how much I still loved him. I wished more than anything that I could take it all back. I just wanted him to hold me again and tell me that everything would be okay. I wanted to hear his laughter. I wanted *him*.

My mother drove me to the funeral home. The minute that we pulled into the lot, I spotted Riley standing a few feet away from the doors, smoking a cigarette. As soon as he noticed me, he tossed it aside and ran to me.

"Lexi, I'm so glad you came. I was afraid that you wouldn't." He grabbed me and pulled me into his arms.

I went limp in his arms as I started crying again. Seeing Riley was almost like seeing Joel. They had always been together. Now that I was with Riley, I almost expected Joel to appear, but of course, he didn't.

"I can't believe he's gone," I choked out.

"I know. It doesn't seem real," Riley said quietly. "I'm really glad that you're here, Lexi. It would make him happy if he knew. He never stopped loving you. He knew how badly he messed-up, and he wanted to make it right."

"I didn't let him. I ignored him, and now, it's too late," I cried.

"Shh…it's okay. He knew that you loved him despite what happened. You were it for him. I never saw him love anyone the way he loved you. He wouldn't want you to feel guilty for how things happened. He knew he fucked up with you."

"I'll never get the chance to tell him that I forgive him."

"No, you won't, but I think he knew. You can't feel guilty about what happened. It'll drive you crazy."

I pulled away, refusing to look at Riley. I *did* feel guilty, and I always would. Nothing Riley or anyone else said would change that. I turned and started walking toward the funeral home. My mother followed a few feet behind Riley and me. When I walked in, I was surprised to see that the room was packed. Most of the faces were familiar. People who we had been friends with and had partied with along with a few of his *clients* were hanging around. Joel had been a hard-ass, but he'd been loved. There was no denying that.

"Why didn't he tell me that he was working with the police?" I finally asked, my voice quiet so that no one except Riley would hear.

"He didn't tell anyone, not even me. I knew he was tired of the scene and that he wanted out, but it's not that easy. He could have left town and started over, but he didn't. He stayed for us and tried to figure a way out of it all." Riley shook his head. "If I had known what he was trying to do, I would have helped him. All he had to do was ask me. I would have had his back."

I could hear the bitterness and the hurt in Riley's voice. He was hurting just as bad as I was, and there was nothing I could do to ease his pain. Joel had stayed and risked his life, so he could stay here with me, and in the end, he'd died for me. I couldn't wrap my head around that. I couldn't believe that he would risk everything for *me.*

"Is his dad here?" I asked finally.

Riley shook his head. "No, the old bastard didn't give a fuck about the fact that his son is dead."

I winced at the bitterness in Riley's voice.

"Who paid for all of this?"

"I did. Well, Joel did. He had me on his bank account just in case something ever happened. There wasn't a ton in there, but it was enough to make sure that everything was taken care of."

"You're a good friend, Riley. Joel loved you, too. I hope you know that."

He gave me a weak smile. "I hope so. He was my best friend. I knew him since we were kids. He meant the world to me. You do, too, Lexi." He took a deep breath. "Come on, I'm sure that you want to see him."

I didn't. I wasn't sure if I could handle seeing Joel in a casket. I was barely hanging on by a thread as it was. If I saw him, I would lose it.

Riley seemed to notice my hesitation. He grabbed my hand and started pulling me through the crowd. "If you don't do this, you'll regret it for the rest of your life. I'll be right beside you."

Even though I knew he was right, part of me still didn't want to see Joel. If I saw him, then all of this would be real. Right now, I could pretend that it was all a cruel joke. I could pretend that if I left and went to his house, he would be waiting for me.

I wasn't good at dealing with death. I wasn't good with emotions, period, except for anger. I had that emotion down for sure. The rest were a mystery to me, something that my brain couldn't process. My mind wasn't equipped to handle the emotions trying to break through my barriers.

Riley didn't let go of my hand until we reached the front of the room. I froze the moment that the coffin came into view. I couldn't do this. I couldn't. I started to back away, but Riley caught my hand again and pulled me closer to him.

"I'm right here, Lexi. I won't leave your side."

I closed my eyes and took a deep breath before opening them. "Okay."

If Riley had noticed how my voice cracked, he didn't comment. Slowly, I walked the rest of the way to the front of the room. Riley kept his word and stayed beside me the whole time. When we reached the casket, I froze again. It was Joel, but it wasn't. He was too pale and too…still. Joel had never sat still. His tattoos that I loved so much looked stark against his now pale skin. If it wasn't for his paleness, I would have thought that he was sleeping. His face was peaceful in death. The expression he had worn to mask his emotions was gone. In death, he had finally found his peace.

I continued to stare at him until Riley nudged me forward a few more inches. Tears streamed down my face as I reached out and touched Joel's face. *He's so cold. This isn't right.* A sob escaped me as I pulled my hand back.

The world started spinning wildly, and Riley caught me just before I hit the floor. I couldn't breathe as the world closed in on me. Riley held me as I screamed out Joel's name. We sank to the floor together and stayed there as my body convulsed from the sobs I no longer cared to hold back.

I wanted to die. Death couldn't be nearly as painful as seeing my first love in a fucking casket. Nothing could be worse than this.

"Why?" I screamed.

"I don't know, Lexi. I don't know" Riley whispered as he held me.

I knew I was making a scene, but I couldn't stop screaming and crying. Riley stood and pulled me up with him as I screamed out Joel's name over and over.

"Get me out of here, please," I cried.

"I've got you," Riley said as he picked me up and carried me from the room.

People moved out of the way, so we could get through. He didn't stop until we were standing outside of his car. After unlocking it, he shoved me into the passenger seat before climbing in on the driver's side. Neither of us spoke for a long time. I waited until my sobs quieted to small hiccups. Once they did, I looked over to see a single tear rolling down his cheek.

"I'm so sorry, Riley."

"Never be sorry for loving him—never."

He reached across the console and took my hand. I closed my eyes as I leaned back into the seat and tried to forget everything. Riley staying with me meant the world to me, but it wasn't enough. I wanted Joel to be the one with me, and despite how sick it made me, I wanted Landon here, too.

Joel was buried in a cemetery across town. After everyone else went home, Riley and I stayed with him. I didn't think that I would ever leave, but Riley made me. The cemetery workers were waiting for us to leave, so they could finish.

I picked up a handful of dirt and tossed it into the grave. "I love you, Joel. I always will."

We started walking back to Riley's car, and I didn't look back. I *couldn't* look back. I couldn't say good-bye to Joel again—not yet. If I did, I was sure that I'd fall apart right in the middle of the cemetery, and no one would ever be able to pick up the pieces.

I would never be whole again. I'd left half my heart with Joel.

CHAPTER 18

After that day, I shut down. I stopped living. While I knew that Joel was gone, my mind refused to process it, so I just stopped…everything. After Riley had dropped me off the day of the funeral, I hadn't left my parents' house. The only time I left my room was when I went to the bathroom. My mom tried to get me to come downstairs to eat, but I refused. Instead, she brought food up to my room for me. I ate enough to survive, but that was it.

My birthday had come and gone two weeks after Joel's death. My mother had bought a cake and tried to get me to open presents, but I couldn't bring myself to do it. *Why should I be celebrating my life when Joel was gone?*

The only plus side had been the fact that I could finally drop out of school since I was eighteen, and my mom couldn't do a thing about it. I never technically went to the school to drop out. I just didn't show up. By the end of the second week of school, I was pretty sure that they figured out I wasn't coming back.

My mom flipped out on me about not going, but I knew she was too worried about me to do anything. She threatened to kick me out, but we both knew that she wouldn't. She knew that I didn't care what happened to me.

The weight I'd gained from living with Gram over the summer quickly disappeared along with a few more pounds. I didn't even recognize myself when I looked in the mirror. I looked sickly. My skin was pale under the tan that I'd received from working outside all summer. Dark circles under my eyes were a permanent feature of mine now. I'd bought hair dye before everything happened, but I'd never used it. Now, almost four weeks after Joel's death, my blonde roots were showing through, making me look ten times worse. It was too bad that I didn't give a shit.

My mom tried to talk to me, and my dad tried over the phone since he was away on an extended trip for work, but I refused to speak to either of them. I knew they were both concerned, but I didn't care. I just wanted the world to stop spinning and end, so I didn't have to feel the pain slowly eating me alive.

Landon called me every day, but I wouldn't speak to him. I couldn't. I missed him so much, but each time I thought of him, guilt crippled me. If it wasn't for him, I would never have let Joel go. I would have taken him back, and things wouldn't have turned out this way. It was my fault that Joel was dead because I had been too busy falling for Landon to come home and let Joel make things right.

I knew I was hurting Landon, but there was nothing I could do to help him. I had moved too fast with him, trying to forget about Joel. I'd had sex with Landon after being with him for only a few weeks. I'd used him as a coping mechanism. He needed to let me go and move on with someone who could be with him. My heart ached at the thought of him with someone else, but I had no right to feel that way. I should be mourning Joel only instead of mourning him and my relationship with Landon.

"I can't handle this anymore, Alexandria!" my mother shouted at me one day. "I know that he's gone, but you're not. You can't just stop living because of Joel. Do you really think that he'd want you to be like this?"

I glared at her. "I don't know. He's not around for me to ask."

She sighed as she sat down on the end of my bed. "I know you're hurting. I get that. But you can't let it control you. If you do, you'll drown in your own sorrow."

"I don't care," I said stubbornly as I rolled away from her.

"At least get up and shower, please. Dye your hair a weird color, get more piercings, go get a tattoo to piss me off. Just do *something.*"

I froze as I let her words sink in. *Go get a tattoo.* I sat up so fast that she yelped and jumped off my bed. I was out of my bed and grabbing clothes out of my dresser before she could ask what I was doing. I left the room and hurried to the bathroom to take a shower. Once I finished, I dressed and hurried back to my room. She was still standing there, looking at me like I'd lost my mind.

"Can I borrow your car?" I asked.

"Where are you going?" She looked unsure about whether or not I was capable of driving.

"To live again."

She studied me for a minute before pulling her keys out of her pocket and handing them to me. "Please be careful."

If this had been a normal day, she never would have let me out of the house without knowing where I was going, but things weren't normal anymore. *I* wasn't normal anymore. I grabbed her keys and hurried out of my room and down the stairs. When I threw the front door open, I was blinded by the sun. After spending the last few weeks in my room with the blinds down, it took me a minute for my eyes to adjust to the brightness. When I could finally see again, I hurried to my mom's car and got in.

My mind was spinning as I drove across town to my destination. When I pulled into the lot, I shut off my car and took a deep breath, trying to calm my racing heart. I stared up at the building in front of me. It was the tattoo shop that Joel's friend worked at. I grabbed my purse and stepped out, never taking my eyes off the building. The minute that my mom had mentioned a tattoo, I'd known exactly what I wanted. It was the perfect thing to remember Joel with.

A bell rang above the door as I walked in. Three people were sitting in chairs in the waiting area, and I could see three artists working behind the counter. I spotted Joel's friend, Zack. He was the one who had tattooed me before. All three of the guys glanced up when I walked to the counter.

Zack's eyes widened when he saw me. "Lexi?"

"Hey, Zack. It's been a while." I tried to smile, but I failed miserably. I wasn't sure that I even remembered how to smile.

Zack glanced at the guy he was working on. "Can you give me a minute?"

The guy nodded, and Zack stood up and walked over to me.

"Hey. I heard about Joel. I'm sorry."

I looked away from him to keep from crying. I wouldn't break down here. I took a deep breath before looking back up at him. "Thanks. I need you to help me with something."

"Anything," he said sincerely.

Joel had always thought that Zack was a good guy. While Zack hadn't hung out with us a bunch, I'd seen him a few times. He looked exactly how I'd expected a tattoo artist to look. He was wearing shorts and a Slipknot T-shirt today. With the exception of his face, every inch of his skin was covered in tattoos. His hair was

175

a dark brown color and styled into a mohawk. There were multiple piercings in his face. In other words, he was the kind of guy who made most people uncomfortable.

"I need a tattoo."

He smiled. "Well, you came to the right place." He glanced behind me at the people waiting. "We're booked today, but I can see if I can get you in for tomorrow."

My stomach dropped. I needed to do this now. I couldn't wait. "Please. It's for Joel. I…I need this."

His eyes softened as he stared at me. He glanced up at the clock. "You'll have to wait until everyone else is taken care of. It might be a few hours."

"That's fine. I'll wait. Can you give me some paper and a pencil? I need to draw it anyway."

"Sure." He walked over to a desk where he pulled a few sheets of paper out of the printer and grabbed a couple of pencils.

"Thank you," I said as I took them from him.

I looked around the room for a place to sit. One open chair was available, so I took it and stared down at the paper in front of me. I knew exactly what I wanted to draw, but I was afraid that I wouldn't get it right. Regardless, I had to try.

I blocked out everyone around me as I started to sketch. I had always been gifted when it came to drawing, even when I was younger. I just hoped that my skills didn't fail me now when I needed them the most.

Hours passed as I worked tirelessly. I ended up tearing up a few of the sheets and starting over, but I finally managed to get the drawing to look how I wanted it.

After using my phone to find a translation website, I added the finishing touches. I wrote the words that meant so much to me above the drawing. I leaned back in my chair and let out a breath. When I glanced around the shop, I noticed that everyone was gone, except for Zack.

"Shit, Zack, I'm sorry. I wasn't paying attention," I said as I jumped up, feeling guilty about keeping him here.

"Don't worry about it, Lexi." He reached out and took the paper from my hands. His mouth dropped open as he stared at my work. "Fuck, Lexi, you're incredible. I had no idea that you could draw like this."

I shrugged, embarrassed by his praise. "Thanks."

"What does this mean?" he asked.

"*Primus amor*—it means first love in Latin," I said quietly.

The drawing was of a motorcycle with flames shooting out of the tailpipes. It was Joel's bike.

"Well, it's an incredible tattoo. I'm honored that you're asking me to do it. Where are we putting it?"

I thought for a moment. Due to the size of the tattoo, I needed someplace with a lot of room. I knew a lot of people put larger tattoos on their backs, but I didn't want it there. I wanted it where I could always see it. I glanced down at my legs. If it wrapped around my outer thigh, that should give it plenty of room. I was glad that I'd worn shorts. While I liked Zack, I didn't want to drop my pants around him.

"Here." I pointed to my leg.

He nodded as he pointed to one of the tables. "Go ahead and lie down there. It'll take me a few minutes to get this ready. Are you wanting color or just how it is here?"

"Exactly like the drawing," I said as I walked back to the table to lie down on my side.

A few minutes later, Zack walked back to me and started setting his supplies out. After he applied the tattoo to my leg and let me look at it, we got started. I knew it would take a couple of hours to complete, so I closed my eyes and tried to relax as his gun buzzed to life. I winced as the tip touched my skin, but I didn't jerk away. After feeling nothing but emptiness for so long, I welcomed the physical pain.

"You doing okay?" Zach asked when we were halfway finished.

"Yeah, I'm good," I said, not bothering to open my eyes.

My leg had gone numb long ago, just like my heart. My thoughts drifted as I listened to the buzz of his gun. Joel had been with me the last time I'd gotten a tattoo. He'd even held my hand at first because I'd been scared. There was no one here to hold my hand now. I was on my own.

My thoughts went from Joel to Landon without me even realizing it. I thought about the days Landon and I had spent together this summer. Even before things had gone bad with Joel, I had leaned on Landon more than I should have. He'd made staying at the farm bearable when I first went there. I'd had so much rage inside of me then, and he'd helped to soothe me. He had been so nice to me, and he'd made me smile when I thought I had nothing to smile about.

I knew now that I had started to fall for him even then. *So, what kind of person does that make me?* I'd had a boyfriend who loved me, and I'd still strayed—maybe not physically, but I had mentally. Then, after everything had happened, I'd let myself get closer to Landon. If I had cared more about my relationship with Joel, maybe he'd still be alive. Maybe I would have been with him that night. Maybe I could have saved him.

I cared about Landon. I was falling hard for him. No, I'd already fallen for him. He'd made me feel things that Joel hadn't. It made me sick to my stomach to think that. It was like I was dismissing Joel and everything we'd ever had together.

I just wanted to forget Landon. I was trying. I'd assumed that not being around him or talking to him would make me forget what I felt, but it hadn't. I hadn't looked at or talked to Landon for over a month, yet he was constantly in my thoughts. I felt as much guilt for missing him as I did for abandoning Joel. Between the two, my heart was in shreds.

"We're done," Zack said as he shut his gun off.

He sprayed solution onto a paper towel. After he wiped the excess ink from my skin, he helped me stand. I walked over to the full-length mirror and turned sideways to see my new tattoo. My breath caught in my throat as I stared at it. Zack was a genius. The tattoo was exactly what I'd drawn for him. I fought to keep the tears at bay as I continued to stare at myself.

"It's perfect. Thank you," I finally said as I turned back to look at him.

"You're welcome." He paused for a second. "Lexi?"

"Yeah?"

"I know I'm probably overstepping my boundaries here, but can I give you a piece of advice?"

"Um…yeah, sure," I said as I looked at him curiously.

"I know how bad you're hurting right now. I…I lost my girlfriend back in high school before I moved here. I thought the pain would kill me. I couldn't eat. I couldn't sleep. I wanted to stop living." He swallowed roughly. "I wanted to join her."

"Why are you telling me this?" I asked softly.

"Because I know what you're going through. It hurts like hell, but it does get better. I knew Joel pretty well, and I know that he wouldn't want you to waste your life mourning him. He'd want you to live. Just live, Lexi."

The tears that I had been trying so hard to hold back burst forth. I lifted my hand and covered my mouth to stifle the sound of my sobs. "I don't want him to think that I've forgotten about him."

Zack walked over and wrapped his arms around me. "He would never think that. Besides"—he pointed to my leg—"you have that to remember him by now. He will always be a part of you. You can't let your grief consume you, Lexi. You have to *live*. If not for yourself, then for him."

I hugged him back for a moment before he released me. "Thank you, Zack. I'm so sorry about your girlfriend."

He gave me a weak smile. "Sarah was my first love. I'll never forget her, but I've moved on. I had to, or I would have lost who I was."

I nodded as I reached into my purse and pulled out the debit card my mom had given me for emergencies. "I'm glad. Here's my card. I don't want to keep you any longer. I know it's late."

"It's fine. Seriously. I would have stayed until tomorrow morning if it meant that you got your tattoo." He took my card and walked to the desk to run it through. Once he finished, he covered my tattoo and gave me the aftercare instruction sheet. He hugged me one more time before I left. "If you need to talk, you know where to find me."

"Thank you." I waved good-bye and walked to my car. It was almost midnight, and the streets were deserted. I hurried across the lot, not wanting to tempt fate. As soon as I made it to my car, I unlocked it and jumped in. After locking the doors again, I stared out at the street across from me.

My mind was trying to process what Zack had said. He'd lost his girlfriend just like I'd lost Joel, and he was okay. He'd survived the pain and the anger that came with death. I hoped that I could be as strong as him. I *needed* to be as strong as him. He had been right. I couldn't let Joel's death control me. I had to accept it and move on. There was no other choice.

I glanced down at my leg and smiled for the first time since his death. I would always have him with me now. No matter where life took me, he'd be by my side. I let my tears fall without regret as I drove home. I was tired of holding them in. Maybe if I let them out, I'd let some of my pain escape as well.

I wasn't even close to healed, but this was a start. As I pulled into my driveway, I decided that I would survive.

CHAPTER

19

My mom was waiting for me when I walked through the front door. Instinct took over, and I prepared myself for the fight that I was sure was about to take place. We'd had it countless times when she caught me coming home late from Joel's.

Instead, she glanced at my leg before looking up at me with a small smile. "I see you made it home."

I nodded, still unsure of whether or not she was about to yell at me for being out late. "Yeah. Here are your keys."

She took her keys from me and hung them by the door. "Can I see it?"

"What?" I asked.

"Can I see your tattoo?"

"Oh! Sure," I said, surprised that she would care enough to ask to see it.

I walked to the couch and sat down before slowly peeling off the bandage. She sat down next to me and stared at my leg as the tattoo came into view.

I stayed silent as she looked it over.

Finally, she glanced up at me. "Will this help you heal?"

I nodded. "Yeah, it will."

"Then, I'm glad that you got it. It's beautiful, Alexandria."

"Thanks." I couldn't hide the surprise in my voice.

"Listen, I know that we don't always see eye to eye on things, but I want you to know that I love you, and I'm very proud of you. It kills me to see you suffering like this. I just want you to be happy. Tell me what I can do to help you, and I will."

I stared at her, unsure of what to say. Her words shocked me. I'd spent the last couple of years assuming that she hated me. Apparently, I had been wrong.

I leaned forward and wrapped my arms around her. "There's nothing you can do to help me. I just need time. I have to let him go, but I can't do it until I'm ready."

"I understand, and I want you to know that I'm here for whatever you need."

"Thanks, Mom. That means a lot to me," I whispered as I released her and stood up. "I'm exhausted. I'm going to bed."

"Night, baby," she said as I walked to the stairs and started climbing. "And Alexandria?"

I stopped and glanced back at her. "Yeah?"

"Will you promise me that when you're ready, you'll go back to school?"

I hesitated for a second, but I finally nodded. "I promise. Just give me time."

When I woke up the next morning, I felt surprised. Lately, my dreams had been plagued with memories of my past with Joel, but I couldn't remember having a single dream during the night before. I guessed I really was making progress.

After a quick shower, I returned to my room and grabbed my brush off the dresser. I brushed the tangles from my hair, noticing just how bad my blonde roots were showing compared to the black dye still in my hair. I could either dye my hair black again, or I could change it. I stared at my reflection for a few more seconds before coming to a decision.

With everything happening in my life, I decided that it was time for a change. I threw my brush down and walked downstairs. My mom was in the living room when I came down the stairs.

"Good morning," she said, smiling from ear to ear.

I knew it was because I was downstairs instead of hiding in my room like I'd usually done.

"Morning. Is it okay if I use your car again?" I asked as I walked toward the door.

"Sure. Where are you going?"

I grabbed her keys and glanced back at her as I opened the front door. "I'm going blonde again."

The trip to the local beauty supply shop was uneventful. I made sure to grab everything I needed to change my hair again. It would take me a couple of hours to do it, and the distraction would be exactly what I needed. If I were busy, I wouldn't think about anything else.

As soon as I made it home, I walked back upstairs to the bathroom. After parting my hair several times, I applied the bleach and developer that would lighten my hair. Once I was finished, I put my processing cap on and set my timer. After almost thirty minutes, I was satisfied that my hair was light enough. I'd changed my hair so many times that I was a professional by now. I rinsed my hair and applied a conditioner.

After I rinsed it out, I pulled the hair dye from the bag. I'd hunted until I found a shade that was close to my natural color. After applying it, I waited again for it to dye my hair. I rinsed it fifteen minutes later and washed my hair. I refused to look in the mirror until I finished drying my hair. I tried to calm myself as I shut the dryer off.

My eyes darted to the mirror, and I froze in shock. Looking at myself with blonde hair was like looking into the past. I hadn't been blonde since right after Joel and I got together. I was still me but softer. It was the change that I needed. Dyeing my hair wasn't just about vanity right now. It was so much deeper than that. I was letting go of the person I'd become and trying to find the new me.

I wasn't sure who the new me was exactly, but she was a mix of the old me and the version I'd become while I was with Joel. I still had my piercings and tattoos, reminding me that I could never really go back, no matter how badly I wanted to.

When I walked back downstairs, my mother's mouth dropped open.

"My God, Alexandria. I barely recognize you."

I gave her a weak smile. "It's...different. I know."

"You look beautiful," she said, her smile genuine.

"Thank you," I said quietly as we stared at each other.

The phone rang, causing both of us to jump. My mother walked over to where the phone was sitting.

After glancing at the caller ID, she looked up at me. "It's Landon." Without giving me time to process that, she answered the phone. "Hello, Landon."

I watched as she talked with him.

"Yeah, she's here. Hang on a second."

Horror filled me as she walked across the room and handed the phone to me.

"It's for you."

"I-I can't," I stuttered, trying to stay calm. I wasn't ready to face Landon—not yet.

She hesitated for a second before putting the phone back to her ear. "She can't talk right now, Landon, but she will soon. I promise."

I closed my eyes as I listened to her say good-bye.

I couldn't handle talking to him right now. I still had so much going on inside of my head, and I needed to sort through it before I talked to him again. I knew it wasn't right to ignore him, but it was the best thing for both of us. Once I could accept Joel's death, I would call Landon and apologize for what I'd done to him.

No matter how much I missed Landon, I knew that there was no future for us. My memories of him were too tainted with Joel's presence. It wasn't fair to either of us to try to save something that couldn't be salvaged. He would move on once I explained that to him, but he would have to wait for my explanation. Maybe he'd save us both some time and move on before I called him.

The next two weeks seemed to move at warp speed. Now that I was learning to function again, it seemed like the world was determined to move faster than ever—or maybe it was just me. I couldn't wrap my head around the fact that someone I loved had died, and the world didn't change at all. If I had expected it to stop, I was sadly mistaken.

I'd visited with Riley a few times. He'd seemed to be holding up, and I could tell that he was pleased with the fact that I was trying to accept that Joel was gone. We'd even driven to the cemetery one day, but I couldn't bring myself to get out of the car. When I was ready to see Joel again, I wanted to do it on my own.

Music was the first thing that I let back into my life. I'd always felt connected to the music that I loved, and now was no different. It was my own special kind of therapy. Music was honest, and it was brutal. The lyrics could make me feel things that

I never thought I could. As I listened to Smile Empty Soul's "Mechanical Rationality," I realized that it was perfect for my life right now. I closed my eyes and let the lyrics take over.

Can I keep it together
Under stress and whatever
Try and pinpoint my problems
But I can never solve them
So I fall into pieces
But nothing releases
And the cycle starts over
While the days get shorter
Push away I'm trying
To separate my findings
And be OK, remind me
That nothing good can come from all this hate
That floods my heart
With endless rain
Can anyone save me now
There's still a heartbeat
Somewhere in me
There's still a heart to find and bring to life
What to do in the meantime
Steady walking a straight line
Till my vision gets blurry
And my head is full of worry
So I fall into pieces
But nothing releases
And the cycle starts over
While the days get colder

I opened my eyes to see my mom watching me from the doorway of my bedroom. I pulled my headphones out of my ears when I saw her lips start moving.

"Sorry. What?" I asked.

She smiled. "I said, I never thought I'd see you listening to music again."

"Oh. I guess I just missed listening to it."

"I can see you slowly coming back, Alexandria. I was so scared that I was going to lose you."

"I'm sorry. I didn't mean to worry you."

"It's not your fault. Death is never easy to deal with. I…I know how much you loved Joel. I can't imagine the pain you feel."

"It took over. It still does a lot, but I'm trying to move forward. I'm trying to let him go."

"I know, honey. And you will." She seemed to think on her next words before she spoke. "I think that you should call Landon."

My chest tightened at the sound of his name. "I can't."

"Why not? He's worried about you. I don't say this to be mean, but you're hurting him. That's not fair to him."

"And if I call him, then what? I would tell him the same thing that I told him the day I left Gram's. I don't want him here. He doesn't belong in my life."

"Why on earth do you think that?" she asked incredulously.

"Because he doesn't. What I feel for him doesn't matter anymore. I cared about him when I should have cared about Joel. Everything we had is tainted."

"Oh, honey, it's not tainted. You can't help that you started to care for Landon. Sometimes, you can't control what you feel."

"I fell in love with him," I whispered, finally admitting the truth.

While it terrified me to say the words out loud, it also felt good to tell someone. I knew that a lot of my guilt came from loving Landon when I should have been focusing on working things out with Joel.

"I never meant for it to happen. It just did." I felt my throat closing off from emotion as I spoke.

"Like I said, you can't control how you feel. From what Gram has told me and from the conversations that I've had with him over the phone, I can tell that he really cares about you, too. What Joel did to you was wrong. You had every right to ignore him. He broke your heart."

"He did," I said.

"And you'll never really be able to get over him until you finally admit to yourself that you did nothing wrong. Even Joel knew what he had done was wrong. He wouldn't want you to feel all this pain. You only live once, Alexandria. Make the best of it."

I let her words sink in. She was certainly right about only living once. Joel's death was proof that you never knew when your last moment would be. It could be today, tomorrow, or years from now.

I looked up at her. "Can I use your car?"

CHAPTER 20

I had no idea what I was doing here. I shouldn't be here. It hurt too much. I stared out the window of my mom's car at the graves surrounding me. I was surrounded by so much death. I didn't want to be here, yet I was. I needed to do this, or I'd never be able to move on with my life.

I opened the car door and stepped out. Despite the sun shining above, the day was cold. I pulled my jacket tighter around me as I started walking past the headstones of the deceased. When Joel's stone came into view, I stopped. It took every ounce of willpower that I possessed not to turn around and run back to my car. I took a deep breath and continued walking until I was standing in front of his grave.

It was late fall, so no grass was growing from the freshly dug grave. With the exception of the now dead flowers on top of the dirt, it looked like he'd just been buried. If I closed my eyes, I could pretend that I hadn't just wasted almost two months of my life trying to remember how to breathe again.

Two months. It really didn't seem like he'd been gone that long. Then again, it felt like an eternity. The world wasn't as bright without Joel in it.

"Hi," I mumbled as I sat down on the cold ground next to his stone. I snorted. "What a fucking stupid thing to say. It's not like you can say it back."

I pulled my knees up to my chest and rested my head against them. Now that I was here, I had no idea what to do. I had assumed that if I came here, somehow, the fog of despair that had been surrounding me for the last two months would disappear. How wrong I had been. It circled me now, trying to push its way into my defenses. I concentrated on breathing as I forced it back.

"I have no idea what to say here, Joel. I'm so lost, and I feel so alone without you. I can't believe that you left me. How could you? *How could you do this to me?*" I shrieked.

The wind was blowing harder now, drowning out my cries of despair. I wished that the wind would just carry me away from here. I wished that it could take me back in time.

"You should have told me what you were trying to do, Joel. I would have helped you. Riley would have, too. You were too damn stubborn and proud to tell us, to ask us for help, and now, we're left with nothing. Nothing! A piece of me died with you, and now, I don't know how to get it back. I don't even know if I want it back anymore."

I stopped talking as tears poured from my eyes. It hurt so damn bad to say all of this to him.

"I know that you're gone, but I hope you can hear me. I hope you know that I loved you. I gave you every part of me. You're gone now, and I'm not whole anymore. I just…I miss you." I wiped my tears away before continuing, "Guilt and pain are eating me up inside. I feel so guilty for leaving you instead of giving you a chance to make things right with me. Instead, I turned to Landon. I let him in, and now, I love both of you. I'm so fucked-up inside, Joel. You've ruined me."

I stared at his name carved into the stone. It felt wrong to see it there.

"I feel like I'm living in a dream. I'll wake up one day, and you'll be with me again, laughing and making inappropriate jokes." I laughed. "You used to embarrass me so bad when we first started dating. I never knew what was going to come out of that mouth of yours. I would give anything to hear your voice just one more time. I'd even let you embarrass me if it meant that you were here with me again."

I stopped talking after that, lost in my memories of happier times with Joel. We'd always had so much fun together. The nights we'd spent together, just the two of us, were my favorite. I would see a softer side, a more caring side to Joel.

I wasn't sure how long I sat there before Landon's face flashed before my eyes. I thought of the way he'd smiled when I said something sarcastic, the way he'd smelled, how it'd felt when he wrapped his arms around me.

"I have to let go of both of you, don't I? That's the only way that I'll truly heal after everything that has happened. I can't let my emotions and my memories control me. I have to let go of it all and start over. If I don't, I'll drive myself mad."

I looked around to see that dusk was starting to settle in around me. I stood and looked down at Joel's grave.

"I want you to know that I will always love you, but I'm letting go of you. I forgive you for everything." I kissed my fingers before pressing them up against the cold stone. "Good-bye."

As I turned and walked back to my car, I let him go. I'd said good-bye. Starting now, I was going to move on.

I still had one more person to say good-bye to though, and I knew he wouldn't be as silent as Joel had been.

I should have called Landon. I knew that, but I couldn't bring myself to do it. Instead, I took the coward's way out.

As soon as I made it home, I walked up to my room and grabbed a notebook and pen. I dropped down onto my bed and opened the notebook to a blank page. My brain shut off, and I wrote what I felt.

Landon,

I'm sorry that I'm doing this via letter, but I couldn't bring myself to call you. Hearing your voice would have been too much for me to bear. I'm sure you realize that I've been dealing with a lot lately. Joel's death destroyed me. I've spent the last two months regretting everything that happened this summer, including you.

What I felt for you was wrong. From the beginning, I knew something about you would draw me in. Instead of running away like I should have, I gravitated toward you. Even before Joel cheated on me, I couldn't help but want to be around you. I ignored my feelings though—until everything went to hell.

You helped me through a lot, and I'll be forever grateful to you for your friendship. You made me feel alive when I thought that I was dead. You made me love you. I'm sorry that I fell in love with you. That was never my intention.

You're one of the kindest people that I've ever met. You're a good person, Landon. You deserve a lot better than me. You always have. So, I'm letting you go. You and I are from two completely different worlds. We both knew it, but we ignored it.

I've felt so much guilt over both you and Joel. It nearly killed me. I can't live like that anymore. I have to protect myself. I have to heal. You will always hold a special place in my heart, but there is nothing left between us.

I ask that you please stop trying to contact me. I have to move on, and I can't do that with you constantly calling me. I just want to be whole again, and I will be. It might not be today or next week, but one day, I'll be Alexandria again.

I'll never forget you.

Your friend,
City

I stood and grabbed an envelope off my desk. I shoved the letter in and sealed it, refusing to let myself think about what I'd written down until it was in the mail. I addressed it and put a stamp on it before walking downstairs and out the front door. After putting it in our mailbox, I walked back up to my room and crashed down on my bed.

Tears sprang to my eyes, and I let myself truly mourn the loss of Landon for the first time. I didn't want to feel the loss of him, but I did. It didn't matter. I'd just told him that I loved him, but I didn't want anything to do with him, so he would have to leave me alone. I knew I had been cruel in the letter, but I had to be. If I weren't, he would never give up on us. He had to let me go. He had to move on.

I was broken, a shell of a girl. He deserved better than that. He deserved someone who could look at him and not think of her ex. He deserved someone who could give one hundred percent of herself to him. I wouldn't bring him down with me.

The next morning, I walked into the kitchen to see my mom sitting at the table.

"Good morning, Alexandria." She smiled at me.

"I want to go back to school," I blurted out before I lost my nerve or changed my mind.

I knew school was going to be different now, but I needed the distraction. I needed to get back into the real world and start living again.

My mother nearly choked on the sip of coffee she'd just taken. After she stopped coughing, she asked, "Are you sure you're ready?"

"No, I'm not, but I never will be. I have to start living again."

She studied me for a minute before nodding. "I'll call the school today."

"Thank you," I said as I turned to walk back up to my room.

"Alexandria?"

I turned to look at her.

"I talked to your father this morning. He'll be home later this week."

A genuine smile spread across my face. "Good. I've missed him."

My dad traveled a lot for his job, but this time had been the longest that he was away from us. I missed him so much, but I'd been so overwhelmed with grief that I hadn't been able to bring myself to talk to him when he called.

I spent the rest of my morning lying in bed, listening to Korn's album, *The Paradigm Shift*. I had it on repeat for the third time when my mom walked into my room. She didn't look happy.

"Get dressed," she said.

I raised an eyebrow. "Why? What's going on?"

"We're going to pay your principal a little visit. It seems that he's not thrilled about you wanting to reenroll."

Oh shit. "Give me ten, and I'll meet you downstairs."

She nodded and left. I stood and pulled the baggy shirt I used for a sleep shirt over my head. I dug through my closet, trying to find something presentable. I didn't want to piss him off by wearing my usual outfits. I finally settled on a pair of jeans that had minimal holes and a plain black T-shirt. I pulled my hair back into a sleek ponytail and headed downstairs. My mom was waiting for me when I reached the bottom of the stairs.

She didn't say a word as she opened the front door and walked out. I followed behind her. I could practically see the anger radiating off of her. I hadn't seen her this mad since…well, since she caught me selling drugs.

The ride to my school was completely silent. Honestly, I felt sorry for my principal. He wouldn't stand a chance against her. I'd been the focus of her wrath more than once, and I wouldn't wish it on anyone.

We pulled into a space marked for visitors and stepped out of the car. She marched up to the door and pushed the button, alerting the office that someone wanted in. After a short conversation with the secretary, I heard the door unlock. My mother threw it open and stormed though. The office was down the first hallway we came to. I'd been there enough times to know the layout. We walked into the reception area and stood at the counter.

The secretary walked up and smiled at my mother. Her smile slipped a little when she noticed me standing behind her. "Can I help you?"

"I need to speak with Principal Groves," my mother stated.

"Sure. I'll let him know you're here." She turned and walked to the principal's door. After knocking, she stepped inside and closed the door behind her.

My mother's foot tapped impatiently as we waited for the secretary to reemerge.

Finally, a few minutes later, she did. She smiled sweetly as she walked up to us. I'd seen that smile a thousand times. It was as fake as a porn star's boobs.

"I'm sorry, but Principal Groves is getting ready to go into a phone conference. It will last a while."

"We'll wait," my mother said.

The secretary's smile slipped for a fraction of a second. "I'll let him know."

Over an hour later, Principal Groves finally walked out of his office.

Out of habit, I groaned. Every single time I had come into contact with this man, things had ended badly for me. Usually, I had been kicked out of school for a week or two.

He glanced at me once before stopping in front of my mother. "Please follow me."

We stood and followed him into his office.

He shut the door and took a seat behind his desk. "What can I help you two with?"

"I spoke to you this morning about my daughter. She wants to reenroll."

"I thought we had come to an understanding this morning, Mrs. Carter. We are already two months into the school year. It would be impossible for Alexandria to make up for all the lost time. Her best option is to get a GED."

"I can catch up," I said before my mother could speak.

He eyed me with disdain. I knew that look on him well. He'd given it to me several times over the past three years.

"You would have to come in early and stay for hours after school."

"That won't be a problem," my mother said calmly.

He sighed as he glanced back and forth between the two of us. "I'm going to be blunt here, Mrs. Carter. Alexandria doesn't have the best track record around here. Truthfully, I think I've seen her more than I see my own kids. Her grades are dismal at best, and the fights…I can't risk my students."

"So, basically, you're denying my daughter an education."

"Not at all. I suggested that she get a GED."

"I understand that she doesn't have the best transcript or track record, but things have changed for her. She's had a lot to deal with over the past few months, but she's doing better."

"With all due respect—" Principal Groves started.

My mother cut him off. "My daughter's boyfriend was killed while assisting the police. She's been through hell and back. Now that she's trying to get her life back together, you refuse to cooperate." She paused for a moment, preparing herself for what was to come next. "I wonder how the press and local community would feel about you trying to deny her a public education—something every child has a right to by law, mind you—after she's suffered so much."

The threat was clear. I almost smiled at the look of shock on the principal's face. Mom had balls—I'd give her that.

"I…" Principal Groves started, but snapped his mouth shut.

"I'm sure that we can come to some kind of agreement. I'd hate to have to take this to the press and the board of education."

"That won't be necessary," he finally said. "I'm sure that we can work something out."

"I'm glad to hear it," my mother replied, her voice like ice.

CHAPTER
21

I stared at myself in the mirror. I still wasn't used to having blonde hair again. I tried to smile at myself but failed. It looked more like a grimace than anything else. I sighed as I turned away from the mirror and walked to my bed where my bag was sitting.

After my mother had threatened Principal Groves, he'd finally given in and said I could come back to school—after making it clear that I would be expelled if I ended up in another fight, of course. My mother had assured him that fighting wouldn't be an issue, but I wasn't so sure. I had several enemies at school, and without the threat of Joel, I knew some of them would be brave enough to face me. I knew I would win, but the fact that I would get kicked out of school was now looming over me. I didn't want to disappoint my mom. I just wanted to go to school and hope that life would slowly start getting back to normal.

I grabbed my bag and walked downstairs. My mom tossed me her keys as soon as I walked into the kitchen. I raised an eyebrow at her questioningly.

"You don't need me to drive you to school anymore. I'm sure you can handle driving yourself to school and back," she said.

"Uh...thanks, I guess. I'll see you later."

I turned and started walking to the door, but she called out to me.

"Alexandria? If things get too hard, call me. I know how hard you're trying, but don't expect things to magically go back to normal overnight."

"I will." I walked out the door and down the driveway to where my mom's car was parked.

I kept my mind blank as I drove to school. I didn't know how today would go. Hopefully, everyone would leave me alone, and I'd be fine. I knew, more than likely, that wouldn't happen, but I could hope. Now that Joel was gone, I had no one to lean on. I hadn't had friends of my own for a long time, and I didn't expect them to suddenly appear before me.

The minute I walked through the doors of the school, the commons area went silent. I glanced up once to see that everyone was staring at me. I stared down at the floor in front of me as I made my way to the office, pretending that silence didn't follow me.

The secretary had been expecting me, and she handed me a schedule the minute I walked into the office. "You need to see the counselor before you go to your first class," she said, her voice like ice. The fake smile from yesterday was nowhere to be seen.

I turned and walked out of the office and down the hall to where the counselor's office was. The door was open, and the counselor, Mrs. Pillo, looked up when I stepped inside.

"Hello, Alexandria. Principal Groves said you'd be stopping by this morning. Go ahead and have a seat."

I dropped my bag in front of the chair before sitting down.

"Principal Groves told me that you're reenrolling in school. I'm very happy to hear that," she said as she smiled at me.

"Yeah, me, too."

She ignored the dead tone in my voice as she continued, "You've been away for two months, so obviously, you have a lot of work to catch up on. I've talked with your teachers, and they are more than willing to work with you, so you can catch up by the end of the semester."

"Great," I mumbled.

Now that I was here, I wished I were anyplace else. *Coming here is a mistake.*

No. I closed my eyes for a second, fighting for control over my emotions. *Coming back is the right thing to do.* It was what I needed to jump start my life back into reality.

"They have agreed to work with you in the mornings and evenings as long as you show that you're serious about getting caught up."

"I am." I looked up to see her studying me carefully.

"Good. You'll start tomorrow with your extra lessons. Be here at seven. You'll leave school at five."

I nodded and stood, hearing the dismissal in her voice. "Thanks."

I turned and walked back out into the hallway just as the bell rang. I looked down at my schedule for the first time and frowned. It was brutal. I had math first followed by chemistry. After that was my one and only art class followed by lunch, then history, English, and gym. At least I would excel at gym after my summer at the farm. Working every day with Landon had strengthened my body. I squeezed my eyes shut, trying to forget Landon. I didn't need to think about him here.

Silence surrounded me as I walked to my locker and threw my bag inside. I grabbed a binder and my notebook out of it before heading to my first class. I glanced around the hallway as I walked, looking for familiar faces. I saw none, friend or foe. As soon as I'd walked in, I'd honestly expected to get jumped by one of the girls who hated me, but so far, no one had dared approach me. Maybe my badass reputation would protect me, even without Joel.

I made it to my first class without any problems. My teacher, Mrs. Adkins, frowned when she saw me walking up to her desk. I ignored it as I handed her my schedule.

"Welcome back, Alexandria. I hope that we won't have any problems this year," she said as she stared at me.

I flinched as I remembered the *problems* I'd caused in her classroom last year. The biggest was when I'd punched Becca so hard that I'd knocked her out cold. In my defense, she'd deserved it. She'd called me a crack whore.

"We won't have any issues, I promise," I said, trying to keep my voice calm.

"Glad to hear it. Take a seat," she said as she handed me a book.

I turned to face the rest of the room. Every single person was staring at me. The silence from the hallways had followed me in here. I walked to the back of the class, not bothering to look at anyone as I went.

I dropped into my chair and put my book and notebook on the desk before looking up. Several of my classmates were looking at me. The silence from before was gone. I could hear whispered conversations coming from all directions.

"Why is she back?"

"I thought she was in jail."

"I heard she killed him."

My knuckles turned white as I tried to control my temper. *I won't let them get to me. No way.*

None of these people were worth getting kicked out. I blocked out their words until the teacher finally called the class to order. I'd never been so glad to get started in my life. A few of my classmates kept looking over their shoulders at me, but I ignored them as I tried to concentrate on the chalkboard. Math had never been a strong point of mine, and it was obvious that it was way over my head now—two months' worth of over my head.

When class finally ended, I gathered my stuff and hurried from the room.

My next few classes went the exact same way. Some of my old friends—or rather, Joel's old friends—caught my eye and smiled occasionally. It was good to know that I wasn't completely alone.

When lunchtime rolled around, I walked slowly to the cafeteria, dreading the task of finding a seat. Hopefully, there would be an empty table somewhere.

Much to my relief, I found a table that was empty near the back of the cafeteria. I dropped down into a chair and started picking at my food. I missed Gram's cooking. She put this crap they passed off as food to shame. Just as I was about to stand and throw my uneaten food away, a chair pulled out beside me, and a body dropped into it.

I looked up to see Lucas, one of Joel's old friends, sitting next to me. Without a word, he smiled before digging into his food.

"Um…hi?" I asked, surprised to see him sitting with me.

We'd talked some before, but we weren't close. I wasn't close with any of Joel's friends besides Riley.

"Hey," he said as he shoved his light brown hair out of his eyes.

"Why are you sitting with me?" I asked.

He gave me a small smile. "You looked like you could use some company."

"Oh. Well, thanks, I guess," I mumbled.

"You're welcome." He studied me for a minute. "I'm sorry about Joel. He could be an ass, but overall, he was a good guy. I liked him a lot."

"Thanks," I said as I fought the tears clouding my vision.

I knew he was trying to help, but I didn't want to casually talk about Joel over bad cafeteria food.

"Look, I know we're not best friends or anything, but I've always considered you a friend. All of our group has. You were Joel's chick, but you were also a hard-ass, Lexi. We're not going to shun you just because he's gone."

We both looked up when the chairs across the table were pulled out. Ryan and Cory, two more of Joel's friends, sat down and gave me a brief smile.

"What's up, Lexi? Long time no see," Cory said.

"Uh...not much."

I stared at all three of them as they started to eat. I hadn't expected this. I'd always assumed that they kept me around because I was with Joel, not because they liked me. As I realized that maybe I did have a few friends around here, I smiled. Maybe I would be okay after all.

The first week had been hard, but I made it through. Lucas, Cory, and Ryan sat with me at lunch every day, and soon, more of my old friends started joining us. No one mentioned Joel again, but I knew they were all thinking about him. I thought that Lucas had told them not to say anything about Joel, and I was grateful. I didn't want to talk about him. I was trying to move forward, and I couldn't do that if people kept bringing him up. I wasn't trying to forget him. There was no way that I could even if I wanted to. I was just trying to move on.

"So, what are you doing this weekend, Lexi?" Lucas asked as we were leaving the cafeteria.

"Uh...nothing. I might hang out with Riley or something."

"Why don't you come to my house tonight? Riley, too. We're having a party."

"Let me see what he wants to do. I'll let you know," I said as we stopped by my locker.

"Great. Maybe I'll see you later then."

I watched him walk away, debating on whether I'd go even if Riley wanted to. I knew Lucas's party would be a lot like Joel's had been. There would definitely be drugs and alcohol, and I was done with that scene. I liked the guys though. If I went, I promised myself that I wouldn't do anything stupid.

I pulled my phone out of my pocket and sent a quick text to Riley.

Me: Lucas is having a party tonight. We're invited. Do you want to go?

A few seconds later, he responded.

Riley: If you're cool with it, I am. Want me to pick you up?

Me: Yeah. I'll be ready around seven.

Riley: See you then.

With a smile on my face, I shoved my phone back into my pocket before heading to my next class. The party was just another way that I was moving on. I could do this. I *would* do this.

CHAPTER

22

I dropped my bag off in my room once I made it home. It was already five thirty, and I needed to hurry up, so I'd be ready by the time Riley stopped by to pick me up. After showering, straightening my hair, putting my makeup on, and dressing again, I walked downstairs to let my mom know that I was going out.

I walked into the living room where she was sitting on the couch, watching television. She glanced up at me, surprise written clearly across her face.

"You look nice. Usually, you're in sweats by now."

"I'm going out tonight, if that's okay," I said nervously. I probably should have made sure it was okay with my mom before I told Riley to pick me up.

"Where are you going?"

"Um…there's a party. I'm going with Riley."

She raised an eyebrow. "Is this party like Jo—is it like the ones you used to go to?"

"It is, but you don't have to worry. I won't get in trouble."

"Alexandria…I don't think that this is a good idea. You've been doing so well, and I don't want you to slip back into old habits."

"I won't. I promise. I just want to get out for the night. Riley knows how I've been lately. He'll watch out for me."

I knew he would. Riley's protective streak seemed to triple after Joel's death.

She nodded, but I knew she was still debating.

"What time will you be home?"

"I don't know. It'll be late, but I can let you know when I get home, if that will make you feel better."

"No, it's all right. I trust you. Just please be careful, okay?"

I nodded, relieved that she was letting me go out. "I will."

I hugged her quickly before grabbing my purse and walking out the door. Riley's car was idling by the curb, and I hurried out to meet him.

"Hey," I said as I closed the door.

"You ready for this?" he asked as he pulled away from my house.

"Yeah, I'll be fine. I need to get out more. I have to start living again."

He nodded. "You do. Whenever you're ready to go, just let me know, and we'll leave, okay?"

"That's fine. I'm not going to drink or anything, so if you want to, go ahead. I'll drive you home."

He glanced over at me. "I don't think that's a good idea. I'll stay sober, too."

"I'll be fine, Riley. Seriously. I want to have fun tonight, and you should, too. You've also had a hard time lately."

"I can have fun without getting drunk."

I snorted. "Next, you'll tell me that you don't want to hookup with chicks anymore."

He laughed. "I wouldn't go that far. I need to get laid. It's been too long."

"Then, go for it. Don't let me stop you."

"You could always join in. I'm sure it'll take your mind off your troubles." He grinned innocently at me.

I rolled my eyes. I'd been around Riley long enough to know that he was only kidding. We both cared a lot about each other but not like that. I had been Joel's, and Riley was...just Riley.

"I think I'll pass, but thanks for thinking of me."

"Suit yourself. Your loss," he joked.

We pulled into a parking space a few houses down from Lucas's. Even though it was barely past seven, the party was already in full swing. We both stepped out of the car and started walking toward the house. As soon as we walked through the door, Lucas appeared with two red cups. He handed one to both of us.

"Glad you guys could make it." He smiled.

I stared down at my cup, unsure of what to say. "Um...thanks for inviting us, but I'm not drinking tonight."

"Why not?" Lucas asked as if not drinking wasn't something he could comprehend.

"I don't know. I just don't feel like it, I guess," I mumbled.

"Lexi, relax. Seriously. Just drink it and have fun. You deserve some fun," Lucas said.

I glanced at Riley, but he shrugged.

"If you want to drink, then drink. I'll watch out for you," Riley said.

I glanced between both of them and finally down to my cup. "Sure. Why not?"

I knew it was stupid to drink, but I did it anyway. My promise to my mother was forgotten as I drank first one cup and then another. I'd forgotten how much alcohol could numb me. As I started on my third cup, I was buzzed and relaxed. I couldn't remember the last time I'd been relaxed like this.

"You doin' okay?" Riley asked from beside me. He'd been by my side the entire night.

"I'm fine. Go have fun, Riley. I can take care of myself."

"Not a chance. You're my responsibility tonight."

I opened my mouth to tell him to get lost, but a girl stepped right in front of me. My vision turned red when I realized that it was Tasha.

"What do you want?" I spit out.

She sneered at me. "I just wanted to come over and see how you're doing." She glanced at Riley, who was now so close to me that his shoulder brushed mine. "But I can see that you're doing just fine. I wonder what Joel would have thought about you and his best friend?"

I didn't think. I just reacted. Before Riley could stop me, I tackled Tasha to the floor. She was the reason that Joel and I had split up. She was the reason that I hadn't been with him that night. She was the reason he was dead.

"How dare you say that to me after what you did?" I screamed as I slapped her hard across the face.

She reached out and grabbed my hair, yanking my head down. I barely noticed as I drew back and slammed my fist into her face. *How many times have I hit this woman?* It didn't matter. I felt no regret over hurting her. Instead, I wanted her to suffer more.

She yanked my hair hard, causing me to fall to one side. I cursed the alcohol I'd drunk as I tried to keep her from climbing on top of me. If I were sober, she never would have had the chance to knock me off. Her fist slammed into my stomach, but I barely noticed as I flipped her off of me and tackled her again. Adrenaline and rage shot through my system as I punched her again.

I felt someone grab me from behind and pull me off of her.

"Stop, Lexi! She's not worth it."

Riley. I sagged into his arms as he dragged me away. He didn't stop until we were outside in Lucas's front yard.

"What the hell, Lexi?" he shouted at me.

"Didn't you hear what she said to me?" I shouted right back. "She accused me of being with you after everything she's done!"

"It doesn't matter! She's not worth it, and we both know it. She was baiting you, and you fell for it. You've got to stop hitting every person who pisses you off!"

I glared at him. "I don't hit everyone who pisses me off. I haven't hit you yet, but I really want to."

He chuckled, causing me to grin, too. "You're an idiot, Lexi. Come on, let's get you home before you start a brawl."

He grabbed my arm and all but dragged me to his car, and then he shoved me inside. Once he was inside as well, he started it and pulled away. Now that my mind wasn't clouded with anger, I realized how stupid I had been to fight with her again. It wouldn't change anything. Granted, it did make me feel better, but still, it wasn't an answer, and neither was drinking.

"You okay?" Riley finally asked.

"Peachy. I'm sorry that I let her get to me. I just…I saw her, and I lost it. Everything is her fault. If she'd stayed away from Joel, we never would have broken up. I might have been with him that night. I could have saved him."

"You wouldn't have been there, Lexi. You were at your grandparents'. There's nothing you could have done. You have to realize that."

He was right, but I didn't want to admit it. Tasha had been the target I needed. My hate could be unleashed on a physical target.

"She screwed everything up for us. If it wasn't for her, Joel and I would have still been together those last few weeks."

"I know, Lexi. Trust me, I know. Joel let her have it, if it makes you feel any better. He refused to be around her, and he told all the dealers not to sell to her anymore. I'm assuming that she finally found someone to sell to her now though."

"I should have hit her harder," I grumbled.

Riley laughed. "I have no idea why you were worried about going back to school. Those chicks would have to be crazy to try anything with you. You go half-crazy when you start fighting."

Neither of us spoke again until he pulled up in front of my house.

"I'll see you later, Lexi. Call me if you need something."

"I will. Night, Riley." I stepped out of the car and closed the door behind me.

He waited until I was in my house before driving away.

I might not have Joel or Landon anymore, but I still had friends. I still had a life. It was a start.

I fell into an easy routine the next week. I was at school an hour before anyone else and stayed until five every night, trying to catch up on my classes. Word had spread about my fight with Tasha at Lucas's, and no one dared approach me. None of them realized that I couldn't fight in school, or I was sure they would have started something. Despite the fact that I was trying to get caught up and staying out of trouble, Principal Groves and my teachers watched me constantly. I knew they were waiting for me to fuck up.

The following weekend, I went to another party with Riley. Tasha was nowhere to be seen—thankfully—and the night was uneventful. I ended up crashing at Riley's place since I was slightly drunk. My mom was pissed off over that one, but at least I had texted her to let her know where I was.

She had no idea that I was drinking again, and I didn't want her to. Besides, I wasn't drinking like I had before. I knew Riley was there for me, but I also knew that I had to learn to take care of myself. Getting stupid drunk at a party full of guys wasn't what I considered taking care of myself.

Things were getting back to normal for me finally. I still had days where I didn't want to get out of bed, but I forced myself to. Joel was in my thoughts a lot, but it didn't hurt quite as bad to think about him anymore. I was finally starting to find peace when it came to him.

Landon, on the other hand, was a problem. Every time that I pictured him in my mind, I wanted to cry. I'd been so cruel to him when he was only trying to be there for me. I thought about calling him once or twice, but I decided against it. I'd told him to let me go, and I needed to do the same with him. I kept repeating that to myself on the nights when I couldn't sleep because he kept popping into my head. I missed him so damn much. If things had been different, I would be in his arms right now. I would be happy. But life never worked that way. Instead, it fucked me over every chance it had.

I spent most of my free time with Riley. I felt bad about it, but he assured me that it wasn't a big deal. He was the only person who understood how much it hurt to lose Joel. He'd listened more than once as I cried over everything I'd lost. I even told him about Landon. I was ashamed that I'd fallen in love with someone besides Joel. Riley didn't judge though. He even suggested that I call and talk to Landon.

Four weeks after I'd sent Landon that letter, the world came crashing down around me yet again. Riley had just dropped me off, and I was walking inside when I heard the phone ringing. I hurried and answered it, unsure of whether or not my mom was asleep.

"Hello?"

"Alexandria?"

My grandmother's voice shocked me.

"Gram?"

"Yes, honey, it's me. I'm sorry that I'm calling so late, but I thought you should know—"

"Know what? What's wrong, Gram? Is Grandpa okay?" I asked.

"Caleb is fine. It's…it's Landon. There was an accident today. He was driving one of the tractors on a steep hill, and it rolled."

I couldn't breathe. I couldn't move. *Landon…accident…oh God.*

It was Joel all over again. My legs gave out, and I slid down the wall just as my mother walked into the room. She took one look at me and rushed to my side.

208

"Alexandria, what's wrong?" she cried as she knelt down in front of me.

When I didn't answer, she grabbed the phone from my hand. "Who is this?"

I watched her eyes widen as Gram spoke to her over the phone. I was breathing again but just barely. It felt like something was sitting on my chest. There wasn't enough room for my lungs to expand.

"We're on our way," my mother said just before she hung up. "Alexandria? Alexandria! Look at me!"

I felt a sting on my face. My mouth dropped open as I realized that my mother had just slapped me. "Did you just slap me?"

"I'm sorry, but you weren't responding. Listen to me, Landon is hurt, but they think he's going to be okay. He was unconscious when they took him."

"They?"

"The paramedics. He was on a tractor that rolled over. Come on, we need to get going. Go grab a few of your things."

I stood and ran to my room. I grabbed one of my bags and starting throwing my clothes inside. As soon as I was finished, I ran back downstairs. My mother was carrying a bag of her own when she met me by the door. She grabbed her keys, and we hurried to her car. Neither of us spoke as she pulled out of the driveway and headed for the interstate.

This couldn't be happening to me again. I couldn't lose Landon. Terror seized my heart as I tried to process what my mom had said. He'd rolled a tractor. I'd seen the tractors my grandpa had. They were huge. And one had rolled over him. He was unconscious. I started sobbing. If something happened to Landon, I was done. I couldn't handle it. I couldn't handle burying someone else that I loved.

"Alexandria, please don't cry. Your grandma said that they think he's okay. He was knocked unconscious, but your grandpa and Kent were both with him when it happened. They got paramedics out there quickly."

"I can't handle it, Mom. I can't lose someone else," I cried.

"Just breathe. Try to calm your mind until we get there. We have no idea what's going on."

The three-hour car ride felt like three years. I kept looking at the clock on the dashboard, expecting an hour to have passed, only to see that it was minutes instead. I nearly cried in relief when we crossed the bridge into West Virginia. After that, it didn't take us long to reach Wetzel County Hospital in New Martinsville. When we pulled into the parking lot, I jumped from the car and ran inside.

It was after three in the morning by the time we arrived, and the emergency room was relatively empty. A lone nurse was sitting behind a desk near the entrance. She glanced up when I stopped in front of her desk.

"Can I help you?" she asked calmly.

I wanted to shake her. *How can she sit there so calm and put together when my world is falling apart around me?*

"There was a guy brought in tonight, Landon Rogers. I need to know what room he's in."

"Are you family?"

"No, I'm not family! Why does that matter?"

"If you're not family, I can't provide you with his personal information."

I ran my hands through my hair to keep myself from reaching across the desk and wrapping them around her neck. "Where is he? Please. I need to see him."

"I'm sorry, but I can't give you that information."

"Are you fucking kidding me right now?" I shouted.

"Ma'am, please calm down, or I'll have to call security," she said as she reached for the phone.

"That won't be necessary," a voice said from behind me.

I turned to see Gram coming through a set of doors on the right side of the emergency room.

I ran over to her and wrapped my arms around her just as my mother walked into the room.

"Gram, where is he? Is he okay?"

"He's still out, but he's going to be okay. Come on, I'll take you up to see him." She spotted my mom and smiled. "Hi, baby girl. I've missed you."

"Hi, Mom," my mother said as she hugged Gram. "I've missed you, too."

Gram pulled away from her and took my hand in hers. "Come on."

We took the elevator up to the third floor. When the doors opened, I all but ran out of them.

"Which way?" I asked as I looked around.

"To the left. Third door down on the right side of the hallway."

I took off down the left hallway and stopped when I reached Landon's door. I looked inside and saw my grandfather and Kent sitting in chairs by the window. Now that I was sure I had the right room, I hurried inside.

Kent noticed me, and I watched as his eyes turned cold.

"What is she doing here?"

"I called her," Gram said as she walked in behind me.

I ignored Landon's dad as I stared at Landon. I started crying again as I approached the bed. He was still unconscious. He was pale and had a deep cut across his cheek. A dark bruise covered the same side of his face that the cut was on. His leg and wrist were both in a cast. But he was breathing.

"Is he going to be okay?" I asked, my voice thick.

"He'll be fine. He broke his leg and wrist, bruised his ribs and his face, but other than that, he's okay," Gram said as she placed her hand on my shoulder.

Tears streamed down my face as I reached out and took his unbroken hand in mine. I could have lost him tonight. Gram pulled a chair over by his bed and pushed me down into it. I never let go of his hand as I sat down. I couldn't. Nothing in this world could tear me away from him right now.

"I've been so stupid," I whispered. "I pushed you away, and I hurt you. I'm so sorry, Landon."

His dad snorted. "Now's a good time to realize that. It takes him almost getting killed for you to show up. I wish you had stayed where you belong. You'll only hurt him more when he wakes up and sees you here."

"Kent!"

I'd never heard my grandma so angry. I looked up to see him glaring at me.

"What? It's the truth. She ran and broke his heart." He glanced over at my mom. "It must be a family trait."

My mother's face turned red, but she said nothing. Instead, she left the room.

"Good job, asshole. I deserve your words, but she doesn't," I snapped at him.

I'd never really talked to Kent that much, but he was really starting to piss me off.

His shoulders hunched forward. "Damn it!"

I watched him stand and hurry from the room. I hoped that my mother ripped him a new asshole.

I turned my attention back to Landon. I couldn't stand to see him like this. It was killing me. *What kind of person am I that it takes a tragedy for me to realize how much I care about someone?*

As I stared down at Landon, I made a promise to both him and myself. No matter what happened, I wasn't going to abandon him again. I couldn't. I loved this man more than I thought possible, and I wasn't going to let him go. I just hoped that he would forgive me.

CHAPTER 23

I must have fallen asleep at some point because I woke up to see the sun starting to rise. I looked down to see that I was still holding Landon's hand. I glanced up to his face, and I nearly cried out when I saw him watching me.

"Landon? Oh my God, you're awake!" I said.

"City?" he asked, confused.

"Yes, it's me."

"Am I dreaming?"

I laughed. "No, I'm really here. How are you feeling?"

I glanced around to see Kent asleep in one of the chairs by the window, but my grandparents and my mom were nowhere to be seen.

"Like I was run over by a tractor," he grumbled as he looked around the room. "What are you doing here?"

"Gram called and told me what happened. I got here as fast as I could. I was terrified. I thought I'd lost you, too."

He stared at me for a moment, his eyes growing cold, just like his dad's had. "Well, as you can see, I'm fine. You can leave now."

I ignored the iciness of his tone as I shook my head. "I'm not going anywhere."

He openly glared at me now. I'd never seen him angry, and it shocked me.

"You should leave, *Alexandria.* You made your feelings pretty clear in that letter you sent me."

I took a deep breath to calm my temper. I deserved his harsh words. I'd hurt him when all he wanted to do was be there for me.

"I'm so sorry, Landon. I was hurting, and I pushed you away. I didn't want to hurt you. I just wanted you to move on and be happy. I wasn't in a good place, and I knew you couldn't be happy with me."

"You never even gave me a chance. Don't you think that I should have had some kind of say in the matter?"

"You're right." I hung my head in shame. "Please forgive me."

"What do you want from me, City? You want me to tell you that it's okay? I can't do that. It's not okay, not even close. You can't just come in here, ask for forgiveness, and expect me to be okay with what you did. You ran, and you never once looked back."

"I'm done running, Landon. When Gram called and told me what happened, I thought my world was ending all over again. It made me realize how much I care about you. I'm done pushing you away." I felt tears forming in my eyes, but I forced them away.

His voice softened when he spoke again, "I'm sorry, City, but I can't. You ripped my heart out, and I'm not willing to let you do it again."

His words crushed me. *How could I have been so stupid?* I'd pushed him away, and now, he wanted nothing to do with me.

"I'm not giving up, Landon. I can't. I know what I did was stupid, but I was hurting. Please. I can't lose you," I whispered.

He squeezed his eyes shut before opening them again. "You should go. As you can see, I'm fine, so you don't have to worry about me anymore."

I shook my head. "I'm not leaving you."

I wasn't going to give up on him, on us. *No way.* It didn't matter how long it would take. Landon would be mine again.

"Just go!" he all but shouted. "I don't want you here."

"Fuck off, Cowboy. I'm not leaving. I don't care what I have to do to prove that I'm serious. I'll win you back. I…I love you. I love you more than I thought possible."

He shook his head. I could see anger burning brightly in his eyes.

"You don't get to say that to me. You know what? Whatever. Stay here. Leave. I don't care. I'm finished with this conversation."

He turned his head away from me and closed his eyes. I didn't try to stop the tears from falling now that he wasn't watching. I deserved this, and I knew it. I'd dug myself into this hole, and now, I had to dig myself out. I wasn't about to give up though.

Landon stayed in the hospital for one more day, and then he was released. I rode back to the farm with my mom and Gram. I smiled as I listened to the two of them catch up with each other. It had been far too long since they'd last seen each other.

"You okay back there, Alexandria?" Gram asked as she glanced back at me.

"I'm fine," I mumbled as I watched the scenery pass by outside my window.

Landon had refused to speak to me after our argument. It hadn't taken long for everyone to figure out what was going on. Kent had even tried to get me to leave, but I'd refused. There was no way that I was going to leave Landon again.

"Want to tell us what's going on with you and Landon?" my mom asked.

I sighed. "I fucked up."

"Well, we figured that much out," my Gram said as she grinned at me. "But what happened between you two yesterday?"

"I asked him to forgive me, and he told me no. He's angry with me for what I did, and he has every right to be. I never should have sent that letter to him."

"What letter?" my mom asked.

"Uh…I sent him a letter a few weeks ago, telling him that I was over him and to leave me alone."

"Alexandria!" my mother shouted. "How could you do something like that to him? That's horrible!"

"I know. I was an idiot. I just…I don't know how to make it up to him."

"It'll take time, sweetheart. You hurt him…badly," Gram said.

"I'm not going to give up. I love him. I didn't realize how much until you called to tell me that he was hurt. I can't lose him, too."

"You'll figure it out. Don't worry. Give him a few months to heal and get back to normal. Then, once school is over, you can come spend the summer here again," my mom said.

My head snapped up to look at her. "I'm not leaving him again."

"What are you talking about?"

"I'm *not* leaving, Mom. I'm staying in West Virginia."

"No, you're not! You just got back into school, and you're doing so well. I won't let you drop out again!"

"I won't. I'll just transfer here or do homeschooling."

"Alexandria, you can't just move out and expect me not to stop you. Think about this before you act. I know you're hurting, but this isn't the answer."

"Mom, I'm eighteen. If I want to leave, I can." I looked over to see Gram watching me. "If Gram won't let me stay with her, I'll find a job and someplace close to rent."

"Don't be silly! Of course you can stay with me!" Gram said, looking offended.

"Mom! Don't encourage her! This is nuts. She can't just move over one hundred miles away from home!"

"Of course I can. Look, you know that I'll be safe with Gram and Grandpa. I won't get into trouble. That's why you sent me here to begin with."

"I…no!" she said angrily.

It didn't matter what she or anyone else had to say. My mind was made up. I was moving to West Virginia.

"Then, it's settled. I have a bunch of my stuff with me already. You can ship everything else to me, or I can go back and get it."

I leaned back in the seat and closed my eyes. Now that I had a plan, I felt better. There was no way that Landon could keep denying me if he had to see me every day. I smiled. He was going to be so pissed off when he found out. I tuned my mother out as she ranted all the way back to the farm.

When we arrived, I grabbed my bag off the seat and carried it into the house. My mother was still grumbling under her breath as we walked in, but I ignored her and headed up the stairs to my room. I dumped the contents of my bag out on my bed and started sorting through them. I'd brought several shirts and jeans along with tons of bras and underwear. Even if my mom refused to send the rest of my stuff, I could survive with this.

I took my time putting everything away. I didn't want to have to go back downstairs and deal with my mom until I had to. I knew she would beg and fight with me to come home with her. She would give up eventually, but until then, she would try her hardest to make me miserable.

Once everything was put away, I lay on my bed and stared up at the ceiling. Things were so screwed-up right now. The past few months had changed me so much. I wasn't the whiny little chick who had come here last summer. I laughed, thinking about how she would have had a fit if she knew that I'd be willing to live here only a few months later. It seemed like years instead of months had passed since Dad dropped me off here.

My thoughts drifted to Joel. I wondered what he would have thought about the new me. I bet he would have liked me. I was still tough-as-nails Lexi, but there were more layers to me now. I didn't see the world the same way anymore. Each day was a gift, and I needed to learn to appreciate the here and now instead of dwelling on the past. The past was the past. Nothing I did could change it. But the here and now was a story waiting to be written. It was time that I started living. Joel would want that. He would want me to be happy even if that meant loving someone else.

My mom came up an hour later to check on me. She closed the door behind her and walked to my bed. I scooted over, so she could sit on the edge.

"Are you sure that you want to stay here?" she asked.

"I'm sure. I have to make this right. I can't lose him again. I know it sounds stupid to uproot my entire life for one guy, but he's worth it to me. I love him."

"I know you do. I've known all along. I was just waiting for you to figure it out. What are you going to do if he refuses to forgive you?"

I shrugged. "He won't. I know it'll take time, but we'll get there. I'm too determined for anything else to happen."

She grinned. "You always were stubborn. I won't fight you on this anymore, but I want you to know that you'll always be welcome at home with me and your dad."

"I know that. And I'm sorry for everything I put you through. Neither of you deserved that."

"You're a teenager, Alexandria. You're young and carefree and bound to screw up from time to time. It happens. Granted, yours was worse than most teens, but still, you're a good girl. I know you learned from your mistakes."

I nodded. "I did. I was messed-up for so long, but I'm better now. I'll always love Joel, but I've accepted his death. I have to keep living and moving forward."

"You're right." She laughed. "When did you get so smart?"

I stuck my tongue out at her as I sat up and pulled her into a hug. "I love you, Mom."

"I love you, too. Now, come on. Your grandmother has dinner ready."

She didn't have to tell me twice. I hopped up off the bed and started walking to the door.

"Finally. I haven't had a decent meal since I left here!"

"Hey! My cooking isn't that bad!" she teased as she followed me downstairs.

Dinner was uneventful. Landon and his dad were nowhere to be seen. My grandpa said that they were at their house. Kent was helping Landon settle in. I could imagine how pissed off Landon must be right now. His leg would keep him from working around the farm for at least six weeks. Once the cast was off, he might have to go to physical therapy. I hoped that he wouldn't have to. Landon was all about the outdoors and working around the farm. He'd go crazy from just sitting around.

"Your grandmother told me that you want to move back in with us," my grandpa stated.

"I do."

"I have no problem with it. Since Landon is out of commission, you can help pick up the slack. You'll have the same chores as before. On top of that, you're expected to go to school every day. If you miss, you better be on your deathbed. Can you handle that?"

I contained the eye roll dying to get out. "Yes, sir, I can."

"Good. You'll go to the school on Monday and enroll."

"Fine with me." I'd hoped that I could have a day or two to myself, but apparently, that wasn't going to happen.

CHAPTER 24

I didn't see Landon for the rest of the weekend. I hadn't really expected to, but I was still slightly disappointed. He was stuck in his house with a broken leg, and the only way I would be able to see him was if I went to visit him. As much as it sucked, I knew that I needed to wait. If he saw me again this soon, he'd make me leave.

After making sure to remind me that I could come home at any time, my mom left late Sunday night. She promised to ship the rest of my stuff down later that week.

Bright and early Monday morning, I woke up and did my chores. Once they were finished, I showered and dressed in a plain shirt and jeans. I left my blonde hair loose and applied only a small amount of makeup. I left my piercings in. I knew that the school probably wouldn't appreciate them, but they were a part of me.

"Is it okay if I use your car to drive to school?" I asked Gram as I walked into the kitchen.

"That's fine. I talked to your mom, and she said that she's going to send some money, so we can get you a car of your own. It won't be much, but at least you'll have something to drive."

"Thanks, Gram. I'll be back soon. Wish me luck." I pressed a quick kiss to her cheek.

"You don't need it. Principal Sanders is a good man. If he gives you any trouble, you tell him he won't get any more of my pumpkin spice cake."

I laughed as I grabbed her keys and headed for the door. "I'll pass it along."

I'd only seen Hundred High School once or twice in my life, but I remembered the general area of where it was. I drove slowly when I was nearing the entrance. The school was just off Route 7. I pulled into the parking lot and stepped out to look around. It was a small red brick building, completely different from the school I was used to.

I nearly fell over in shock when I walked to the front door, and it wasn't locked. My old school had locks on all entrances and a metal detector right inside the doors. This school had neither. I followed the signs down a hallway to where the office was. An older lady sat behind the desk. She looked up and smiled when she saw me. Unlike my old school's secretary, this one's smile seemed sincere.

"Can I help you?" she asked as she stood and walked over to the counter separating us.

"Uh…yeah, I just moved to the area, and I need to enroll."

"Are you over eighteen? If not, you need a parent or guardian with you."

"I'm eighteen," I confirmed.

"Great. Let me get the paperwork you need to enroll."

I waited as she dug through folders in a filing cabinet. Once she found what she was looking for, she turned back to me and handed me a packet full of papers. "Just fill these out for me, please."

I grabbed them and sat down on one of the folding chairs. I took my time filling out each form, wincing when they asked about my previous grades and suspensions. I finally finished filling out the forms and handed them back to the secretary.

"Thank you, sweetheart. Give me just a minute to get you put into our system. I'll have to call your old school and get your transcripts from there."

I nodded and sat back down in my chair as she started adding me into the computer system. I hoped that this didn't take long. It wasn't like I had anywhere to go, but still, I hated sitting around.

"Dear, who are you living with?" the secretary asked.

"Uh…my grandparents, Caleb and Lily."

"*You're* their granddaughter? I haven't seen you since you were just little. I remember you coming to church with Lily on Sundays during summer break."

"Oh yeah. That's me." I smiled weakly at her.

"Well, I'm sure they're excited to have you back," she said as she went back to typing. As she turned the page to the one asking for my grades and record, her fingers slowed on the keyboard. She opened her mouth to say something but stopped herself.

I knew what she was thinking. My record on paper wasn't the greatest. I knew that. I just hoped that it wouldn't get me kicked out of here before I even got my foot through the door.

"I'll let Principal Sanders know that you're here. He'll be with you in just a moment." She stood and walked to a door near the back of the office. After knocking, she disappeared inside. A few minutes later, she reemerged and told me he was ready to see me.

I stood and walked around the counter to his office door. As soon as I was inside, the secretary closed the door behind me. I turned to see Principal Sanders sitting behind his desk. I raised an eyebrow in surprise. No offense to him, but he was older than dirt. His hair was completely silver, and his skin was wrinkled with age. His eyes though were bright and clear.

"Hello, Alexandria. It's nice to meet you," he said.

"Uh…it's nice to meet you, too."

"Why don't you have a seat?" he asked as he gestured to one of the chairs in front of his desk.

"Nancy informed me that you will be enrolling at our school. She also told me that you have quite a history with fights and suspensions and that your grades are horrible."

"I can explain. I know it looks bad, but I'm not like that anymore. I messed up—a lot. I know that, but I want to start over. I swear that you won't have any problems from me."

"Alexandria, breathe. You didn't let me finish," he said as he smiled at me.

"Oh."

"Everything that's on your record? I'm going to throw it out the window. As far as I'm concerned, you're a model student. We all make mistakes, Alexandria, and everyone deserves a second chance. Our school is small, and I think you'll like it. We rarely have issues with students fighting, and the classes are small enough that the teachers can help you if you're having trouble with the material."

"So, I don't have to beg and grovel for you to let me in?" I asked doubtfully.

"You don't have to beg or grovel. Welcome to Hundred High School, Alexandria."

"Thank you. I promise, you won't have any issues with me while I'm here."

"Good. Now, we are in the process of getting your information from your old school. We should have it by tomorrow. Once we do, we can get your schedule set up, and you'll be good to go. I'll see you bright and early tomorrow morning."

"Thank you." I stood and walked to the door. "You won't regret this."

I left the school feeling lighter than I had in a while. I had a feeling that things were going to work out for me. School was just a small hurdle compared to Landon, but it was a start.

I almost stopped at Landon's house that night after I finished my chores, but I stopped myself. I needed to give him space. I would wait until this weekend to see him. I could handle that. *Who am I kidding?* It was going to drive me nuts to wait, but I had to. I didn't want to push him.

The nervousness I'd felt about returning to my old school wasn't there when I walked into Hundred High for my first day. I wasn't nervous or scared. I was calm, relaxed even. I was shocked when I saw just how few students were in the school. If I had to guess, I would say no more than a hundred were enrolled. I guessed the principal hadn't been kidding when he said the classes were small.

Most of the kids were like Landon—farm kids. I stood out like a sore thumb with my tattoo and piercings, but no one seemed to mind. No one judged me. A few students even came up to me and introduced themselves to me. They all seemed to share Landon's down-to-earth, small-town personality. I had no doubt that I was going to love it here. All of my teachers were friendly, too. That was probably because they hadn't seen my transcripts. I hoped to keep it that way.

Once school was finished, I drove home in Gram's car. When I made it home, I went up to my room and started working on my homework. I was behind here, too, but the teachers assured me that I could get caught up quickly. Once my homework was finished, I headed back downstairs and out to the barn to do my evening chores.

Over the next week, I fell into a schedule—chores, school, homework, chores, dinner, and finally bed. I was exhausted most of the time, but I was happy. I called Riley a few times to let him know how I was doing. He had been pissed at first when I told him that I'd moved again, but he understood why I was here. I called him every few days, promising that I would come up to visit him soon.

Landon was constantly on my mind. By Friday night, I felt like I was going to lose my mind if I didn't see him. Unfortunately, I knew his dad would be home. I waited until Saturday afternoon to finally visit him. I made sure that his dad was gone before I drove the four-wheeler down to his house. I could handle one pissed-off male but not two.

I shut off the four-wheeler in front of his house and grabbed my bag off the back. I'd stuffed it full of movies, hoping that he'd give in and watch them with me. I'd brought a little of everything—action, romance, comedy, thriller. Surely, he would like some of them.

I knocked on the door and waited. I heard a muffled shout telling me to come in. When I opened the door and walked through, I spotted Landon on the couch.

His eyes widened when he saw me. "What are you doing here?"

"I thought I'd stop by and keep you company," I said as I kicked off my shoes. I walked into the living room.

"No, I mean, what are you doing here—as in, on the farm?"

"Your dad didn't tell you?"

He shook his head.

"I moved back in with Gram and Grandpa."

"Since when?"

"Since the day you came home from the hospital."

"Oh. I figured you were back home by now. You shouldn't have stayed," he stated firmly.

"Oh, shut up, would you? I'm not going anywhere. You'll just have to deal with seeing me all the time."

"That's not fair, City, and you know it. I told you that I wanted you gone."

"We don't always get what we want," I taunted as I sat down on the couch next to him. "How are you feeling?"

"Like shit. My leg and wrist are itchy as hell."

"How are your ribs?"

"Sore, like the rest of me."

I lifted my hand to his face and grabbed his chin, tilting his head to the side. "Your face looks a lot better. The bruise is already starting to fade."

"Lucky me," he grumbled as he pulled away from me.

"You're grumpy today, aren't you?"

"You would be, too, if you were stuck on a damn couch for six weeks."

"Well, I brought something that might help." I put my bag between us and started pulling movies out. "I brought a bunch of different ones for us to watch."

"Don't do this."

I looked up to see him watching me. "Do what?"

"Don't come in here and act like everything is fine between us."

"I'm not acting like everything is fine. I figured you were bored, so I thought I'd come over and keep you entertained for a while. I know you're still mad at me, but that doesn't mean that we can't be friends."

"I don't want to be friends with you, City. I want you to go home and leave me alone."

"Sorry, but I'm not leaving. I already told you that. Now, pick a movie, so we can watch it."

He glared at me for a few minutes before finally giving up and staring down at the movies. "That one."

"Good choice. I love action movies." I stood and walked over to the TV. I popped the DVD into the player and sat back down. "Do you want me to make popcorn or something?"

"No."

"Alrighty then," I mumbled. I pushed play and then curled up in a ball on my side of the couch. I rested my head on the armrest and stared at the TV.

As the movie played, I kept glancing over at Landon. Most of the time, his eyes were glued to the TV, but occasionally, I noticed him watching me. When I caught him staring, he'd quickly turn his attention back to the movie. I couldn't help but smile. No matter what he said, he still cared about me.

When the first movie finished, I put another one in, a comedy this time. I curled back into a ball on the couch and watched it. I felt my eyes growing heavy, but I fought to stay awake. Finally, I couldn't take it anymore, and I let them close. I wasn't sure how long I'd slept, but when I opened my eyes, I saw Landon watching me. I glanced over at the screen to see that it was on the main menu.

"Shit, sorry. I didn't mean to fall asleep," I said as I sat up.

"It's okay. I'm sure you're tired."

"I am. Between school and chores, I'm always exhausted."

"You're in school?" he asked.

"Yeah, I started on Tuesday. Hundred is different from my old school, but I like it. There isn't a bunch of drama here."

"I never thought I'd see the day when *you* attended Hundred."

"Why?" I asked.

"You're so different from everyone else around here."

I shrugged. "No one seems to mind. I do my work and stay out of trouble, so no one pays me much attention."

"So, let me get this straight—you *moved* here, a place you hated this summer, *and* transferred schools?"

"Yep, that pretty much sums it up."

"But why?"

"Because I wanted to be with you," I answered truthfully.

"Shit, City. You can't just say stuff like that to me and expect me not to respond. You're making this a lot harder than I thought it would be."

"Good. The best things in life are never simple. I don't want you to forget about me, and I don't want you to give up on us. I told you that I love you, and I meant it."

He closed his eyes and took a deep breath before opening them again. "I think you should go back to your grandparents' house."

"You're right. It's getting late, and I need to get the chores done. I'll come back tomorrow."

"You don't have to."

"I know. I want to." I stood and threw my movies back into the bag. Before he could stop me, I leaned down and kissed him on the forehead. "I'll see you tomorrow."

He grinned. "I'll be here—probably in the exact same spot. And, City?"

"Yeah?"

He hesitated for a second. "I like your hair like that. You look good as a blonde."

"Thanks," I said as I grinned at him.

"Why did you change it?"

It was my turn to hesitate. "Because…because I'm starting over. I'm not who I used to be."

He frowned at that, but I ignored him. I walked to the door and opened it, but then I turned back to him instead of leaving.

"You know what? I'm kind of glad you broke your leg."

His eyes widened. "Why?"

"Because you can't run from me now."

CHAPTER
25

Over the next few weeks, I spent every evening with Landon. Neither of us mentioned what had happened between us. Instead, we focused on the present. He was slowly turning back into the old Landon—my Landon. While he had his moments of being a complete asshole to me, overall, things were slowly progressing. He was smiling and joking around with me a lot more. I knew his walls were crumbling. I just needed to have patience.

"Want to tell me what happened when you went home?" he asked one night as we sat on the couch together.

I'd started bringing my homework with me when I came to his house, and tonight was no different. We'd spent the last twenty minutes trying to figure out my math homework.

My head jerked up, my homework forgotten. I was shocked by his question. "What do you mean?"

"You know exactly what I mean. When you left, I didn't hear a word from you for almost two months. What happened?"

"I don't really want to talk about it, Landon," I said quietly. I didn't want to focus on the past anymore. I wanted to focus on the here and now. Lately, I'd been doing a pretty good job of it, too. I was proud of myself.

"Why? Do you want things to go back to the way they were? Then, talk to me, open up to me."

I could hear the anger and hurt in his voice. I didn't want to talk about the time I'd spent wasting away, but he had a point. *How is he supposed to forgive me if I won't open up to him?*

"It was rough, Landon. I had a breakdown at his funeral. After that, I just shut down. I didn't care about anything or anyone. I…I didn't want to live anymore. I felt like his death was my fault. If I had been there, maybe things would have been different. Instead, I'd focused all of my attention on you. The guilt nearly killed me."

"City, you have to know that you couldn't have done a thing to save him. Joel was mixed up in some really heavy stuff. He knew the risks. He knew what could happen. It wasn't like he walked blindly into that lifestyle."

"I know that now, but back then, I truly believed that his death was my fault. I stopped functioning."

"So, what changed?"

"My mom finally sat down and had a long talk with me. It made me realize that I was wasting my life. Joel wouldn't have wanted that. He would have wanted me to live. It took me a long time to start living again, but I finally did. Riley helped me a lot. He was feeling the same grief that I felt."

Landon raised an eyebrow. "Riley? Is that why you told me to stay away?"

"What? No! Of course not! Riley is my friend, nothing more. He's been my friend for a long time, and we both knew what the other was feeling. He took care of me, helped me. He forced me to get out and live again. I enrolled back in school and started hanging out with some of my old friends. I started going to their parties. I went to see Joel, and I finally said good-bye. I let him go."

"Then, why did you run from me?" he asked.

"I felt like what we had was tainted. Besides, I was messed-up for a really long time. You deserved better than that. You deserved someone who could make you happy."

"What would you have done if you had rushed to the hospital that night, only to find out that I had moved on?"

I was quiet for a moment, debating on what to say. "Truthfully? I probably would have hit her. I don't think I could handle seeing you with someone else. You're mine. I know that sounds like a crazy ex-girlfriend, but it's how I feel. You're mine, Landon, and no one else's."

That earned me a smile.

"Don't I have a say in the matter?"

"Nope. Don't you know by now that girls always get what they want? Especially me. And right now, I want you more than anything. It's like a physical ache. *But* I know that I have to earn your trust again. I screwed up."

"You did. You screwed up so bad, but I understand where you're coming from. You're only eighteen, City, and you had to deal with losing someone you truly loved. That messes with a person. I just…I don't know if I will ever be able to move forward. I'll always wonder if you're still thinking about him when you're with me."

"Landon, I can promise you that I don't think about him when I'm with you. Do I think about him? Yes. I'd be a heartless bitch if I didn't, but I never think about him when I'm around you. You make things better. You make *me* better."

"I'm glad that you feel that way. I still care about you, Lexi. I care about you more than I should."

My heart soared. *He does care.* "I care about you, too." I paused for a second, thinking over my next few words. "You know how I said that girls always get what they want?"

"Yeah?"

"Right now, I want to kiss you more than anything. Will you let me?"

His eyes widened for a fraction of a second. "I don't think that's a good id—"

Before he could finish his sentence, I threw my math book down on the floor and lunged at him. I was careful to avoid his injuries as I settled myself half-on and half-off of his lap.

"It probably isn't, but I don't care. I still want it."

I slammed my mouth down on his. He hesitated for a split second before finally caving. I moaned as he started kissing me back with as much aggression as I was using. Our lips melded together as I clung to him. I savored every taste, unsure of when I would experience this again.

His good arm wrapped around me, pulling me tighter against him. As I settled further into his lap, he groaned again. I slid my tongue into his mouth, teasing him. His breath grew shallow as he fisted the back of my shirt. This moment would forever be seared into my brain.

I finally pulled away to catch my breath. He stared up at me, lust and uncertainty both clouding his eyes.

"What was that about, City?" he asked, his voice gruff.

"I told you that I wanted to kiss you."

"You didn't mention anything about molesting me." He glanced down to where my hand was resting on the inside of his leg.

I pulled away hastily. "I didn't molest you."

"Sure you didn't." He paused. "I'm not ready to jump back into something with you just yet. Just give me time, okay?"

I nodded. "I told you, I'd wait as long as it takes, and I meant that. I'll wait forever for you, Cowboy."

He smiled when I used his nickname. "Good. Now, let's get back to your homework. Your grandpa will skin my hide if you start failing classes since you're spending so much time with me."

"Um…I'm not failing anything for once in my life. I have all As and Bs, except for math, and I have a high C in there."

"Then, let's keep it that way." He smiled as he squeezed my arm.

Yeah, things were starting to look up for once in my life.

Thanksgiving break came faster than I'd expected—not that I minded. It was nice to have a week off from school. Between the farm, Landon, and school, I had a full plate. I took advantage of the time off to spend even more time with him.

Landon finally got both of his casts off two days before Thanksgiving. I went with him to the doctor's office and waited in the waiting room as he had both of them removed. The smile on his face when he came out had my heart beating at twice the normal speed. He limped a little as he walked, but that was to be expected after being in a cast for so long. He would have to go to physical therapy once a week to help him get back on his feet, but the doctor didn't think that there would be any problems. Both his wrist and leg were healing nicely.

We stopped in New Martinsville on the way home and grabbed something to eat. Landon still wasn't allowed to drive, so I took us to the Mexican place we'd gone to so long ago. It seemed to brighten his mood even more when I pulled into the parking lot.

I helped him from the car and kept my arm around his waist as we walked into the restaurant. We both knew he could walk on his own, but I used the excuse that I was afraid he'd fall so that I could hold on to him longer. I knew he saw through my lie, but he didn't pull away. I hated when I had to let him go. The warmth of his skin and his smell made me want to cling to him even longer.

I nearly laughed when the waitress from before walked up to our table. Her eyes landed on me and narrowed. I knew she recognized me from the last time we had been in here.

Completely ignoring me, she turned to Landon and smiled. "Landon! It's been a while. I heard you got hurt. I tried calling you, but your dad said you weren't talking calls."

I coughed to cover a laugh, but I must not have done a good job because she turned back to me and glared.

"Did I say something funny?"

"Well, yeah. You keep saying that you try to call him, but he never calls you back. Take a hint," I said as I smiled sweetly at her.

It was Landon's turn to cough.

"What are you talking about?"

"He's taken, sweetheart. He has been for a long time."

She looked back and forth between the two of us. "I see."

I watched as she turned and walked away without another word. "I think I pissed her off."

"You shouldn't have done that," Landon said.

I turned to look at him. "Why?"

"Because she'll probably spit in our food or something." He grinned at me.

"Oh, I didn't think about that. Maybe we should go someplace else," I said, feeling guilty.

"That's probably a good idea. Come on."

I stood and helped him rise from the booth. He limped a little as I wrapped my arms around his waist and led him out the door. When we reached Gram's car, I opened the door for him to get in.

"We're doing things a little backwards here," Landon said as he looked down at me.

"Why?"

"Normally, I open the door for you."

I laughed. "I like taking care of you."

He studied me for a moment before leaning down to kiss me on the cheek. "Don't get used to it. I'll be back to my old self before too much longer."

I stared at his lips as he pulled away. Unable to stop myself, I stood on my toes and brushed my lips against his. He grabbed the back of my head and pulled me closer against him. I smiled against

his lips, loving the feel of his body against mine. When he pulled away, I was still smiling.

Neither of us said a word as he got in the car and closed the door. I hurried to the driver's side and got behind the wheel. We were both quiet as I drove us to a fast-food restaurant and ordered our lunch in the drive-through.

The ride home was silent as well, but neither of us seemed to mind. It had always been this way for us. When we were together, it was enough. No amount of useless chatter would change that.

After dropping him off at his house, I drove to Gram's. She took one look at my face and smiled knowingly. I blushed and quickly hurried to my room without a word. I knew Gram was hoping that I worked things out with Landon. From the beginning, she'd hoped that something would happen between the two of us.

I lay in my bed and stared up at the ceiling as I thought about kissing Landon. If I were to die today, I would die happy.

Thanksgiving was a huge event at Gram's house. She'd started working on dinner and desserts two days before the actual holiday. Gram was a miracle worker in the kitchen. She tried to teach me how to cook, but I failed miserably at just about everything she showed me. At least I could boil water. That was something.

On Thanksgiving morning, I laughed when I walked into the kitchen and saw every inch of the counters covered in food.

"How many people do you plan on feeding, Gram?"

She gave me a guilty smile. "Thanksgiving is my favorite holiday. I tend to get a little carried away."

"A little?" I teased.

"Oh, hush up, you, and help me put this food on the table," she scolded.

We had everything on the table, except for the desserts, when my grandpa, Kent, and Landon walked in. None of them batted an eyelash at the huge amount of food. Apparently, this was normal to them.

I took my usual seat at the table, but I was surprised when Landon sat down next to me instead of where he normally sat across the table when he and his dad ate dinner with us. His dad frowned at him but said nothing. Gram could barely contain her smile as she took Landon's usual seat.

After my grandfather said grace, we all attacked the food in front of us. I moaned when I took my first bite of turkey.

At the sound of my moan, Landon stiffened beside me as Gram laughed. I felt my face heat up, knowing what Landon was thinking. He surprised me when I felt his hand rest on my knee under the table. I glanced at him, but he ignored me as he continued to eat.

"So, how's school, Alexandria?" my grandfather asked.

I looked away from Landon to see everyone else looking at me. "Uh…it's going good so far."

"How are your grades?"

"Mostly As and Bs. I have a high C in math. I'm working on it though."

"Good. I talked to your principal at church on Sunday. He seemed pleased with you. I'm glad you're fitting in well."

My mouth hung open in shock. *Is my grandfather actually trying to carry on a conversation with me?* "I am. I like it here," I mumbled as I looked away.

I never thought I'd see the day when my grandfather and I could carry on a real conversation without throwing insults at each other. It took me a moment to realize the dislike I'd harbored for him for so long was now gone. It hadn't been with me for a while. I guessed Landon had been right when he said that my grandfather wasn't so bad.

"How are your injuries, Landon?" Gram asked.

"They're healing. I'll be back to normal in no time," Landon said.

"Well, take your time, and don't push yourself. Let Alexandria help you."

Playing matchmaker much, Gram?

"She's been great, but I'm tired of being an invalid." He squeezed my knee under the table.

I glanced over at him and smiled. "I'll be your nurse anytime."

The pressure on my leg increased, but he only smiled.

For the rest of dinner, none of us spoke much. We were too busy shoving Gram's food into our mouths. Once we finished with dinner and then dessert, I helped Gram clear the table and then wash the dishes by hand.

Landon walked into the kitchen just as we were finishing up. "Hey, City. Want to go on a ride with me?"

"Uh…sure," I said as I dried my hands. "Just let me change first."

Gram had informed me that holiday dinners were a formal occasion in their home, so I'd worn khaki pants and a baby-blue button-up shirt. I wasn't sure where Landon wanted to ride, but I figured mud would be involved. I hurried upstairs to my room and pulled a tank top and shorts on. Even though it was November, we were in the middle of a warm spell. I'd even worn flip-flops to school the previous week.

I walked back downstairs to see Landon waiting for me by the door. I followed him as he walked out to the barn and opened the doors. He climbed onto the four-wheeler without my help, and I smiled. His leg was healing fast.

"Come on," he said as he scooted up so that I could climb on behind him.

Once I was situated, I wrapped my arms around him. "I'm not hurting you, am I?" I asked, remembering that his ribs still hurt him from time to time.

"Nah, I'm fine. You might want to hang on tight though. I haven't been riding in a while. I need to let loose."

I smiled as I scooted up closer to him. "You don't have to tell me twice."

He started the four-wheeler and backed out of the barn. Once we were turned around, he tore down the driveway. I squealed and clung to him as my hair blew everywhere. He hadn't been kidding when he said he needed to let loose. I would have been terrified to go this fast before, but now, I loved it. Adrenaline pumped through my body as we flew down the driveway and then onto the main road. He turned off on the side road leading to the mud hole we'd gone to before.

He slowed as we reached the field. When we were only a few feet from the mud hole, we came to a stop, and he shut off the four-wheeler. I kept my arms around him as we stared at the now dead field. The silence continued until I couldn't take it anymore.

"What are we doing out here?" I asked as I laid my head on his shoulder.

"I just wanted to get away for a while. I've been stuck in that damn house for over a month."

He stood, forcing me to let him go, and he hopped off the four-wheeler. I opened my mouth to ask him what he was doing, but he slid back on, facing me this time.

"And I kind of wanted to get you alone for a while."

I looked up to see him smiling at me. "Is that so? How come?"

"I wanted to talk to you."

"About what?" I asked, suddenly nervous when his expression turned serious.

He reached up and cupped my cheek. "I miss you."

"How could you miss me? I'm around you all the time."

"I miss being with you. It's driving me crazy to be around you all the time and not be with you."

"You're the one who's keeping us apart, Landon, not me. You know how I feel," I whispered.

"I know. I'm just scared, City. When you left and told me not to contact you, it nearly broke me. I can't go through that again," he said as his eyes clouded over with pain.

"I'm so sorry. You'll never know just how sorry I am. What I did to you was wrong." I raised my hand and ran my fingers along his jawline. "I swear that I'll never hurt you again."

"What if things get rough? I don't want you to run again."

"I'm done running. I know just where I want to be, and nothing on this earth can keep me away. You're it for me, Cowboy. You're *it*," I said as I stroked his face. "I love you."

He sucked in a shocked breath. "You have no idea what that means to me. I love you, too, City. I think I've loved you since the moment I saw you. There was just something about you."

"I know what you mean. I tried to stay away from you when I came here, but I couldn't. I was drawn to you. People rarely find their one in a million, but I know I've found it with you," I whispered as I leaned up and brushed my lips against his.

"You're here to stay? Even when things get rough?"

"You couldn't get rid of me even if you tried," I teased.

"I can't stay away from you anymore, City. I'm done trying."
He ran his hand down my body and rested it on my thigh. "I love
you."

Tears filled my eyes as I stared up at him. His eyes trailed
down my body to where his hand rested. I looked down as he
pulled my shorts farther up my leg to reveal my tattoo.

"When did you get this?" he asked.

"Right after Joel died."

"It's for him?"

I nodded.

"And you're over him now?"

"I am. I let him go a long time ago, Cowboy. He'll always be
with me, but my heart belongs to you now."

His eyes found mine as he leaned in and kissed me gently.
"That's all I needed to hear. All I've ever wanted was for you to be
mine."

I smiled against his lips. "It's your lucky day. I'm officially
yours."

He laughed as he pushed me back on the four-wheeler. My
head rested against the travel bag tied to the back rack.

He leaned down and kissed me forcefully on the lips. "I love
you so damn much."

"I love you, too."

We ended up on the ground next to the four-wheeler. His
hands roamed my body, causing me to moan and call out his name
over and over again. My shirt and bra disappeared. I lifted my hips
as he pulled my shorts and underwear down. I pulled his shirt over
his head and started working on the button of his jeans. When we
were bare, he pressed against me, resting his weight on his hands.

"I don't have anything, City."

"It's fine. I'm on the pill, and my mom took me to the doctor
before I started school and I got tested. I'm clean. I haven't been
with anyone since you."

"Me either."

He leaned down and kissed me again as he slid inside me. I
moaned as he filled me. My legs wrapped around his hips as he
started thrusting into me. He didn't start slow like last time.
Instead, he pounded into me forcefully as I clung to him. He was

using sex as an outlet to release all the emotions that had been bottled up inside of him.

"You're my everything. I'd die for you, City," he said as he nuzzled my neck.

Unable to speak, I wrapped my arms around him and met him thrust for thrust. Sweat coated our bodies, and we joined together over and over again. I felt myself building and building until finally I came. I clung to him as wave after wave of pleasure took over my body.

No matter what happened, I would remember this moment forever. This was the beginning of everything for us. I closed my eyes as Landon called out my name when he found his own release.

This was it for me. Landon was my happily ever after. No matter what happened, I knew that we were destined to be together. I loved him more than anything else in this world. We had to fight like hell to get here, but all that mattered was the fact that we were finally together.

I'd thought for so long that my life was over, but I'd been wrong. It was just beginning.

The End

ENJOY THIS
EXCERPT FROM
K.A. ROBINSON'S

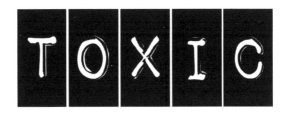

COMING MAY 12, 2014

PROLOGUE

I stared at the room number on my schedule and then looked back at the classroom door in front of me. *312.* I was in the right place. I took a deep breath before opening the door and walking in.

Several students looked up to see who had entered. I ignored their stares as I focused on the teacher sitting behind her desk in front of the classroom.

She smiled as I approached. "Can I help you?"

"Uh…yeah, I'm a new student," I said nervously.

I had no idea why I was nervous. It wasn't like I hadn't moved to a new school before. My mom had moved us around a lot—so much that I'd lost track of how many schools I'd been to. She promised me that this time would be different. This would be the last time we moved.

Yeah, right.

That was what she'd said every single time. I just hoped that my freshman year would be the year that she really meant it. I was tired of moving all the time, and now that I was in high school, it wouldn't be as easy to make friends.

I held out my schedule, and the teacher glanced at it.

"It's nice to meet you, Logan. I'm Mrs. Jenkins. Let me grab you a book."

She stood and walked to a door a few feet away from her desk. Once she disappeared inside, I glanced over my shoulder to see two-dozen students staring at me like I was the most interesting guy in the world. I sighed, hating how this happened every time. Being the new kid sucked, but what could I do?

The teacher reappeared and walked back over to me. "Here is your book. We're starting on chapter three today. Why don't you take a seat next to"—she glanced at the seating chart on the desk—"Chloe Richards. Chloe, will you raise your hand, please?"

I turned to face the classroom and saw a girl raise her hand. I walked toward her, ignoring everyone else as they continued to stare at me. I sat down next to her without even looking her way. I knew my new neighbor would be staring at me like everyone else.

"Class, let's give Logan a warm welcome. Now, if you'll open your books to chapter three, we can begin," Mrs. Jenkins said.

Once Mrs. Jenkins turned away from us to start writing on the board, I glanced over at my neighbor. My mouth dropped open as I stared at her. *Damn.*

She glanced over at me and smiled before turning her attention back to the front of the room.

The girl was gorgeous. Her hair was a light blonde color, and her eyes were bright blue. I noticed she was wearing a shirt with some rock band on the front. She was tiny, but she had more curves than most girls our age. She looked like an angel.

She glanced over and caught me staring at her. She leaned over closer to me and whispered, "I'm Chloe."

I smiled at the sound of her voice. It was as sweet as the rest of her.

"Logan," I whispered back.

"Where are you from?" she asked.

Where am I from? I sighed and decided to go with the last state we'd moved from. "Missouri."

"Cool. I've lived here my entire life. I'll warn you now— there's nothing to do around here. It's boring as hell."

I smiled. *I don't think I'll be bored with you around.* "Good to know."

We both turned back to pay attention to what Mrs. Jenkins was saying. A few minutes later, Chloe poked my arm. I gave her a questioning look.

"Do you think her hair is real or a wig?"

I snorted in laughter, but I quickly covered it with a cough when the students in front of us turned to look. "Uh…I don't know."

"I vote wig. There is no way she could get her natural hair that high on her head."

I glanced up at the teacher and then back to Chloe. "I think you're right."

"Finally! Someone agrees with me!" she snickered.

I spent the rest of class glancing in Chloe's direction. I couldn't get over how pretty she was. Sure, I was a teenage guy, so I noticed things like boobs and ass, but there was just something about this girl.

When the bell rang, she turned back to me. "Let me see your schedule."

I handed it to her, and she glanced over it.

"You have a couple of classes with me. Our next one is together, and we have lunch together, too. I always sit with my friend, Amber. You're welcome to sit with us if you want."

She smiled at me, and I knew right then and there that I was fucked. This girl was already under my skin, and I wanted her more than anything. I would make her mine.

"Sounds perfect," I said.

CHAPTER ONE

Four Years Later: Fall

I deepened the kiss and started slowly sliding my hand under Chloe's shirt and up her stomach. She froze at the touch and pulled away.

"What's wrong, babe? If we're going too fast, just tell me. I thought after the other day…" I looked at her with concern in my eyes.

I'd thought that we were in a good place, but her body language was telling me otherwise. We'd been together for a few months now. Plus, I'd known her for over four years, so I knew when something was wrong with her.

"Logan, remember how I wanted to talk to you the other day?"

I nodded, but I stayed silent as I tried to ignore the sinking feeling in my stomach. Something was seriously wrong.

"Well, there's something I need to tell you." She closed her eyes and took a deep breath before opening them to look at me again. "Something happened between Drake and me. Right after we got together, I went over to his house to hang out and study for a couple of our classes. Neither of us intended for anything to happen, but we ended up having sex. I am so sorry I didn't tell you. I just couldn't stand the thought of hurting you. It was an accident."

I froze as I looked down at her. Drake was the local rock star and someone she'd become good friends with since we came to West Virginia University. While she had sworn that nothing was going on between the two of them before, I'd noticed how he was always watching her. My gut had warned me about him, but I'd refused to listen. Instead, I'd blindly trusted her, assuming that she would never lie to me.

"*An accident*? What? You just accidentally fell on his dick?" I yelled, losing my temper.

How could she do this to us?

We'd been doing so well together. I was happy. She was happy—or so I'd thought.

I took a deep breath, trying to calm myself. "Why are you telling me this now? Why wait all these months and then dump this on me?"

"I don't know. I guess I just couldn't take the guilt anymore. I don't want to keep lying to you." She stared into my eyes.

"I'm glad you told me, Chloe. I want you to be honest with me. I don't really know what to say, but I'm trying to understand here. You said this was right after we got together?"

She nodded.

"Okay, well, as long as it was just once, I am willing to look past it. I know how confused you were about us then." I pulled her into a hug as she burst into tears. "What's wrong, Chloe? I forgive you, baby girl. I forgive you."

She continued to sob as she managed to gasp out the few words that would seal our fate. "It wasn't just then. It happened again a couple of weeks ago. I went to his house to try to work things out because we hadn't really talked since it happened, and things got carried away."

My body tensed as I tried to fight the rage building inside me. "You had sex with him two weeks ago? What the fuck, Chloe?" I dropped my arms from around her like I'd been burned, and I stood up. She was still crying as I continued yelling, "That son of a bitch! He knew you were mine, and he still went after you. Twice! Un-fucking-believable! I'm going to kill him!" I stormed across the room to the door and threw it open.

She jumped off the bed to go after me. "Logan! Logan, stop! Where are you going?"

I glanced over my shoulder at her, and I headed for the stairs. "I'm going to teach that bastard a lesson. I knew something was up between you two. I just never thought he would pull that. I never thought you would do this to me! How could you, Chloe?" I continued to yell as she chased me down the stairs.

All around us, students stopped dead in the hallway and stairs to stare at us as we passed.

"I'm so sorry, Logan, but please just stop."

She reached for my arm, but I threw her hand away.

"Stay away from me, Chloe, or God help me, I won't be responsible for my actions."

We had made it down the stairs and out into the parking lot. I quickly unlocked my car and jumped in. Chloe tried to open the passenger door, but I kept it locked as I put the car in drive. I left black marks as I screeched out of the parking lot. I glanced back in my rearview mirror to see her running for her own car and jumping in. I turned my attention back to the main road.

I drove straight to the bar where Drake played, knowing he would be playing on a Friday night. As soon as I shut off my car, I jumped out and ran toward the building. I heard Chloe calling my name as she chased me across the lot, but I ignored her as I went into the bar.

Drake was up on stage, playing with the band, when I entered. I headed straight for the stage with Chloe on my heels. Before she could stop me, I jumped up on the stage and punched Drake in the face. She screamed as Drake's head jerked back with the force of it. Blood started trickling down onto his lips from his nose. The crowd started screaming, and the other band members quickly grabbed me as I lunged for Drake again.

"What the fuck?" Drake yelled as he glared at me.

He glanced up and went pale when he saw Chloe standing in front of the stage, crying and shaking.

"You stupid son of a bitch! Did you think I wouldn't find out that you've been fucking Chloe behind my back?"

I lunged again, and Adam, one of Drake's bandmates, was caught off guard, letting me go. Drake saw me coming and jumped back before landing a punch of his own in my stomach. I grunted and dropped to one knee before standing back up and going at Drake again.

"Come on, pretty boy, I'm standing right here. Come and get me," Drake taunted me.

I threw another punch that Drake wasn't quick enough to dodge, and it landed in his rib cage. I threw myself at Drake while the pain distracted him, and we flew backward into the drums, sending them flying. I could hear Chloe screaming at both of us as we continued to throw punches before Adam and Eric could pull us apart.

Eric pried Drake off of me and held him tight as Adam twisted my arm behind my back and held me in a death grip. I struggled to get loose, but it was no use.

Jade—another one of Drake's bandmates, who had been standing on the end of the stage the entire time—put her fingers in her mouth and whistled. "That's it! Grow the fuck up, boys, or at least take it outside!"

I looked at Drake with pure hatred in my eyes. "How could you, Drake? I asked you that day at lunch if there was anything between the two of you before I went for her. You told me nothing was going on, and nothing would. You promised me that you would leave her alone, and look what happened. You fucked her not once but twice behind my back."

Drake glared right back at me. "Yeah, I did fuck her twice because once just wasn't enough for me, and I'd do it again if I could."

I tried to lunge for him, but Adam was prepared this time, and he held tight.

"All right, guys, both of you outside now," Adam growled as he held me back.

He marched me offstage and across the bar to the door. Eric followed closely behind, still holding on to Drake. With their arms wrapped around each other, Jade and Chloe followed behind them at a distance.

When I stepped out into the cool night air, I breathed deeply, trying to control my rage. *How did my life come to this?*

Chloe was everything to me, and she'd betrayed me. She might as well have stuck a knife in me. It wouldn't have hurt as bad as this.

Once we were far enough away from the bar doors, Eric and Adam released Drake and me, and they stepped back.

"All right, you want to kick the shit out of each other, be my guest. We're not going to stop you, but you guys need to get your shit together. Fighting over a girl is fucking ridiculous, and you know it. So, do what you want. Just get it out and over with before our drums suffer anymore," Eric growled as he and Adam made their way over to where Jade and Chloe were standing.

Drake and I faced each other, both of us glaring at the other. We both glanced down when Chloe stepped forward to stand between us.

"Listen to me, both of you. This is so stupid, like Eric said. This is all my fault, and the two of you beating the shit out of each other isn't going to fix anything. I fucked up, not you two. So, if you want to take your anger out on someone, take it out on me. I ruined everything." Tears ran down her face as she looked at both of us. "You both mean so much to me, and I will never forgive myself for what I have done to you."

She quickly turned away from us and headed across the parking lot to her car before either of us could say anything. We watched in silence as she pulled out of the parking lot and disappeared around the corner. Once she was out of sight, I turned my attention back to Drake.

"You destroyed everything!" I shouted at him.

"Fuck this. I'm going back inside. As much fun as it would be to watch you two idiots beat the shit out of each other, it's cold out here," Adam muttered as he turned and walked back to the bar.

Eric and Jade watched us for a second before turning and following him. I didn't miss the pity in Jade's eyes, but I ignored it. I didn't want anyone to feel pity for me.

"You think I don't know that, asshole?" Drake said as he glared at me. "I know this is my fault."

"Then, why did you do it?" I shouted.

"Because I love her!" he shouted back, stopping me in my tracks.

Of all the responses I'd expected, that wasn't one of them. Drake used women. He didn't love them.

"You what?" I asked incredulously.

"I love her. I've tried to ignore it—believe me, I've tried—but I can't. I love her, and I don't know what the fuck to do about it."

"You're incapable of love, Drake. I've watched you screw every woman in sight for months!"

"I haven't touched another woman since I figured out how I felt about Chloe. I wouldn't do that to her." He ran his hands through his hair. "Look, I think we need to talk and not in the middle of a parking lot. My house is right around the corner. Let's go there and figure shit out, okay?"

247

I stared at him, debating on whether to go with him or punch him again. Finally, I decided that talking was the only thing that would solve this whole mess even if punching him would make me feel better. "Fine. Let's go."

Neither of us said a word as we walked to his house. He hadn't been kidding when he said he lived right around the corner. I waited impatiently as he unlocked his front door, and then we walked inside. Once he flipped on the lights, we walked to the living room and sat down across from each other.

"So, now what?" I finally asked after several minutes of silence.

"I don't fucking know. I *do* know that I want Chloe more than anything else in this world," he said as he stared at me.

"Yeah, well, so do I. I've loved her since the moment I laid eyes on her. It's taken me five years to get up the nerve to tell her how I feel, and then you come along and sweep her off her feet in a few months."

"I didn't mean for it to go down like this. I'm not a complete asshole. I just…I can't control myself around her."

"I've noticed," I growled as I clenched my hands into fists. "If I had known she was sleeping with you and me both at the same time, I would have—"

"You would have what? Left her? Told her you hated her? Called her a slut?" he asked.

"I don't know what I would have done, okay? I've spent most of my teenage years in love with her. I don't know what to do."

He sighed and ran his hands through his hair. "This is so fucked-up! I actually care about one girl, and she's with someone else."

"We have to let her choose. That's all we can do," I said.

He looked up at me and smirked. "And the loser does what? Walks away and pretends that none of this happened?"

"I guess so. What other choice do we have?"

"I can't just walk away from her, Logan."

"You have to. And if she chooses you"—I took a deep breath—"I'll walk away. We're ripping her apart."

"You're right." Drake stood and kicked the chair he'd just been sitting in. "Why the fuck can't I let her go?"

"For the same reason I can't—you love her. Chloe is special."

He smiled, the first one I'd seen all night. "Yeah, she is."

I frowned as he stared off into space with that damn smile on his face. He pulled out his phone and started typing on it.

"What are you doing?" I asked.

"Texting her to see if she's okay. She was really upset when she left the bar."

"So, what do you want to do? Go talk to her now, or wait until she calms down?" I asked.

"Let's wait. I doubt if she'd speak to either of us right now," Drake said as he looked at me. "Look, I know you don't like me, and I sure as hell don't like you, but let's try to be civil with each other until this is sorted out. Once she chooses, we can go back to hating each other. I don't want to upset her more than she already is."

"Fine with me," I mumbled.

We spent the next hour texting Chloe, but she didn't respond to either of us. I started to worry, especially with her psychotic mother trying to contact her again.

"Maybe I should go check on her," I said as I stood and started walking to the door.

"You're not going over there without me. I don't know what you'll say to her. I'm coming with you."

I rolled my eyes. "Whatever. I just want to make sure she's okay."

I ignored him as I walked back to the bar where my car was parked. I climbed in and drove back to the dorm, refusing to think about anything. I would deal with everything when I was in my room by myself. If I thought about it now, I'd lose my mind and probably hit Drake again.

I pulled into the dorm parking lot and shut off my car. I stared at the dorm in front of me, unable to move. I didn't want to face Chloe right now. I loved her more than anything, but I also hated her at the moment. We'd finally found happiness, and she had to go and screw it all up. If she had stayed away from Drake, we'd still be in her room together right now.

I opened my door when I saw Drake walking past my car. I followed as he walked into the dorm. I wasn't about to let him see her alone either. I couldn't handle that yet. We were both silent as we walked up the stairs and onto her floor. Once we reached the door, Drake knocked. A minute later, the door swung open, and Chloe was standing in front of us. Even though I was pissed, the mere sight of her took my breath away.

She smiled at both of us as soon as she saw us. "Hey, guys! How are you?" She giggled. "Actually, never mind. You're both pretty damn fine, like always."

She turned without another word and made her way back to her bed. She fell on top of it, and she glanced back at us, still smiling.

"What the hell is wrong with her?" I mumbled to Drake as I stepped into the room. "Are you all right, Chloe?" I asked, my voice louder.

"I'm great! I had a couple of shots, and now, I'm all set." She smiled brightly at us. "What are you guys doing here? Wait, you're together, and there's no blood!"

Both of us continued to stare at her. I glanced around the room to see a bottle of vodka on her nightstand. *Shit, she's drunk.* That was what the warm welcome had been all about.

I leaned down beside her bed and looked into her glassy eyes. "Just how many shots have you had, love?"

"Only a couple." She motioned to the bottle on the nightstand. "See? It's still full. I just opened it tonight."

Drake glanced at the stand before looking back at her. "Uh, Chloe, the bottle is empty."

She stared at the bottle, realizing that he was right. She slapped her hand across her face before laughing. "Whoops! Guess it's a good thing it was the cheap stuff. Otherwise, I'd be seriously drunk right now."

Drake and I exchanged looks with each other, both of our expressions filled with concern. She was past drunk and moving into wasted.

"Chloe, honey, you *are* drunk, excessively drunk actually," I said as I watched her.

She rolled her eyes. "Seriously, guys, I'm fine. Why are you here?"

Drake spoke up from his spot in front of the bed. "Look, Chloe, you're trashed, so I don't think right now is a good time to talk, like Logan and I planned. We'll come back tomorrow"—he glanced at the bottle again—"or the day after. I'm pretty sure you aren't going to be up to any talking tomorrow."

"I said, I'm fine!" she grumbled as she sat up.

Two seconds later, she grabbed the garbage can beside the bed and threw up violently into it. I jumped back a couple of feet as she continued to throw up. It seemed like hours passed until she finished.

Jesus. I'd never seen her like this.

Finally, there seemed to be nothing left in her stomach, and she rolled back onto her bed, groaning, "Fuck. Maybe I am drunk."

Drake chuckled quietly. "No shit, Chloe."

She glared at him. "Just say what you came here to say, asshole."

"We came to tell you to decide who you want. Both of us want you, but who you want is what really matters. Whoever you don't choose will back off—no questions asked."

She looked back and forth between us. "What if I want both of you?"

And then, she passed out.

Fuck.

ACKNOWLEDGMENTS

To me, this is the hardest part of a book to write. There are so many people who have helped me, and I know I will miss a few.

To my husband—Without you, I would never have finished any of my books. You're my rock.

To my parents—You listen to me and help me with everything I need. I wouldn't be who I am today without you.

To my blogger friends—Gah! I can't say thanks enough times to all of you. You're not *just* bloggers to me. You're my friends. Without you, no one would even know who K.A. Robinson is. No one would know who Drake is. (That would be a damn shame right there, wouldn't it?) Your support means so much to me.

To my "real-life" friends—Thank you for dealing with my constant absence. I know it's hard to get a hold of me. I get so into writing that I forget to live sometimes. You're always there to drag me back to reality. I love you!

To my author friends: Tabatha, Katelynn, Sophie, Tijan, Teresa, Sara, Jamie, Debra, L.B., and several others I know I'm forgetting—I love you. Seriously. You guys keep me calm, help me when I need it, and remind me to eat. I feel so blessed to call you my friends.

To my readers—Your response to my books has been overwhelming. I *never* imagined that so many of you would care about these characters the way you do. You guys continue to rock my world on a daily basis. I love you all to pieces.

To Letitia—You make the best covers. Ever. Thank you!

To Jovana—You deserve a medal for dealing with my crazy self and for reading the unedited mess of a book that I send to you. You rock!

ABOUT THE AUTHOR

K.A. Robinson is twenty-three years old and lives in a small town in West Virginia with her toddler son and husband. She is the *New York Times* and *USA Today* Bestselling Author of The Torn Series and The Ties Series. When she's not writing, she loves to read, usually something with zombies in it. She is also addicted to coffee, mainly Starbucks and Caribou Coffee.

Her latest novel, *Twisted Ties*, was released on February 12, 2014.

Facebook: www.facebook.com/karobinson13

Twitter: @karobinsonautho

Blog: www.authorkarobinson.blogspot.com

Made in the USA
Lexington, KY
30 May 2014